PRAISE FOR FLYAWAY BY KATHLEEN JENNINGS

"An unforgettable tale, as beautiful as it is thorny."
— *The New York Times Book Review*

"*Flyaway* is a nearly perfect novella. It sings with pain and roars with power. Although it is short, it is neither spare nor unfulfilled. Kathleen Jennings has a voice unlike any other, and I long for more."
— Alex Brown, Tor.com

"In spellbinding, lyrical prose Jennings lulls readers into this rich, dreamlike world. Lovers of contemporary fairy tales will find this a masterful work."
— *Publishers Weekly,* starred review

"I love the imagery, the atmosphere, the incredible tactile quality of the world as described, the structure. . . . Some of the best prose I've ever read."
— *Smart Bitches, Trashy Books*

"It should be no surprise that Kathleen Jennings's debut novel is splendid and unusual, that it feels like a dispatch from another, finer world, that it frightens and enchants in the same breath."
— Katharine Coldiron, *Locus*

"Part ghost story, part murder mystery and part fairy tale, *Flyaway* feels like a perfect combination of all Jennings' experiences and imagination."
— *Book Page*

"An entrancing and unforgettable debut."
— *The Southern Bookseller Review*

"An impressive mixture of gothic and folklore."
— *Canberra Times*

"Jennings's debut novella is pure, poetic Australian gothic, filled with haunting emotions, fairy-tale action, and sharp prose."

— *Library Journal*

"A deliciously mysterious Gothic fairy tale wrapped in elegantly descriptive prose."

— *Booklist*

"Half mystery, half fairy tale, all exquisitely rendered and full of teeth."

— Holly Black, author of *Book of Night*

"A fairytale wrapped about in riddles and other thorny bits of enchantments and stories, but none of them quite like any you've heard before. Kathleen Jennings' prose dazzles, and her magic feels real enough that you might even prick your finger on it."

— Kelly Link, author of *White Cat, Black Dog*

"A superbly told tale of folklore-infused fantasy, full of rising dread, set in a sharply observed Australian outback town."

— Garth Nix, author of *Sabriel*

"I feel as if a very new voice has whispered a very old secret in my ear, and I'll never be able to un-hear it. Nor will I ever want to."

— C. S. E. Cooney, author of *Saint Death's Daughter*

# KINDLING

# KINDLING

## STORIES

Kathleen Jennings

Small Beer Press
Easthampton, MA

This is a work of fiction. All characters and events portrayed in this book are either fictitious or used fictitiously.



Small Beer Press
150 Pleasant Street #306
Easthampton, MA 01027
smallbeerpress.com
weightlessbooks.com
bookmoonbooks.com
info@smallbeerpress.com

Distributed to the trade by Consortium.

Library of Congress Cataloging-in-Publication Data

Names: Jennings, Kathleen, 1980- author.
Title: Kindling : stories / Kathleen Jennings.
Description: First edition. | Easthampton, MA : Small Beer Press, 2023.
Identifiers: LCCN 2023024859 (print) | LCCN 2023024860 (ebook) | ISBN 9781618732132 (paperback) | ISBN 9781618732149 (ebook)
Subjects: LCGFT: Short stories.
Classification: LCC PS3610.E5585 K56 2023 (print) | LCC PS3610.E5585 (ebook) | DDC 813/.6--dc23/eng/20230623
LC record available at https://lccn.loc.gov/2023024859
LC ebook record available at https://lccn.loc.gov/2023024860

Hardcover (9781618732170), trade paper (9781618732132), & ebook (9781618732149).

First edition 1 2 3 4 5 6 7 8 9

Set in Bembo with titles in PT Sans.

Printed on 30% PCR recycled paper by the Maple Press in York, PA.
Author photo: Ngaire Naran.

*For Angela Slatter*

# Contents

# *The Heart of Owl Abbas*

Once, before the great Empire of Else enveloped the land between the red mountains and the quiet sea, the city-state of Owl Abbas was a mere bird-haunted forest temple. But protected by treaties, suffocated by safety and benevolent neglect, it had swollen and grown in upon itself, roiling and fomenting, so slowly that only (perhaps) a few dust-dry wraiths of abbots hanging motionless in enclosed footings of the Palace Aster would have marked the change from one century to another.

The gains and losses of its citizenry had been gradual. Its resentments and injustices oozed like moisture down the dank wall of a forgotten reservoir, unremarked by either the clustered, crushing commonality or the Little Emperor, cloyed and gorged in his great gilt chambers. *Drip, drip*, until the dark water was high against its bowed, ill-repaired walls. Until it lapped at the foundations of palace and hovel alike.

In all Owl Abbas, before it burned (after the Falling but before the Cartographer's War and the Recurrence of Owls), there were among its many windows only two that need concern us.

The first was fogged with spiderwebs. It belonged to a garret, precarious above the spring-carts and spirit-lamps of Petty Street. Behind it was installed a wretched scribbler, who eked out a living writing songs for the populace. Let us call him Excelsior, for that is the name with which he signed his work.

Across the cobbleskulls and flints, and a full other storey over that abyss of jam merchants and glove-skinners that was Petty Street, above the hanging signs of teahouse and slop house, workhouse and whorehouse, higher even than the knotwork of laundry-, bell-, delivery- and ladder-strings, was another, airy casement.

The tenant of that room was only recently arrived to Owl Abbas—itinerant, mendicant, but admitted at the Mountain Gate because of the journeyman's seal it bore on one exquisite brass shoulder. Even had the gate guards consulted the annals of the Elevated Guild of Horologists and Artificers, they would have found no reason to turn aside the masterpiece of an obscure craftswoman whose exile was self-imposed. Wonders, then, were a daily import of the palace, and—hemmed in as the city-state was by ancient vows and the benign disregard of the Empire of Else, in whose armpit it festered—the peace of the Little Emperor of Owl Abbas was threatened by nothing but thieves.

Excelsior, who seldom ventured even to his window, let alone to the street, had never seen this neighbour, whom time would call the Nightingale. From his lower garret, Excelsior could glimpse only a ceiling painted with blue dove-shadows and rose-gold candle glow.

He could, however, hear the Nightingale's voice. Pure and high, discs of spinning glass singing against chamois, it fell like tumbling bells, like spilled silver wires.

It sang "Love Like the Guillotine," "The Too-Taut Heart," "When I am Duke of Petty Street (You Shall Be the Clown)"—all the choruses bawled by rampant youth loitering over gutters below, trilled by the delivery boatmen in the oily, olive canals, hummed even by agued ancients scrubbing the pearl-floored halls of the Palace Aster. Cheap songs. Excelsior's.

He could have written a dozen more like them in his sleep, for his scribbling of lyric and melody, accompaniment and refrain was a mechanical task, calibrated to please the fecund and fickle tastes of the crowds of Owl Abbas, their perennial lusts and losses.

And what appetites for music that city-state had then, for all its decay and poverty! Forgotten were the bone groves and the quietude of owleries that once nested where the city had grown. The last owl-abbots were long starved in the gutters where they had begged, their skulls cambering the roadway. The owls had departed the sleepless streets for the zoological gardens of Else and the monk's-fringe forests of the red mountains. Now, though the finest delights were reserved for the Little Emperor, balladuellists caterwauled on roofsheets; ladies' cantating parrots swung in brass rings; lovers in teahouses threw coins into the throats of cheap songboxes, to wind the gears that set the teeth that struck the notes from the spinning metal tongues, sending slivers of copper to Excelsior, that he might buy ink and nibs and spirit-oil, cheap paper, wine hard as a fist and, when he remembered, a little bread.

Rough songs he wrote, like all the lesser scribblers of Owl Abbas. Raw songs, tunes to dull sense and sensation, ditties to hem in a little portion of pleasure between hunger and the grave.

Excelsior had never crept out of his garret to crouch at the outer palace walls to hear rare notes escaping from an Imperial Performance. Nor had he attended the Collegiate Academy of Guilded Instrumentalists, which existed to supply the artful music of the palace: formal stylings for sleep and dressing and every course of a dozen served at each of the eight tables laid daily for the Little Emperor. Even had Excelsior done so, he would not have heard anything to match the Nightingale's abilities.

He listened to the deconstructed threads and parts, the wheeling, rewriting rehearsals, the little broken, mended, rough-edged fantasias with which the Nightingale warmed and amused the bright apartment, there above Petty Street, in that merryloud quarter of Owl Abbas where surely no one who mattered could overhear. The Nightingale, learning the music of the streets, the heartbeat of the city.

Bells and wires and strings, keys and barrels and tumblers, reeds and pipes, skin and wind. Melody, harmony, disingenuous discord. The hearts and throats of caged larks, of free birds, of trained choristers. All these were in the voice of the Nightingale.

But the voice carried, as the bounty of the palace never did. From Petty Street to the knotted alleys of the Maresnest, from Agnes Lane where once a disgraced clockmaker had kept her stinking workshop, to the last nested hovel before the avenue of guildhalls. Though neither understanding nor caring, the denizens of Owl Abbas stepped a little more lightly, laboured with an ear half-turned, unwitting, to those strains.

Excelsior eked out the end of the daylight, the nightlight, the moonlight, the ghostlight. He scrimped and slaved until he gathered courage and words enough to light a fire-inch and burn a whole pennyweight of ground copper. He offered the coin to the Phantom of the Window-sash, and summoned that obscure spirit almost to its full weight of feathers and claws.

The Phantom of the Window-sash was not a shade that embraced change. It had once had its own antique, unmusical views on such matters as songlust and bodymusic. But those, like the shade itself, were the shabbiest of memories.

Summoned by the soul of coins, it obeyed its commission without remark. Clustering Excelsior's rolled onionskin to its vanishingly sharp breastbone, the phantom fell from the garret sill—fell, then lifted on a gust of oil-spiced laughter to the glowing window opposite and there dissolved before the Nightingale could question it, leaving its dry burden to flutter on the floor.

Excelsior could not watch.

He hauled closed the leaning shutters and pulled down the sash, cross-latched it and rubbed drawing gum along the edges. He etched more webs into the panes, spitting glass like flour from beneath his good penknife, that his garret might look tenantless. He raked the curtains across, pinning pumice-cloth and blotting paper over the moth holes.

Then for good measure he put out writing-lamp, hearthglow, bed-candle and moth-pilot, closed his eyes, and waited.

He waited for three clock-unwinding days, feeling the long springs of his world loosen, while the ink crusted in the glass well and the nibs began to rust in the little moisture from the breath of creeping rats or spiders.

On the third day, a thrill stirred the dull panes, the curtains. Excelsior could not have told when it had begun. He crouched, resolutely unhoping.

The insinuation became a hum, a melody. Excelsior heard what had never been heard before, except in the signs and symbols of his dark garret, in his private equations: the song he had composed in the light of the last of his lamp-spirits, for which he had burned the last coin; the paper words for which he had sent the phantom winging.

The Nightingale's voice, now, was a high, thin curling, like the frost on a glass of Abbas-White, or like red snow ribboning off the tops of the mountains. It was melody uncomplicated by harmony or the thrilling trills of ornament, tentative only in its simplicity, the singer's questing guided by all the confidence of the supreme master of an art.

Over and again that voice followed Excelsior's script, the words seeking notes, notes seeking paths as water flows across a dry land. Then gradually that glass-and-golden voice found a pattern, gathered force, rilled and frothed along the edges of its new-cut banks, built undertows and laughing sprays of sound. It poured down through the alleys where craftsmen and labourers starved, trickled through Agnes Lane where a young clockmaker had once studied the grafting of metal to splintered bone, funneled into the inlooped ways of the great warren of the Maresnest.

High over Petty Street, the Nightingale sang for the first time Excelsior's composition—not a commission, not a command, but . . . Well, even the scribbler could not have said whether it had been gift or tribute or sacrifice.

The Nightingale sang and Excelsior, weak with waiting, listened.

He wrote another, immediately he had revived. It was unworthy. Dissatisfied, he broke it apart into bare penny-shave popular ditties. Ragged and rancid, he did not care to take them down himself, but sent them by errand urchins to the punch-shop, where they were pricked relentlessly into parchment rolls and delivered to tea shops and pleasure warrens, fed into mere pinching, playing songchests, which nipped fingers as well as paper, and singly-minded cranked out Excelsior's abandoned tunes.

"*Love, love,*" sang the high-painters in their blood-dipped, paint-dripped hats.

"*You are a far dying star,*" sang the menials toiling with bow-bent spines and mole-fur cloths along the Palace Aster wainscoting.

"*You test the hearts of the court, and find them wanting,*" sang the xylophone-ribbed parrot trainers, chorusing from cage to cage, that their clients' birds might have the newest tunes.

Excelsior, having ill considered how his words might be mis-sung, covered his ears against the rattle and racket of the streets, uncovered them again in terror that he might miss the Nightingale's next effusive variations.

The copper slicings rattled up in the delivery basket. *There,* thought Excelsior. He could fit a new song to that high, rhythmless beat.

The ghost of a sigh is a weighty thing. The Phantom of the Window-sash unfolded itself heavily into the haze of the copper-burnings, not in the least elevated by music.

It gathered up the onionskin in layers of ether and slunk to Excelsior's window, sagged over the sill, bore itself by grudging degrees up layers of garlic breath, pipe smoke, midden scent, fresh soap, crushed leaves, and wet feathers to the higher floor, opposite.

If Excelsior could have seen, he would have watched in affront as it uncoiled, graceless, and spilled on the ruddy tiles his heart's offering, his hope of immortality.

Now, ghosts are little more than animate nostalgia. New songs in old patterns were a sop, a soporific, and old songs by new singers no more than reinforced the rule of the city. But so fine a thing as the scribbler and the singer together might make was a danger to the unquestioned squalor, the eternal twilight, the restlessness without ambition, the struggle over no more than bread and beds, which were the groundwork of the Little Emperor's reign, the foundation of the false peace of Owl Abbas.

The phantom lay unspooled on the cool tiles until the Nightingale, shod in shell and horn, clicked and bent to it and lifted spirit and onionskin together.

The sheets of music, raw as bone, fresh as blood, lured the singer, but the spirit was a tragedian. How it dangled and feinted.

Sensibility is the stock-in-trade of any performer, long dead or unliving. The Nightingale set the song aside and attended the messenger.

Burnt feathers revived the spirit a little, burnt copper restored it, a dusting of finger-chalk to better reveal its form the phantom found quite unnecessary. It arched itself grateful and looping around the bronze joints, the magnificent alabaster throat of its benefactor.

"Strange spirit," said the Nightingale. "Were you bird once? Are you, then, the heart of Owl Abbas? If so, I have been overwrought, and you were easier to capture than my maker thought."

*No*, its spasm of ghostly laughter implied. It was a humble ghost, dusty and old. Far below the notice of such as the Nightingale.

The Nightingale's maker had never been interested in spirit, only in the melding of metal with flesh—had, indeed, taken her leave of Owl Abbas when the Guild mocked her designs for a Patent Brass Hip, a Magnetic Hand, a Better Limb, as an affront and bastardisation of their craft. The phantom's claim therefore satisfied the Nightingale. It turned to the onionskins and began to try the first notes, the melodies.

*How great, how grand*, the lingering spirit insinuated with little shivers and purrs. *How* marvelous *to be heard as one was intended to be. The homage of the scribbler is only to be expected, but your voice was not designed to be let fall where it might, on night-dust-carter and tea-carrier alike. You are a creature of artifice and ambition, your voice made to refract from mirrored maze and chandelier.*

*Turn away*, the phantom's mummery suggested. *Turn your back on this window, with its view over bird- and ghost-encrusted roofs to the ghastly blue fields and untrustworthy scarlet mountains. Turn instead to that opposite. Look to the chimney-forests, the peacock-strutted valleys of lead and copper, the waxen glowing domes of the Palace Aster, set like a weight of jewels at the centre of the city.*

*One might,* it implied, draping affectionately about the mark of the Nightingale's distant maker, *one might even say the Nightingale had been purposed and designed for such delights.*

*Sing Excelsior's little offerings in* that *direction.*

The Nightingale saw the force of the argument. Its throat, the chords strung within, these articulations of wrist and jaw, had been crafted and calibrated for a high purpose: to seize the heart of Owl Abbas. Where else might a city's heart be found?

So it was towards the Palace Aster that the Nightingale sang.

Excelsior, having at last in hope opened curtain, sash and shutter, did not at first notice the added distance in the Nightingale's voice. He lingered, nib held clear of the thirsty paper, and drank in the tentative, tender explorations, the strengthening resolve, the removal of magnificent veils of possibility to reveal the song more truly than he had written it.

Petty Street had proved an impassable chasm before this, even to those robust enough to dare its buffeting. It was possible, in the scheme of the city, with its streets like the whorls of an ear, branching like veins, looped like a brain, that Excelsior might never see the Nightingale. He believed he did not care. It was the *voice* that captured him, reverberating in the hollows of his thin chest, fluttering and rebounding there like a second soul.

Abruptly anxious, he cleaned the crust of ink from the pen, the settling dust from his paper, and began again.

*Hark how glory falls,*
*Tumbling from Owl Abbas walls.*

No.

*Send gold-and-silver crowns*
*Tumbling in the street,*
*Enough to cover the copper path*
*Laid at the singer's feet.*

Again, he scratched out the words.

*Aster and rose will never bloom*
*Like the light in my love's room . . .*

That was awkward, presumptuous, and wrong. Excelsior nearly tore up the paper, but the thought of copper arrested him. Coins meant ink and nibs, castor oil and onionskin and the services of a courier.

Out went the lesser tunes, into the kettle-arcades and the dance-alleys, out to the earnest, workaday singers who would seek no subtlety or layers in words that had been dreamed up for nothing *except* nuance. Out to listeners who, unwitting, had already been half-woken by the Nightingale's art, and whose nascent hunger other scribblers, other singers—themselves starved—hastened to fill with words not of old complacencies but in mimicry of Excelsior's dim longings.

At last, like the heart of a thistle, the pure, bitter core of a song emerged from the peeled-back pages. This, thought Excelsior, was fitting tribute and sacrifice.

Out in the streets, languishing, lusting idlers and iron-bitten, fire-calloused labourers hammered out his ballads with all the delicacy of a beam on a bell. Excelsior took his thin levy of their trade and burned it to the Phantom of the Window-sash, which, for once, appeared with alacrity, an eager whiplash of air.

"Take this to the Nightingale," Excelsior bid it, as if the spirit did not know where all his thoughts were trained.

The Nightingale's voice had been borne by breeze and breath in through the windows of the Palace Aster, where it reached the ring-heavy ears of the Little Emperor, as he lay on his back in his vast bed at owl-light, as was his custom, weighted with ennui, calcified with alarm. The fears of the Little Emperor were many: that he might never know delight again; that the vast Empire of Else would outstrip him in its discovery of luxuries; that emissaries from a distant land, consumed with envy, would break into the storerooms of the Palace Aster and find a jeweled gown, a pearl cup, a marvel from which he had not wearily drained the last honeysuckle spasm of pleasure.

"That music," he said, startling the doctors who, beaked and embroidered, bent over his bed, tempting him with rarities. "I want *that*."

"It is the windharps in the hanging gardens," said his courtiers. "It is the song of the cocoon-tenders lulling their charges to sleep. It is the breeze in the vines where Abbas-White is grown."

The Little Emperor was become petulant and particular with a surfeit of pleasures. "Then bring it to me!" he said.

They sent runners out into the streets, the gardens, the acre-width of tilled treaty-land that bordered Owl Abbas, and had windharps, silk-herders, vine cuttings brought to the palace. All fell silent in the presence of the Little Emperor, but the miraculous voice continued.

The nobles went out themselves, questing and questioning, soft and perfumed and quilted, pomandered against the exhalation of rotting lungs, parasoled against the filth that spilled from windows. The grimy populace, more sullen and shouldersome than had been their wont, would not or could not tell them whence the song came. Above them, the soot-lunged chimney-urchins leaped and leered. So many shifts of them had tumbled and burned since the clockmaker of Agnes Street had proposed, to denouncement by the Guild, her Mechanical Bellows Suitable to Reside Within the Living Chest. But Excelsior's words and the Nightingale's song rang in their boxed and smoke-blocked ears, and as they spat down on the velvet caps fluttering with imported owl-feathers, the shining, circleted heads of the prim nobility, the urchins thought among themselves that *those* heads would never fall to form the smallest cobbleskulls.

At last, as the Little Emperor grew restive, voicehounds were sent out. They went about the streets, leaping runnels of beery bravado. They heard, dismissive, Excelsior's adulterated choruses rousing bottle-room and tap-house, they ducked unperturbed beneath the debased and stirring phrases whistled by rat-cullers and spring-winders. They clicked up the fingerstairs and along the cobbleskulls until they crowded together on Short Street, which runs beneath Petty Street, all their ears cocked to the sky, their small, weeping eyes turned to the garret where the Nightingale sang.

Arpeggios and wandering scales spilled like largesse, rich and fragrant on their collars and livery.

The Phantom of the Window-sash, delivering its latest commission, let the onionskin spill like so many kitchen-sweepings over the Nightingale's unclenching hands, to catch in the breeze and flicker out into Owl Abbas.

*There*. The little ghost coiled meaningful at the pulsing throat of the Nightingale, although each tremor, each tremolo shook it a measure further out of the world. *Make ready*.

The Nightingale had little to prepare. The tiled room was already bare of all but the meanest necessities. The red lamp was put out, and brick and tile thus returned to their native pallor, all Petty Street and no memory of the far red mountains.

And thus, to the satisfaction of one insignificant spirit, the Nightingale was quit of Petty Street, and Petty Street was rid of the Nightingale.

All would be as it ought to be, as (to the frail, fond memory that was the phantom) it always had been. The singer would go to the Palace Aster, be admired, neglected, rusted out, and thrown into some storeroom, as is the fate of all fine things; the scribbler would go back to composing his cheap, satisfactory songs. At least, of these futures the ghost convinced itself.

Excelsior gripped the sill like the jasmine-hawks in the highest towers of the Palace Aster, and listened. He tinkered a trumpet out of an abandoned horn, the better to funnel down to his garret the thinking murmurs, the trialled whispers of the Nightingale. He turned to that higher floor like a koncheomancer pressing against a shell for some rumour of the sea.

He heard the thin thunder of doves under slate, the earthquakes of spring-carts striking cobbleskulls, the rising roar of barter and banter, flattery and fatuous talk, threaded throughout with the discontenting repetition of his own words (tankards beating time like marching feet, lungs breathing defiance of harmony and melody alike, a formless rising tide). But no Nightingale.

Excelsior wore out his hopes and heart, burned all oil, spilled all ink. He crafted song after song, and even through his desperation he knew he had never written anything so fine. But the rare and blessed music was ashen beneath his pen.

Had it been this word, this note, this barest suggestion of weight or fire? In some way he had miswritten, misjudged.

Cautious even in despair, Excelsior shredded the gossamer spell into cheap sentiment and tramping rhythm, and sent it by nip-fingered courier below where, unintended, the words fell like fire-inches, like sparks in kindling.

*The rooms of roses burn,*
*The lanterns are turned high.*
*Petty Street, long starved for light,*
*Lifts a ravening eye . . .*

Few souls huddled in the dense miseries of Owl Abbas had ever mustered the will, the flash of flame, to strike out against the rule of the Palace Aster. What else, after all these centuries, had they to compare it to? They laboured, and they died. Even the clockmaker had only left, the better to complete her masterpiece: a singer that would conform faithfully to the restrictions and requirements of the Guild.

And then she had sent the Nightingale into the heart of Owl Abbas.

Oh, Petty Street and Agnes Lane, the Maresnest and the guildhalls had not *listened*. But they had heard. The Nightingale's voice had threaded through the work of commoner singers, lulling and lilting, softening the singeing qualities even of Excelsior's misdirected ditties.

The abrupt absence of that voice was like a sinkhole in a street, a sucking emptiness tearing the fabric of Owl Abbas. The citizens did not know what they had lost, but they knew it was something vast: the view of the red snows which only the nimblest chimney-urchins had seen from afar, the rustle of star meadows through which none of them would stride, all the miles and idly strewn space the clockmaker had seen on her journey out of the city, the bright air and the silences of hills.

Through Owl Abbas, the rumour of loss spread like the slow groaning of an overburdened beam, the creak of a rookery from whose footings one stone too many has been scavenged. The city-state, close-pressed, was a bone-pile at the base of which one littlest vertebra, or smallest knucklebone, had crumbled to dust, with a breathy sighing-out of its ghost, threatening to bring the whole tumbling down. And into the silence, the strident notes of Excelsior's thoughtlessly outflung songs rattled like dice.

"Where *are* the rose rooms? Whose are the star walks?" asked brewers and road-wives, wakening to the words. The catacomb-filers, who saw the paintings on the deepest, oldest walls, said,

"Surely these images aren't a dream. They are just there, within our reach. Did not we have them once? When the city was owl-quiet and the stacked houses were groves, when the Little Emperor's Council was a parliament of birds, and their auguries guided us more fairly than *this*?"

The workhalls, the orphan-rows murmured with Excelsior's songs—not the only songs of the city, but sudden-sharp and bracing—and pennies rolled into the mouths of the crank-singers. Barwashers hummed even as they watched their wakening clientele askance. Gross-bakers stamped the words with chalk-gravel and sawdust and the heels of their hands into the heavy half-day bread. Petit-bakers stretched and rolled them into the cobweb expanse of their thousand-layered sugar-dough. Seamsters and oxen-harriers who had never seen Petty Street built the words into the pattern of their bitternesses, knotted them into the whipstring lacing of coats, threaded the lyrics through the murmurations they took from door to door with barrelled oil and saffron.

"*The rooms of roses burn*," they sang.

The words had been handed down with no thought to discontent and discord, untrimmed for any fire but that which lit Excelsior's midnights.

Those who sang them did not look to the Nightingale's room above Short Street and Petty Street (home now to three little starved seamstresses such as might have welcomed a Mechanical, Light-Widening Eye like that the clockmaker had once proposed, and the Guild had rejected). The populace looked instead to the towers where the jasmine-hawks dozed and the Palace Aster peacocks preened themselves ghost-bright on the patterned tiles; their hands tightened on the tools of their many ill-paid, bloodied trades, and their eyes grew keen.

Meanwhile, Excelsior's dulling nib and clotting ink scraped on, as if they could abrade the imagined offence.

But when Excelsior next burned his coppers, the phantom, slippery as a cough, refused the commission. The Nightingale had gone too far away. Even if Excelsior had set fire to pearls and gold—even had the reluctant ghost known beyond rumour what they were—it was too thin to waft the distance to the Palace Aster unaided, let alone freighted with music.

The banks the Nightingale's voice had carved in Excelsior's soul grew dry and the riverbed parched, weeds of ditties rank where willows of song had trailed.

Even the customary rattle and beat of Owl Abbas had grown sick and strident. The overwound springs of cart and boat shrieked, the middens steamed and smouldered.

A fever found its way into Excelsior. He could not rest. The ink dried, but he scribbled on in oil and soot; the nibs broke, and he scraped out staves with wire and nail; the paper slid from his table, the copper lay neglected on the floor and the music went to seed, etched on board and beam, glass and door.

The Phantom of the Window-sash watched, dispassionate. This would pass, and if it did not, then this scribbler would die and another take his place. Madness took scribblers just as falling took pigeon-gatherers, as cogs took mill-workers, and time took phantoms.

Once a simple temple in a grove, the Palace Aster had grown decadent and cancerous over grass and tree, over its own simpler stylings, over even the first streets of Owl Abbas.

Through gates and corridors, ballrooms that had been market squares and parlours that had been common greens, where silk and wax flowers hung now in silver baskets from gilded gallows, the Nightingale was led.

The faint messenger-spirit was wise, thought the Nightingale. This, and not the citizenry, was what the Nightingale had been designed to capture.

Through corridors the walls of which were lined with facades of plundered houses, under arched roofs painted like forgotten skies, the voicehounds brought their quarry, and handed the Nightingale over to the nobles.

They brought the Nightingale to the heights of the Palace Aster—galleries and balconies, lace bridges, the roof-walks where the denizens of the Imperial Aviary strutted and fluttered to the accompaniment of flautists imported to teach them better musicality.

Into a chamber scrubbed clean of its last inhabitant the Nightingale was taken, and there washed and oiled, polished and gowned, clad in velvet the colour of the mountains, the tint of the light that had burned in the little room above Petty Street.

"We have found the voice you sought," the courtiers told the Little Emperor, while the voicehounds, ignored, circled and grumbled among themselves, gnawing out their bitterness in the words they'd heard sung in the streets.

The finest composers (brought long since to the Palace Aster and left to languish in corners and gardens) were discomposed and discommoded, divested of sheets of chorales and anthems.

These were finished, polished things, every nuance of voice directed, and for all the Nightingale's powers the music had the staid elegance that Excelsior's lacked.

Only the voicehounds noticed anything amiss. The Little Emperor was already bored.

Lust and love and loss; hopeless naïveté and ground-down wisdom; soot-etched, fire-branded, blade-cut, wheel-crushed, ill-rested, underfed. Thus the merry folk of Owl Abbas.

To them, the high, dying falls, the heart-cries Excelsior had intended for the Nightingale, took new meaning. This is what the songs proclaimed: the lily-towers, the jasmine-hawks, the Little Emperor and the Palace Aster must, should, *would* fall.

Excelsior, racked by sickness, heard voices raised in Petty Street. It was music, he realised, of a sort. A passion greater than that of youth, more violent than that of love.

*I could write for this,* he thought, tracing twitching marks in the dust of his garret floor, barely alarming the little spiders that had begun to blanket him.

Excelsior, so poorly fitted to be a revolutionary, such an unwitting conductor of dissent, tapped on the floor a martial drumbeat that only the Phantom of the Window-sash, frowning, felt. If a musical affair high above the streets might have disturbed the rooftop dwellers, a burning of roofs—whether in a fit of revolutionary enthusiasm or political retribution—was infinitely more to be deplored.

The ghost was dimly aware that this, after untold years and hauntings, might be its end: sifting as ash down on broken spring-carts. That this was likely also to be Excelsior's end did not overly concern it.

But oh, this had been too great a mischief.

Having mustered a faint discontent, it slipped out by the window and wafted over the greasy canals, through slums and barricades, borne on the breath and voices of marchers, lifted by the songs of bakers (their long, heat-hardened breadboards carved to spears), tossed by the shouts of dungmen redolent with ire.

Through gardenia paths waxen with bodies and over palisades spiked with sabres, it drifted into the Palace Aster. It blew like the dust of cobwebs among marvels and mosaics, unmoved by the unmaking of wonders.

Withering, it thought at last of the view from the room in Petty Street, and of the high widowing-walks of the palace, where one might see a mountain glowing red as a lantern.

Finer than thistledown, the phantom tumbled in the currents of bonfire-warmed air up the twisting stairs, and sighed, finally, against the finely turned ankles of the silent Nightingale.

Set free to haunt the Palace Aster with every other creature, curiosity and concubine marked with the Imperial seal, fragmenting its talent in the mirrored arcades of the Palace Aster, the Nightingale knew nothing of revolution.

It had been sent to win the heart of Owl Abbas. First, yearning back to its maker's mountains, the Nightingale had believed itself shaped merely to capture that heart with beauty.

Then the singer had thought itself to be kidnapper and assassin, but here it had reached the centre and found nothing to bear away. The Little Emperor was merely a man, and could contain the city-state only by letting it slip endlessly through his hands. An ear and heart so lightly lifted were as easy to grasp as smoke. Ringed as they were by flame and riot, they would soon become smoke in truth.

Now, the Nightingale lifted its visitor like a snowflake, save that a snowflake would not have melted moment by moment on the cold brass of the singer's palm.

"Strange spirit," said the Nightingale, tuneless. "My maker-mistress sent me to bring back the heart of Owl Abbas. But it is too vast for me to carry, and too bright. See how the walls shine, like my lantern."

The voice that had never before spoken without singing scraped the phantom's being like steel on porcelain. It writhed a little, weakly.

"I listened to you once, and here I am," said the Nightingale. "I will not say you led me astray. It was I who was not adequate to my task. Am I to follow you again?"

They left the Palace Aster of the heights and followed the groaning of draughts through tower and tunnel. They departed the halls and salons where mirrors splintered and paintings bubbled, and crept into the lowest palace, that composed of cellars and basements, new and old and ancient, and each filled with the surfeit of every beauty, every luxury, every excess, and somewhere—who knows?—the dusty reliquary that contained the bones of the last idle owl.

"Perhaps the heart is here," said the Nightingale. But there was riot and looting overhead, and no time to search those unnumbered cells and dungeons.

Through storeroom and oubliette, sewer and gutter they hastened, phantom and Nightingale. They slipped past the guards, the crowds, they elbowed through mob and melee. Buildings burned around them, the cobbleskulls ascended in bone-smoke while spirit-lamps, bursting, gave up their ghosts. Once only they paused, on the street of guildhalls, to take the great signet of the Elevated Guild of Horologists and Artificers from the rubble. Then they hastened on.

Fire melted the Little Emperor's seal on the Nightingale's shoulder, and wisped shreds from the phantom like steam. And as they fled, they heard, beaten into blunt weapons, into anthems and banners, the songs of Excelsior.

Excelsior did not know what he had wrought.

*There are feet upon the stair*, he thought. *People will want words.* But he had none left. The ink in its well had dried to dust, the nibs rusted on the floor, spiders spun in his hair. *It is chill. Perhaps they want paper for their hearths*, he thought. *They will not find enough here.* For all the fire below, he saw frost in the window, curling from the webs he had etched there in his first passionate shyness.

*They will take the copper-shavings*, he thought. *Let them, someone may get use of them.* He did not even have strength, now, to burn them for the faithless ghost as a last legacy.

The door latch lifted, and a creature walked in.

The Nightingale's palace robes had been eaten away by spark and flame, threads of precious metals imparting the briefest of strength to the Phantom of the Window-sash, which clung still around the throat of silver and mahogany pipes.

The bonfire light danced like drums through the Nightingale's hollow cage of ribs, the sliding sheets of ebony and quartz that shielded bellows and bells.

The Nightingale looked about the garret, read singingly the ravings etched into bench and board.

"This is the hand that wrote the songs you brought me, strange spirit," said the Nightingale. "Yet these are the words the people with torches sang, all through the streets. I heard these in the idle-rooms of the Palace, and this in the tearooms past which the voicehounds brought me. You led me a dance, spirit, but perhaps this is the room on which Owl Abbas now centres, after all, and I shall have earned the signet seal we took."

Kneeling with a beautiful spinning of weights and wires, the Nightingale peered at Excelsior and said, "It cannot live longer, I see, as people live. Can it live as you?"

The phantom undulated impolitely.

"No," agreed the Nightingale, without reproach. "I see it lives as you do even now. Wishing nothing to change, wishing power beyond what it was built for."

The long decorative fingers, designed to accompany music and elaborate a beat upon the air, now probed the skull, the throat, the diminishing softnesses that still enclosed Excelsior.

"How does one get in?" the Nightingale asked the phantom. "How were you drawn out of your shell?"

It could not answer the question, even if it had cared to. Hatred, love, unstretched wings, habit? They had all eroded so long ago.

The Nightingale calculated. It had never had cause to be fitted with the knowledge of where ghosts came from. They infested the city in much the way of the seasonal senates of ash-pigeons and the sub-kingdom of rats, but now all the nests and roosts were in disarray. The city was rearranging itself, and who knew what would pour into its new emptinesses, as a singer stretches the air to let the listener's heart fall in.

"Ah, that at least I have done before," the Nightingale said. "It is all I have ever done."

Among the broken nibs, the slivered coins, the fraying quills, the Nightingale sought fragments that would fit its need: glass shards and a penknife not entirely rusted.

"You will understand," the Nightingale said to Excelsior. "There is fire below the stairs. Owl Abbas is shedding all that was. So, too, are you. But like a clock I must hasten time a little."

"Are you death?" murmured Excelsior. "I thought death would be an old thing. But for all the soot on you, you shine."

"You know me, songwriter," said the Nightingale. "Listen, and hurry."

"I cannot move," said Excelsior. "What can I do?"

"You will understand, and know the urgency," said the Nightingale.

Carefully, counting the seconds, the Nightingale unpicked the lock in its own breast, and opened first the cage of its ribs, and then the cabinet its mistress had installed there. It drew out the little drawer, cushioned in velvet. And as it did so, the Nightingale sang.

It was only a slight essay in scales, simple and hampered by the smoke in the bellows, the discord in a wire that had been jangled in the crowds.

"I know that music," sighed Excelsior, and his fingers wandered over the dust of the floor. "I had meant to write such songs for you as would spill the city over with meaning, and pull hearts from their moorings."

"You did," said the Nightingale. "Now, I must unmoor your heart."

"You already have," Excelsior began to say, with no more volume than the watching ghost. But the Nightingale parted his ragged shirt and with careful, unshaking hands opened flesh and muscle and bone. How little blood, and how thick, spilled on the floor. Not enough to save even a small phantom, though it chased several even older wisps, of the sort that flutter in the dust about bedposts, away.

"Your heart alone would fulfill my errand," said the Nightingale, lifting out that flinching organ, "but we might make something new entire, you and I: a thing I was not built to invent and you would not live to try. What my maker will make of that, I do not know."

To the third member of their company it said, "Will you show him how to *be* as you? For he must learn quickly."

The Phantom of the Window-sash, however, had no interest in further expiating its sins against Excelsior. It rumpled itself to the sill and floated in the air above the fires, breathing for the deaths of coins, ascending to the garrets-above-the-garrets, to bother pigeon-parliaments and rat-scouts a little longer, before it vanished altogether from sight.

The Nightingale stowed Excelsior's gory heart and gathered up the trailing threads of his horrified, bewildered spirit, tucking them neatly in place amidst the staining velvet that it had once, mistakenly, intended for the heart of the Little Emperor.

Then the Nightingale latched closed the cabinet of its chest. "There," it said, patting the metal and the panels of quartz and beaten horn. "Rest a little. I shall carry us for now."

In time, new scribblers would arise from the ashes, as would a new city and a new emperor, of whatever stature, to take the place of the one who (it would be said) had lain in state, arms full of treasures, while the Palace Aster blossomed into flame.

But for now, the city rioted and burned, and neither then nor later did it know or care that the author of its rebellion was carried out of its bounds, rocked within the ribs of the Nightingale.

"I shall learn to write songs through you," murmured the Nightingale to its little burden, as it strode out of the city gates in the shining night, and between the blue fields at dawn, "and you shall grow to sing them through me."

They reached the foothills in a glowing afternoon, where the leaves flamed copper. And it was in an evening that, singing softly a song entirely new, they climbed into the scarlet haze of the mountains and vanished at last from the history of Owl Abbas.

# *Skull and* Hyssop

"Get out of here!" shouted Captain Moon from the door of the *Helmsman's Help*. "Go on, clear off!"

As the captain's thin, dark form lurched into the Port Fury street, several urchins fled, leaving their victim—a young woman in a blue weatherfinder jacket—to stagger in confusion. At the corner, they turned back to shout imprecations at the captain, but he ignored them. Instead, he caught the woman by the sleeve of her jacket and towed her out of the drizzling rain. In the brown tobacco-fog of the Help, he propped her up on one of the tall stools at the high table where Eliza Blancrose, with whom he had been enjoying a quiet rum and a discreet bet, waited.

"This is Eliza, journalist and travel writer for the *Poorfortune Exclamation*," said Moon, beaming. Eliza, arrested in mid-sentence by the captain's abrupt departure, doubtfully studied the new arrival before looking back at Moon. He was already a tall man—taller than Eliza—but altitude, adventure and (in Eliza's expressed opinion) lack of feeding had attenuated him. Under Eliza's gaze he became suddenly aware that he loomed like a crane above the stranger, and backed away. Eliza patted the woman's hand, beneath the blue cuff of the rain-spattered jacket. "There, there," she said, as if she doubted anything would be all right.

Moon called to the barman for buttered rum.

"My luck's turning," he said, as he returned to a tall stool. He hitched one leg through its bars and put a pipe, which he did not light, between his teeth. "It's not every day I get to help a weatherfinder. I'm sure you're much obliged, you needn't mention it. Those gutter-rats would have had every coin out of your pockets, wouldn't they, Eliza? Well, gutter-mice. Assuming you had coins to begin with. Safer aloft, you know. Above the clouds." He nodded upward with all the wisdom his thin, incautious features could display, but a touch of yearning had crept in with those last words.

"You're a terrible liar, Moon," said Eliza affectionately. "Port Fury isn't large enough to sustain a criminal element."

The young woman had a long jaw which made her look both familiar and pugnacious, but she kept her gaze lowered and her chin tucked in below her raised collar. "Thank you for your assistance," she said firmly, "but I shouldn't be in here."

"It's an airman's pub," said Moon, "And there's no man more truly an airman than a weatherfinder, is there, Eliza?" The journalist raised one eyebrow, a feat Moon had never achieved although he had practised since childhood. He turned back to the other woman. She looked promisingly hungry.

"Do you need a job?" he asked.

"No. I'm here searching for my brother."

"Can't say I've seen him," said Moon briskly, without pausing for a name or description. "Look here—I've got a fine ship headed for Poorfortune, that jewel of the seas," ("Jewel of the sewers," put in Eliza with the loyalty of a true native of that city), "and I could do with a weatherfinder. In fact," he added, his eagerness to be in the air again soured by the recollection, "I have a passenger who insists on it."

"If I can find my brother, he could assist you," said the woman. Her speech suggested education, and a good one, but it had not eradicated her accent—an inland drawl from the country regions beyond Port Fury where the towns were too small to merit dock-towers. "This is his coat, not mine." She rolled up the sleeves of the regulation Academy jacket to show her lower arms. They were bare of the tattoos in which weatherfinders, for all their arrogance, gloried as much as any common salt or breezy. "His name is—he went by the name of Evan Arden—" she began.

"Not a bell," said Moon. "I don't run with weatherfinders as a rule."

"He calls them glorified wind socks," put in Eliza.

"No offence meant. Cally—he's steersman—and I get on just fine. My passenger, however, is very insistent, and he can pay."

The woman who wasn't a weatherfinder slipped down from the wooden stool and folded the collar of her jacket up further. "I'll brave your gutter-rats, captain. I haven't anything they can steal. But thank you again."

She'd made it to the door before Moon had an idea. "Wait!" he called.

The woman glanced back. When he met her gaze, she looked older, but her eyes were lit with a flicker of hope.

"I'll buy that jacket," offered Moon.

When he returned to the table, Eliza said, "Well?"

"In luck," said Moon, bundling up the jacket.

"The trick with luck," said Eliza, lifting her glass, "is holding onto it."

Mr Fuille was a Level 7 State Scientist (according to his papers, his card, the labels on his luggage and his self-introduction). Grey-suited and -featured, he stood on the platform of the middle docks and regarded the *Hyssop* closely. After a morning of being loaded with crates labelled FRAGILE, LIVE BEWARE and BIOLOGICAL SPECIMENS, the *Hyssop* hung heavy from her supports, trapped in the sluggish shadows of the docks and out of the high crisp winds. Her holds were pungent with crowded boxes, and Port Fury sparrows and the odd raven perched and flew from spar to strut to gangplank.

To Captain Moon, fidgeting beside his passenger and willing the ravens away, Fuille's patient inspection seemed malevolent.

"I must be satisfied, sir," continued Fuille, "that all codes and authorities are, have been, and will continue to be complied with. Especially as we are to make the crossing in a single stage, in such a diminutive vessel."

Moon was anxious to be away from Port Fury, with its codes and laws and Imperial interests, and had hoped that his passenger shared that eagerness. Now, choking down his impatience, the captain forced himself to conduct Mr Fuille once more around the ship, directing the scientist's attention to orderly preparations and regulation outfitting—rubberised equipment to prevent sparks, correct ice insulation and sighting-glass—and steering the man deftly away from the freshest paintwork.

"I saw three deckhands," said Mr Fuille at last.

"Two," said Moon, as he watched the scientist's ashen fingers tap a beat on the railing. "Cally is steersman. Tomasch and Alban are more—everything-hands."

"A very small crew for a vessel of these specifications. Possibly the minimum required for compliance with the *Poorfortune People's Aviation and Elevation Cargo and Vessel Handling Code*, which being declared by the port of destination is, I must accept, the applicable document. But I observed no weatherfinder. It specifically says in the *Imperial and Transcontinental Standards and Accord* that—"

"—and this is where we keep him," said Moon, pointing to his showpiece. In truth the storeroom was the size of a coffin, but the blue regulation-issue weatherfinder jacket was artistically draped over a hook on the door. "I'm afraid he is somewhat, er, under the weather. As they say. Landsickness. He'll return to us shortly. You said you were anxious to make good time?" He shepherded Fuille back to the single passenger cabin at the rear of the *Hyssop*, already crowded with Fuille's luggage (elegant and extensive luggage, viewed beside the canvas ditty bags and matildas the crew had slung across from the docks). Having installed his passenger there, Moon stepped onto the dock to sign, with Cally, the last forms standing between the *Hyssop* and freedom.

From this spot, he surveyed his little ship. The canvas and rubber of her gas cushions was striped red and yellow. He had painted the hull garish black and red, with long blue luck-eyes on the sides. The figurehead, which held a heavy lantern suspended by chains from her hands, was picked out in mercilessly lifelike colours. Moon looked at her with love. Underneath the paint and canvas, for those who had eyes to see, she had the bones of an elegant and venerable vessel, the soul of a more romantic age. Only the knowledge of the passenger sitting like a canker in the cabin dulled his pride in the *Hyssop*.

"If you ever gaze at a woman like that, dear Captain, I'll eat my hat," said a merry voice from above.

"That would be a shame, Eliza," said Moon. He looked up. She was leaning over a railing, on her way to the highest level of the docks. From where he stood Moon could see the sleek curve of the *Orient*, the long, swift cruise ship on which she had a berth. "It is a very smart hat."

"And that," conceded Eliza, touching one gloved hand to her hair, "is a particularly stylish paint job. Your taste is remarkable, the more so considering your, ah—finances, my poor Captain. You should have been a pirate."

"There is time yet," said Moon. "Besides, 'no man is poor or alone who owns a ship.'"

"Or otherwise acquires one."

Moon added as an afterthought, "You, of course, are always welcome aboard. The boys took a liking to you. We're taking the direct route—I will arrange a thrilling voyage for your readers."

"The colours would clash with my dress," said Eliza. "Besides—" She broke off with pointed tact.

"I told you, the *Hyssop* can make the voyage, easily. She was flying before they ever thought of making your fine cruise ships. I'll wager we'll have a smoother trip."

Eliza tossed her head. "I was going to say, you couldn't afford me."

"You take payment for favourable reviews?" he asked.

"It would take payment to get a favourable review of that tub," said Eliza. "It's no pleasure craft. Get me a good story one day, Captain Moon, and a ship that's steadier on the stomach, and maybe I'll fly with you. Till then, find me in Poorfortune, for I have news to tell you when you get there."

"I'll race you," said Moon rashly.

Eliza went on up, laughing.

"News of what?" he shouted up, after a moment.

"It will keep!" Eliza called back, and then the next platform of the dock tower hid her from his sight.

On the second day out from Port Fury, and already well clear of the seaports and land, the *Hyssop* caught a bitterwind. Ice crackled on the rails and glass shieldings, and vanished again like smoke. The ship had been designed to sail with the wind, and refitted by previous owners to be propelled by modern power and manned by a very small crew, currently made up of Cally and his sons. Moon, who believed that sense, experience and attention would beat an academy-trained weatherfinder any day, and cost less, was standing at the tiller, planning further renovations and contentedly watching the sky through the glass dome of the steering deck when Mr Fuille flushed out the stowaway.

The sounds of pursuit began below Moon's feet, became accompanied by the cries of Tomasch and Alban, rose up through the bowels of the *Hyssop* and spilled onto the deck. The steersman remained carefully deaf, and there were no shouts of fire or leakage, so Moon waited until the tumult died. Then he tucked his unlit pipe into the pocket of his fur-lined coat, regretfully handed the tiller over to Cally, and wandered out to see what had caused the fuss.

Mr Fuille, his face greyer than usual, his shoulders hunched against the cold, confronted Moon amidships. "I am a Level 7 State Scientist," he said. "Their Majesties' Government will not be at all pleased to know that my cargo was being rifled through by ship's rats!"

"Rats?" said Moon.

"Vile, vagabond—" said Fuille, beginning to sputter.

"Ah," said Moon.

Tomasch was leaning over the side, a gloved hand raised against the swirl of ice-air which peeled around the wind shields. Moon joined him. For a moment his attention was caught and whipped away by the wind, the vast blue sphere of the empty world in which the ship hung suspended. Then he saw a flutter of cloth disappear around the curve of the hull.

"Over the side!" Fuille choked. "The cowardice—Their Majesties' Government—"

"What Their Majesties' Government doesn't know won't hurt it," said Moon thoughtfully. He turned to Mr Fuille. The scientist did not improve the view. "Hazard of shipping. But the problem has gone. Disposed of itself. Short duration. Remarkably."

"Send your men after him!"

"To what end?" said Moon, noting the alarm of Alban, who had not inherited his family's head for heights.

"There has been a violation of Government property!" said Mr Fuille, his grey eyes protruding. He shook with anger or cold, and his skin was chalky. "My experiments are delicate, carefully calibrated. If your crew has been nurturing a stowaway—"

"Get something for Mr Fuille to drink," Moon told Tomasch. "And get him a warmer coat." When they had gone into Fuille's cabin, Moon stood scratching his jaw. He looked at the clear sky (such a warm dark blue in spite of the ice) and the indicator flags all fluttering stiffly as they should, then went to his own small cabin, set at the front of the little ship. He opened the shutters over one round window. Through the uneven glass he could see sky, ropes, chains, billowing gas cushions, sky again and then the upswept arms of the figurehead, holding out the unlit lantern to where the endless blue arched into oblivion.

Moon ran a careful calculation of time and infrastructure in his mind, then opened the next shutter along and forced open the window itself. It slammed against the timbers with a report like a gun, and the ice wind poured in.

Moon, pleased, glimpsed the stowaway crouched behind the figurehead, clinging to the iced ropes and staring out into the void. He closed his own eyes against the blinding cold and, climbing half out the window in spite of his stiff leg, reached down, seized a double handful of hair and shirt and hauled the stowaway back aboard.

Someone hammered heavily on the cabin door, but Moon ignored the noise and frowned down at the stowaway who sat on the bed, wrapped in Moon's blankets. He suspected she was the young woman he had met in Port Fury, although the windburn was new, as was the ancient coat which had replaced her brother's jacket.

"That was a foolish thing to do," he said, conversationally. He had succeeded in pouring a quarter of a bottle of brandy into her before she'd revived enough to protest, and he didn't think she'd been out in the bitterwind long enough to lose any fingers.

"Getting thrown over the side?" she asked, indistinctly. Her eyes were closed and her lips chapped and bleeding.

"Not even pirates throw stowaways over the side," he said bracingly. "Not without enquiries. You're lucky you didn't fall. Unless you were frozen there?"

"I was going to jump," she said.

"Unnecessary, and a long way down. Keep your eyes closed, I can't get anything to put on them until I go out on deck, and I'm not inclined to yet."

"At first I was terrified of falling," the woman went on, "and then the wind cut through me. I could hear it in my head and my bones, howling inside them, and I thought, *I won't fall, the wind will bear me up*. I think I went a little mad."

"That implies you were sane to begin with," said Moon.

"Will I see again?" she asked.

He nodded, then remembered she couldn't see him. "With luck, the ship and the figurehead between them cut the worst of the wind."

"Captain!" roared Mr Fuille, outside the door. "I know you are in there."

"Lie down," said Moon. He pushed her back onto the narrow bed and draped his handkerchief over her face. "Try to look like you have a headache."

"Everything aches."

"It won't be hard then," said Moon. "Come in, Mr Fuille," he added grandly, unlatching the door. "Please try to be considerate."

"Considerate!" exploded Mr Fuille. "I will have you know—Who is that?"

"Evan Arden," improvised Moon. Livid spots stood out on the scientist's cheeks and brow. "Ivana Arden," Moon amended. "My weatherfinder."

"I received the distinct impression your weatherfinder was a man," said Mr Fuille.

"You would be surprised at the prejudice one still encounters," said Moon.

Mr Fuille narrowed his eyes and swelled slightly. "Women have not been admitted into the Academy for a sufficiently extensive period of time to permit any graduate to have acquired the experience necessary to inspire confidence!"

"As you say," said Moon mildly.

Fuille took a deep breath, then demanded, "What was your weatherfinder doing in my cargo?"

"Probably looking for brandy. Not to worry, I've dosed her up and she'll be herself in a few hours." The stowaway groaned convincingly.

"A weatherfinder should not be drinking on duty," said Fuille. "The third amendment to the *Navigator's Ordinance*—"

Moon wanted to say "You're just making up legislation now," but merely shrugged. "Old air dog, new tricks, no harm done."

Fuille glared at Moon, whose heart sank at the scientist's next words. "I will be giving information to Their Imperial Majesties' Ambassador and the Poorfortune Aerial and Aerostat Governance Department when we dock."

When Fuille was gone, Moon stepped out to inform the steersman of the addition to their crew. When he returned to the cabin, his stowaway lifted a corner of the handkerchief and regarded him foggily. "Well, one of us is lucky," said Moon. "I thought I was buying an empty coat." Then he sighed and looked regretfully at his pipe. "I also hoped to get to Poorfortune unremarked, Ivana."

"That's not my name."

"It is until we get to port," he said and put his pipe between his teeth. "You'll have to act like a weatherfinder."

"I've never been taught how!"

"I'm not asking you to read the winds. I can do that as well as any Academy-approved wind vane. Just—prance around and pretend to make calculations. Act like your brother."

"Evan's a very good weatherfinder," she said angrily.

"Then he should be able to take care of himself. Which of all the blue devils made you pull a trick like this, anyway?"

"You were going to Poorfortune," she said, and put the handkerchief back over her eyes. "That's the last place anyone heard Evan was going."

"You would have been more comfortable on the cruise ship," said Moon.

"Your security was worse," said Ivana.

Moon thought of his crew and conceded this. "What ship was your brother on?"

"*The Ravens*," said now-Ivana. She touched the wall of the cabin as she spoke. Moon had run out of paint, and the walls here wore their original colour. Her fingernails—short for a lady's, although her hands were uncalloused—caught on the grooves where fine copper wires were still set into the wood.

"This is the *Hyssop*," said Moon quickly. "No one's seen *The Ravens* for a year or more."

"I know," said Ivana from underneath the handkerchief. "I'm not the only person looking for it."

"What do you mean?" asked Moon.

Ivana paused before she spoke. The silence was filled by the throb of engines, and Tomasch shouting instructions to his brother. "That grey man is looking for it too," she said. "I heard him mention it when the cargo was being loaded. And there were papers in the boxes he brought. Records and schematics."

Moon winced. He didn't want Government trouble. "I'll kick you both off in Poorfortune," he said. "You can look for it together."

"I don't like him," said the woman. She took the handkerchief off her eyes. "I wish you hadn't told him my name was Arden."

"And I wish you hadn't stowed away on my ship," said Moon, but he was even less fond of the idea that Fuille had some connection with *The Ravens*. The sudden acquisition of this extra passenger, with less ship-sense than Alban, did not unsettle him as much as that.

"So your brother was—is a weatherfinder," he mused.

"A trained one." She turned to the wall. He could see her shoulder blades sharp under her ragged coat. Her fingers traced the lines in the timbers where the wires lay.

"They don't make the other kind anymore," said Moon with a smile, but she gave no indication of amusement.

Moon sighed. He preferred conversations with people who gave as they got. He would look up Eliza when they reached port.

"What do you do when you're not hitching rides to Poorfortune, Ivana?"

"I work in a doctor's surgery," she said.

"You're a secretary?"

Ivana made a noncommittal sound.

"I don't need a secretary," said Moon. "It's a small ship. Everyone needs to be useful."

"Even the scientist?" asked Ivana.

"He pays our way," said Moon. "Do you know anything about ships?"

"My family traditionally avoids the ports," she said loftily.

"Well, do you do anything useful? Can you cook? Otherwise I'm going to have to put you out the front again."

"No!" said Ivana, grasping his arm. "Wait, look." She rolled back and struggled to sit upright, then leaned against the wall.

"If you pass out, I'll use you for ballast," said Moon, freeing himself from her grasp.

"I work with doctors. I learn quickly. I know a few things—surely I can be useful. You have a habit of injuring yourself." She made a quick gesture towards his leg and Moon, who prided himself on his ease of walking, was hurt that she had noticed.

"The question is," said Moon, "Can you act?"

"I learn quickly," she repeated. "I'll play your weatherfinder, Captain, and I'll fix injuries if I can, but don't make me stand in the wind. When I was out there, it went through me as if I were made of flags, and all my nerves and organs were flying away. That frightened me more than falling."

Moon had felt the summer breezes and the bitterwinds, but they had never cut through him in such a way, and he envied Ivana.

"Well, don't tell Fuille that," he said at last.

Ivana, tidied, stood in the corner of Moon's cabin. He had helped her back into the too-large blue coat, and rolled one sleeve so that the ink would dry on her arm. "Fuille is particular," said Moon, setting down the pen and stoppering the ink bottle. He kept hold of her wrist and turned back to blow on the ink. Her fingers twitched. "All weatherfinders I've seen have tattoos," he continued. "I don't want him to notice anything odd and cause more trouble before I get him to Poorfortune."

"And after that?" asked Ivana. "He will notice, if he hasn't already."

"Notice what?" asked Moon, releasing her arm and putting the ink away.

"That under the paint there are ravens carved all over this ship. And I've seen what's left of the older paintwork, here and below decks. It's . . . telling."

"All ships have histories," said Moon, cleaning the pen. The ship lurched in a sudden gust and the captain swayed against his desk.

"And the figurehead should be beautiful, and pale," continued Ivana, adjusting to the turbulence as if it were a summer wind. "It's made of bone and ivory, did you know that?" She gestured to the books and charts in the cabin, the carved tobacco pipes, the creditable botanical tracery of a hyssop stem which he had drawn on the inside of her arm. "But I'm sure you did. You like beautiful things. You wouldn't have painted that figurehead like a dockside . . . like that, if you didn't have a very good reason. Did you steal this ship? Are you a pirate?"

"Not yet," said Moon. "Just lucky. But she is, as you said, a very beautiful ship, and old. This era of ships—well, they aren't around much any more. They were built to respond to every change in the weather, and a fine degree of understanding of it, and that doesn't suit modern methods. She wallows under engines, but she would have been fast in her youth. She could be again, with a true weatherfinder on board."

"But you don't have one," said Ivana.

"I live in hope that can be remedied," said Moon, settling back and filling his pipe using long deliberate fingers.

Ivana, still holding her inked arm away from her side, walked easily around the cabin, studying the charts with a gaze both intelligent and bewildered. "I thought the journalist said you didn't like weatherfinders, but there's always the Academy. These maps are the same territory at different heights, are they not? They're very handsomely drawn." She traced a pattern of weather-currents thoughtfully.

Moon waved one hand. "If I'd meant an Academy weatherfinder, I'd have said that. A blue coat and a degree isn't evidence of an ounce of real talent. The old weatherfinders, it's said, could feel the wind in their blood."

Ivana met his pointed gaze, and her own did not waver. "I didn't tell you that so you could use it against me. Besides, it was a—a madness. Altitude sickness. I've never even been as high as the port tower before now."

"Your family avoids the winds?"

"Maybe your scientist had hallucinogens in the cargo."

Moon was not distracted. "Most people don't believe that born ability still exists, or ever did. But what you said you felt—look at that book over there, the brown one, *Lives Aloft*. Eliza says it could do with an editor's hand, but it's an old book and that's what it talks about: 'a knife of blue freedom.' If I'd thought to look in doctors' offices . . ." He stood up again and began sorting through his books. "You'll have plenty to learn, I daresay, you can't just tell a steersman what to do by vague feelings, but books and experience will teach you that. As far as I can make out, it should just be a matter of translating for the laity. Do you know what it would mean to have a true weatherfinder? With that and a good old ship, a man could have the run of the skies. I had hopes of the money Fuille's cargo would bring, but this has turned out better than I could have hoped. You could be a legend, Ivana Arden. We both could."

"Captain!" said Ivana shortly. He looked up from his visions and books. "I'm only here to find my brother," she said, slowly and clearly. "He left us and changed his name and went to study of his own accord, but he's been missing too long. I'm sure Fuille knows something. I want to look in the cargo hold again."

"I don't think that's wise," said Moon, briefly diverted. "I'd rather not upset him further. He might still declare himself. Let's ask him to dinner instead."

Both the meal and the conversation were cool, for heating was minimal on an old gas-ship and Fuille's rage had settled to a peevish disgruntlement. The scientist only once mentioned Ivana's brandy, bitingly, as she hesitated over the simple Poorfortune table-service, but he watched the captain and the weatherfinder steadily throughout the meal.

"You have a broad experience, Arden," he said to Ivana sardonically. "Such an illustrated past."

Ivana looked at the single stem of hyssop drawn on her arm. The ink had bled lightly into her skin.

"She's articled to the *Hyssop*," said Moon, to draw Fuille's attention from the ink. "Everyone has to start somewhere."

"Indeed," said Fuille. He glanced around the cabin before narrowing his eyes at Ivana. "You have the look of someone about you, and your name a certain ring. Tell me, this penchant for cloud-watching—does it run in the family?"

"My brother—" said Ivana and Moon kicked her under the table. Her face was already too windburned to betray a blush.

Moon supplied glibly, "Her brother said she never has her feet on the ground. Old friend of mine. Took her on as a favour."

"Hmm," said Fuille. "One can be too high-minded. You should widen that experience of yours, before you get walled in. One can be . . . limited, staying too long on a small boat, or so I understand. It is not, of course, my sphere."

Ivana did not have Eliza's speed of reply, and Moon took pity on her.

"What is your sphere, Mr Fuille?" he asked.

"Aerodynamics," said Fuille. "It is a vitally important work, though often looked over or, perhaps, under. As you know, the lifeblood of Their Majesties' Empire and, indeed, of the nations streams through the currents of the sky. I have sacrificed my life to that work—the interaction of the organic with the atmospheric, that delicate interplay of wing and wind, bone and billow, mind and the mellifluosity of flight." He seemed lost for a moment in some glorious vision. Then he reached across the table and took Ivana's hand in his large, colourless one. Moon saw sudden distaste convulse her mouth, although a heartbeat later she had concealed it. Fuille, unaware, turned her hand over clinically, and said, "I should like to examine you, my dear. It is always charming to add new data to my research. My collection would, I think, fascinate you."

"You don't like him," said Moon, after Fuille retired and before Ivana escaped to the storage cupboard she had insisted upon occupying. His cabin was now uncomfortably cluttered with evicted buckets and pulleys, stored in the few corners and under—and on—his bed. "I can't say I don't sympathise, but in the interests of getting to Poorfortune peaceably, and getting paid, perhaps you could conceal it better."

"He touched me," said Ivana, leaning against the cabin wall, her arms folded across her body. "It was like shaking hands with a walking corpse."

"Just a bureaucrat," said Moon.

"Not that," said Ivana. "He's . . ." She shifted and fiddled with the latch of the window. "Unsavoury," she finished at last, as if the word did not satisfy her, and then added hastily, "I wouldn't trust him."

"You don't have to. Just don't let your nerves make you so chatty!"

"Don't assume I'd tell him more than I must!" sniped Ivana.

Moon was tempted to return in kind, but long experience with Eliza's robust company had taught him circumspection. He sat on his desk, crossed his ankles and waved one hand. "Perhaps he was fascinated by something more than your conversation." His evil genius prompted him to add, "You think sailors get bad, it's nothing on bureaucrats. Inviting you to 'see his collection.'"

"I'm not a fool," said Ivana, witheringly. "He was serious about his collection, but I don't believe he would really care to have it seen. So I want to see it."

"I don't," said Moon. "And I don't want you to go prancing about the ship with him either."

"I don't intend to prance with anyone," said Ivana. "Or be any nearer to him than I have to. I'll go on my own. You invite him in here again for drinks."

"Not until you tell me why."

Ivana glared at him. "Feminine intuition!"

"You haven't any," said Moon. "You took against him like—like a judge that just heard evidence. Like a journalist spotting bad grammar. Pure professional hatred. He's on my ship, and your job is to keep me out of hard weather, so tell me: What put the wind up you?"

He held her gaze. She did not blink, but her expression was searching rather than hard.

"I pulled you out of the street," said Moon. "I paid you for that coat, I didn't throw you off the ship. I might even want to help you again, though I don't know why. I don't believe you've told me any more of the truth than suits you."

At last, with an air of acceptance rather than capitulation, Ivana left the wall and took a step towards him. "Give me your hand."

Moon obliged, and felt his hand folded between her rope-burned palms.

"Fortune teller?" he asked, wryly.

"Not quite," said Ivana. Her hands were not otherwise work-roughened, but her cool dry fingers felt strong. If she was a secretary, the only ink he had seen on her hands was from his pen.

"That's odd," she said after a silence during which Moon sat and felt her pulse beat against his.

"What?" said Moon.

She nodded at the pipe in his pocket. "You don't smoke, and you never have. You get a cold foot at night, though, and the other foot—ah." She glanced at him with almost a smile. "You don't have the other foot. You're not quite used to that yet, but you hide it well; I thought before that you only had a slight sprain. And it explains the bruises. Your liver isn't all it could be. And you have an ingrown fingernail on your other hand and it's getting unpleasant, but I saw that at dinner."

She released his hand. "I don't know if any of that's useful."

"Nothing I didn't know," said Moon. He stared at her and she looked down at her own hands. "But I don't know how the hell you know it. What was that?"

"I showed you so that you'll believe me when I say there is something I don't like about Fuille," she said.

"Maybe it was a lucky guess," said Moon. "Maybe you're a—a charlatan. Or maybe you really are a doctor's secretary and can guess when someone is liverish. Try it on someone else. I'll get Alban, there's got to be something wrong with him."

"Please no!" said Ivana. "I only showed you so that you'll believe me about Fuille. I'd much rather nobody else know."

Her alarm was sincere enough that Moon subsided back onto the desk. "It could still have been a lucky guess," he grumbled, to keep the curious mix of discomfort and excitement at bay.

"Your journalist!" said Ivana abruptly.

"Eliza?"

"Yes. She took my hand back in Port Fury. She has a tearing scar, up her side, and her hand will ache from writing, at times. She wears shoes that are too small—"

"She's vain," supplied Moon.

"And she's pregnant."

"Hell," said Moon, mildly. He took out his pipe and held it meditatively.

"She didn't tell you," said Ivana, her face falling. "I thought—"

"I was distracted by weatherfinders," said Moon. "She promised me news in Poorfortune." He raised his eyebrows in thought, then returned the pipe to his pocket. "I shall have to endeavour to appear surprised." He supposed he ought in good conscience to have been preoccupied by Eliza's interesting predicament, but was more intrigued to find he did not doubt Ivana.

"How do you do it?" he asked.

Ivana, taken up by her own thoughts, answered almost without noticing. "I see the patterns in blood," she said. "More clearly than in air." Her focus returned to him and she said, "Not destiny, or fortune, or any of that, and I can't heal anything. At least, only by ordinary means."

"Doctor's secretary," murmured Moon.

Ivana ducked her head. "I see paths and eddies, what's going right and what's wrong. I feel it the same way I felt the wind, only people are so much smaller. You said experience and books would teach me about the wind, and I'm not a fool. I've studied to understand what I see in a man's veins. But the wind was so huge. I felt as if my mind was being scoured."

This revelation, beyond the legends of weatherfinders in his books, was too important for Moon to take in all at once.

Concentrating on the immediate issue, he said, "And you don't like Fuille."

She shook her head. "He's got chemicals—things in his blood that embalmers use, and anaesthetists. Not a sudden concentration, but little pieces, all the way through, as if he uses them all the time. Drugs that must alter the way he moves and sleeps and thinks. That's why I don't like him, together with the things he said, and—other reasons."

"He's a Government scientist," said Moon, but the explanation sounded poor besides Ivana's recital. He told himself he was put off-kilter by Eliza's news, but that wasn't it. It struck him that a Government scientist might be interested in Ivana's broad talents. But it was too late in the evening to worry about mad scientists, or the confidence Ivana had given to his keeping.

"What happened to your leg?" she asked at last.

Moon shook himself, glad of a lighter turn to the conversation.

"The People's Poorfortune Hospital cut it off," he said. "I don't have time for doctors—always saying you should have gone looking for them after every fight, instead of waiting to be carried in. I think they amputated out of spite. But I got out of it with a bulletproof leg, which isn't something to sneeze at."

"Do you get into a lot of fights?" asked Ivana.

"Not for want of trying," said Moon. His thoughts were straying again. "What you did isn't normal. People might be interested. To the tune of State Interests, and money."

"I know," said Ivana quietly. She did not say that she trusted him not to betray her. Her silence was more persuasive than words might have been.

Moon thought a little longer, until Ivana said, "You're looking at me like you look at your ship."

"Apologies," said Moon, pulled from his reverie. He stood up to show her out of the cabin and to her closet. There was much he felt he ought to say in parting, but he settled for "Just don't tell Fuille."

Fuille had indicated a preference to eat alone in his cabin for the past two days, relieving Moon of the need to be civil to the man or observe Alban and Tomasch's attempts at table-waiting.

"Where is that weatherfinder of yours?" the scientist demanded, as soon as he had taken a seat in Moon's cabin. His careful grey fingers toyed carelessly with the delicate glass Moon had provided. The port wine moved in it like old blood.

"About some atmospheric business," said Moon. It could even have been true. His small library was outdated, but Ivana had applied herself to it single-mindedly in the preceding days. Alban and Tomasch were incapable of conversing with her, so meals were silent, and she proved to be a faster reader than Moon, who had sat across from her at meals, his own plans unrolled on the table, trying to guess her thoughts from her expressions while she read.

She had stood, too, beneath the *Hyssop*'s glass dome, talking to Cally and staring at the clouds. When the bitterwind fell, she borrowed Moon's glass eye-mask, belted the fur-lined over-jacket and clambered about the sides, always too close to falling. She had gained her airlegs quickly enough, Moon hoped, to convince Fuille she had always been only an ordinary weatherfinder after all, and not an untrained prodigy. Still, neither he nor Alban, who shut his eyes each time, liked to see her going over the side of the ship again.

"We will make Poorfortune the day after next, all going smoothly," said Moon.

"I count on you to make it smooth," growled Fuille. "There will be lawsuits enough if any of my cargo has already been damaged by the events of this voyage, let alone by further delay. It does not pay to thwart the plans of Their Majesties' Government, Captain."

Moon did not answer. As he had bowed Fuille into his cabin, he had seen Ivana descending through the grilled hatches. Fuille pushed back his glass now and stood. As he did so, he brushed his hand against a line in the timber of the cabin wall, almost idly. "It is a very old ship, is it not?"

"The builder would be flattered," lied Moon glibly. "She's a replica. The colours are based on a pleasure ship from the last century, but I'm afraid she's all modern, and cost considerably more than she's worth. Let me pour you another."

"How did you come by it, then?" asked the scientist, not sitting down. Suspicion lined his pallid face. "Even this copper in the walls is not cheap."

"Very accurate, isn't she?" said Moon. "On the surface at least. Underneath I'm afraid she has new bones. Still, I call it good luck that brought her to me. Won her in a game of squares." He spoke quickly, but it was clear Fuille was inclined to leave. Moon did not know if he worried more that Fuille would find Ivana in the cargo hold, or that she would blame Moon for not holding Fuille longer.

"You know a lot about the era?" went on Moon, brightly. He crossed to the front of the cabin. "Perhaps you could give me advice on these window fittings. My friend on the *Orient* says they should be brass but I think it would be more accurate—"

"Window fittings," growled Fuille, "are beneath . . ." then stopped, slammed open the door of the cabin and left.

*I'm going to be down a weatherfinder,* thought Moon. While he waited for the shouting to begin, a shadow flickered through the light from the cabin window behind him.

Moon turned. The window showed blue sky and then a flurry like black wings. *Cursed ravens*, he thought, and then, *We're too high for birds.* He opened the window and caught a fold of heavy blue cloth as it swung once more towards him. It was anchored by something below, and the icy wind struck dull the sound of Ivana's voice as she shouted, "Pull me up!"

For the second time, Moon hauled her in, his foot braced against the wall. As he dragged her over the windowsill she yelled, "It's murder!"

"Not yet, but it will be," said Moon through gritted teeth, thinking of Fuille.

He set her on her feet as she said, "Necessary sacrifice, then? Hazards of employment? Those who live by the wind—" Her voice broke.

"Calm down," said Moon. "No-one's died. Everyone's at their stations."

Before he could close the window fully, Ivana gripped the edge with a thick-gloved hand. "There's something ugly coming," she said, and tugged down the fur collar of the coat to speak more clearly. Her voice was flat. "I'm only warning you because I'm on this ship too, or else you might have your fate and welcome to it. There's a coiling twisting in the air, a big storm. And I need something hard and heavy." She darted past Moon to get the rubber-dipped line hook. He grasped it as she returned.

"Are you going to stop the storm with this?" he asked.

"No," said Ivana. "Fuille." She pulled the line hook free and opened the window again fully.

Moon put his hand up against the cold air. "Fuille didn't go that way."

Ivana stopped with one leg over the windowsill. She tugged up the heavy goggles and looked at him, no merriment left in her eyes. "No, Captain. My brother did," she said. "He won't be coming back." Then she shook herself and added, with bitterness and no sincerity, "Not that you have reason to care. I'm terribly sorry about your precious figurehead." She folded herself out the window.

"No, wait, what?" said Moon, but Ivana had already dropped and scrambled to the base of the figurehead. One hand gripping the lines, she swung at the graceful figure with a will.

"No!" said Moon. "This is my ship! Ignore everything I said. I will throw you over the side!" The wind choked the words back into his throat. He slammed the window shut, latched it and turned, fuming, to find himself face-to-face with Fuille.

"Is everything in order, Mr Fuille?" he asked, with a reasonable facsimile of calm.

"I could ask you the same," said Fuille.

"Mere nothing. Difference of opinion," said Moon. "With the steersman. Can I help you?"

"I should not have thought he could hear you from here," said Fuille. "I went to my room to fetch my commonplace book—I keep a record of . . . intriguing artefacts. I thought I might have something relevant to your window latch. May I have a closer look?"

Moon stood, back to the window. He hoped Ivana would not try to get in again, and at the same time that she would not need to, and would not freeze to death. *You found one weatherfinder, there must be others*, he scolded himself, *you only have one* Hyssop. "I wouldn't ask a scientist of your standing to trouble himself with such trifles," said Moon.

"Nonsense," said Fuille. "You were so insistent before. It is the least I can do to repay your hospitality."

He opened the book and flipped through it. "It so happens that I have seen some ships not unlike this one. Less festively coloured perhaps." Moon, taller than Fuille, looked down to see a rough sketch not of a window latch but of a figurehead of unmistakable elegance, pale and long-jawed, with a lantern in its outstretched hand. Where it should have joined the ship, the drawing disintegrated into a network of carefully labelled lines.

Moon leaned against the window. "You should secure your cargo," he said. "I'll send the boys to help. Weatherfinder says there's a storm coming."

"It's as blue a day as you could care to see," said Fuille. "The rigours of this crossing have been exaggerated. You should secure your brandy—it has addled your woman's brains."

Moon thought he heard the slap of cloth against the window once more. He hoped his shoulders blocked the glass. If Ivana had not already damaged the figurehead beyond recognition, he did not want to give Fuille the chance to study it.

"Sky's deceiving," said Moon. "Said there's a bad storm coming. Could be here anytime. Small ship. Very good weather-finder."

"You think I cannot tell the fresh marks of a pen from the ink of a tattoo?" said Fuille smoothly. "This is very gallant of you, and I'm sure she's sufficiently grateful, considering it is as you say such a small ship, but I must insist, Captain, that you permit me—"

"My weatherfinder went down to the cargo hold earlier and hasn't come back up the hatch," said Moon.

Fuille's forced pleasantness evaporated. He spun on his heel and ran out of the cabin. Moon latched the cabin door and turned back as glass shattered behind him. Reaching the window, he wrenched it open and caught the line hook.

"I will . . . throw you . . . over . . . the side!" he shouted into the wind, punctuating the sentence by shaking the hook. He let go. Ivana, who had been pulling down, fell backwards and slipped. Moon saw her fall into the wind, only to jerk to a halt. She still held onto a line by one gloved hand.

Moon did not later remember how he got himself out the window.

The wind hit him like white fire. He gripped a line and dropped down into the slight shelter of the ravaged figurehead. The cold stung his eyes to tears, but he reached out, caught the front of Ivana's coat and towed her back to the ledge. "I didn't mean it!" he shouted as he hauled her upright. He couldn't hear her reply. He pushed her up towards the window. She went in with a convulsive struggle. One boot, or the dangling line hook, struck him in the side of the head.

The sky was growing dark. Dazed, Moon risked a glance at the figurehead. A panel had been broken over a narrow door at the base of the carved skirts—a boarded-over exit from the belly of the ship, but that was easily repaired. The true damage was to the figurehead herself—the paint had broken away in great chips where Ivana's first few blows had glanced, and the elegant folds of the back of the figure's robes were splintered and shattered open. Within the dark hollow behind them was something curled and pale—like a bird's talon, or a clawed hand. Moon started back and looked up at the window. His vision was blurring and he could not tell whether his grip held on the line.

Ivana, still goggled, leaned out the window, both hands out. Moon jumped up, caught them and fought both elbows over the window. Ivana pulled him in by the back of his jacket, head-first among the broken glass.

"I've got frostbite," he said, through lips that were nearly immobile. "I'm going to lose my face and my fingers. Do you destroy everything?"

Ivana put her bare hand on his face. He could not feel it. "You'll live," she said. She stood up, closed the window and took the eye-mask off.

"There's a body in my figurehead," said Moon. He had seen its empty eyes, the clinging strands of black hair. Skin and cloth had been dried to the bones, the skin mottled with tattoos.

"I'm going to kill him," said Ivana.

"Whoever it is, he's already dead," said Moon.

"Not him," said Ivana. "Fuille. He knows we exist now." Her face looked like Moon's felt. She held the line hook and looked at Moon as if she wondered what would show up if she broke him open. "How did you come by this ship, Moon?"

"A game of squares!" he protested. "I won it in a game. Fairly! A year ago! I was just out of hospital and a chance came—"

"Then why hide its real name? The missing *Ravens*—you must have known the bargain was tainted, you who wish to be a pirate. Did you also know my brother was dead inside the figurehead—your own private skull and crossbones?"

"No!"

"Were you going to do the same to me? You could have. All those little wires running through the ship into my veins, into my head so I could fly it for you—the fastest ship in the world? You were so happy to find what I could do."

"No!" said Moon. He was thawing enough to sit up. Ivana and the ship were slipping through his fingers, and he did not know how to choose. "I swear! I knew—I knew there were probably shady dealings, but there always are and I played fair. I didn't know." Behind her, the lines of the wires fanned out across the walls of the cabin, spread through the ship. He felt ill.

"Left there to die," she went on. "Staring endlessly into the well of the wind."

"It was a Government ship," said Moon, although he did not really think Ivana was listening to him. "I swear—I didn't think anyone would miss it. Not after a while. She was just an old tub, and—" *And beautiful,* he was going to say, but it was harder to think that now. "I swear on the ship—on my life. I didn't know." And he didn't know if Evan Arden had been still alive in there. He couldn't have known.

"There were papers in the cargo—very technical," she said in a colourless voice, rubbing her hand as if to rid it of a stain. "Experiments, formulae. And I know—I touched him. They kept him alive. They used the same drugs as were in Fuille's blood, but by the end he would have had more chemicals than blood. I didn't always get on with my brother, but still—"

"Fuille had a drawing of a ship very like this," said Moon. His lips were chapped. Blood came away on his hand when he touched it to his mouth. "His life's work—"

"'Mind and the mellifluosity of flight,'" echoed Ivana. She looked down at Moon, unseeing.

"Help me up," he said, holding out his hand. She looked at the darkening window and turned away to the door.

"Wait!" said Moon. He tried to scramble to his feet but, still half-frozen, had more control over his wooden leg than the other one. "Fuille went down to the hold. I told him you were down there."

"He'll be angry then," said Ivana placidly. She hefted the line hook, stepped out and closed the door behind her.

Moon could not bring himself to lean against the cabin wall with its tracery of wires, and did not think calling for help would simplify matters. He levered himself up to sit on the edge of his desk and waited for life to return to his limbs. The wooden shutter banged in the ice wind. Moon lunged across the cabin and slammed it closed. Luck couldn't be out forever, it would turn and he could get another ship—besides, he told himself, this one was losing its charms. The thought did not comfort him. He was leaning his forehead against the shutter, seeing again the weatherfinder plunge backwards into air, when Cally entered the cabin.

"Pardon me, Captain," he said, "But I wasn't sure all was well. I was singing-out before, and no answer, and Tomasch said he saw someone out on the figurehead. Again. Wouldn't have believed it if it had been Alban said it, but there it is."

"I'm fine," said Moon, straightening. "Is that all?"

"Storm's coming. And passenger's not best pleased," said the steersman.

A shot rang out on deck.

Fuille's pistol was a heavy one. The shot had thrown Ivana to the deck like a fist. She lay sprawled on the darkening timbers, hand clutched over what was left of her shoulder.

Tomasch had already seized Fuille, but before Alban could, at his direction, secure the pistol, the scientist fired again. Moon fell, nearly at Ivana's side. The steersman sprang forward and dashed the gun from the scientist's hand. It skittered across the deck to Moon's feet.

The shot stunned Moon, and he was numb to the feel of blood slick beneath his hand, but he had fallen too often in the early days of his wooden leg to be much dazed by the fall itself. He was conscious of a gathering anger—Fuille would not take his leg too. It had been too hard-won.

Moon sat up, felt splinters where the bullet had struck and reached for the gun.

"I'd better get to the tiller, sir," said Cally, and made himself scarce.

"It was self-defence!" said the scientist. "I did not shoot to kill. I could have, but I did not. I requisition this woman on the authority of Their Imperial Majesties' Government—!"

"On my ship, I'm the government," interrupted Moon. He stood up stiffly and limped towards Fuille, who gaped. Moon put the muzzle of the pistol to the middle of the man's forehead. Fuille stopped pulling against Tomasch's grip.

"This ship is stolen," whispered Fuille, his skin turning greyer. "It was part of a project of national—international!—significance. Don't think that by uncovering what may very well be a genuine weatherfinder, the consequences to you will be lessened. By your actions you interrupted and destroyed a very delicate and long-running Government operation, which, if disclosed to our enemies—"

"I am tempted to conduct a delicate operation of my own," said Moon, tapping the muzzle lightly against Fuille's forehead. He found he did not enjoy doing so, although Tomasch looked appreciative. "The only reason I won't is that I know it's a capital offence to carry loaded firearms on a gas-ship." He took the bullets out of the pistol and went to thrust it into his belt, then changed his mind and threw the weapon over the side. It was a more dramatic gesture, but it only relieved his feelings a little. "Besides, we're nearly in the Republic's sky, and what loyalty is it of yours that takes you and your precious experiments out of the Empire?"

Whatever joy Fuille's helpless rage might have given him was taken away by the sight of what lay ahead, piling up in what had been blue sky.

"Shut him in his cabin," he told Tomasch. "Lock him up and tie him to something. Don't let Alban tie the knots. There's going to be a storm."

"No!" said the scientist. "No, no, you must let me secure my specimens."

"Gag him, for preference," added Moon. Tomasch hauled Fuille away, struggling again.

He knelt down again next to Ivana. Alban had his bare hands clamped over the wound, blood welling between his fingers. Together they dragged her upright, but she passed out before she was standing. They towed her back into his cabin and propped her on a chair.

"Go do what your father tells you," Moon told Alban. "Heavy weather's here." Alban acquired a sickly expression but obeyed.

Moon got the sleeve of Ivana's coat cut away and had his own jacket against the wound before Tomasch, eyes averted from blood, arrived to report the scientist secure. When he was gone, she opened her eyes and murmured, reproachfully, "You were shot."

"It didn't take," said Moon cheerfully. "The good news is you're not bleeding to death. He really had quite good aim—that, or the deck gave a fortunate tilt. Or possibly, though I never thought I'd say this, you owe a little thanks to Alban. The bad news is that your storm is here, and I'm going to pour the rest of the brandy into you until you're able to get up and tell me how to get through it."

"I don't want to get through it," murmured Ivana. "Do you know what a bullet tastes like in blood?"

"Never tried it," said Moon. "Anyway, it's not in you. It went straight through, more or less, and into my cabin door—you can see it if you like. There's probably another in my leg, but I think I'll keep it as a souvenir. Drink up."

"Why?" said Ivana.

"Because Fuille is still furious and alive, and I'll let him out if you don't," said Moon. "I'm only asking you to report on the storm. He wanted you to fly the whole ship. Like your brother."

That had the effect he wanted. "You should have killed him," said Ivana, weak but angry.

"I want him to stand trial," said Moon, although privately he agreed with her.

"He's Government," said Ivana. "He won't."

"There are other sorts of trials. Tomasch reported some choice selections from his luggage," said Moon, securing the bandage around her body and under her other arm. "I plan to let the newsmongers make what they will of it. Their Majesties' precious ambassadors will have conniptions. Eliza would love to interview you—almost his next victim, and all that, and it's pleasant when she's grateful." Moon knew he was talking too much, and still he could not bring himself to say what he wanted to say, or to think clearly about what that was. "Well," he continued, "it doesn't happen all that often. Or at all. But I think it would be nice. And then I'll be properly surprised about her news, and a model uncle to the poor creature when it's born, and everyone will be happy."

"Uncle?" said Ivana.

"I know, and it makes me feel very old, but that's better than not getting to be old," said Moon, then realised that Ivana's brother would never have the chance to say that. He cleared his throat and went on, "But we have to get to Poorfortune first, so have another drink, please, quickly, then come out on deck and tell me the way through."

"How long have you been flying?" asked Ivana, her voice stronger although her words were slurred.

"I like to think we would survive," lied Moon. "But there's a reason small ships don't fly this way. Besides, I've never flown with a real, born, weatherfinder, and I'd like to say I've done it once in my life. I might not get the chance again."

"I think I'm drunk," said Ivana.

The *Hyssop* limped over Poorfortune, ragged and battered, listing where gas cushions had burst, her spars and lines tangled, but still aloft and still bearing its crew—all bone-weary, save for the captain. He was exhilarated by survival and their neck-or-nothing passage through the great storm. When they cleared the last shreds of cloud and broke through into clear air, when Ivana—shaken—had silently pointed to the horizon while Cally corrected their course, he had wanted to take her by the shoulders and dance her in a circle. He had remembered in time that she was wounded and he could not dance, so had simply pulled out his pipe and folded his arms, grinning towards the distant port until Tomasch shouted for help with the most urgent repairs. Moon said, sadly, that he saw no need for efforts beyond those, and as Cally, given long acquaintance with Moon, had insisted on full pay in advance and suspected there was no future on the *Hyssop*, there was no objection from the crew.

When Moon returned to his cabin, he had found Ivana asleep on his bed, Alban watching anxiously over her. He dismissed Alban, and stood a moment looking down at his weatherfinder. Her face was an unhealthy colour, but she was breathing and so he left her while he salvaged the few books and papers he could carry in a canvas matilda. He righted a chair and sat to compose a letter which would inspire the necessary curiosity and urgency in an ambitious journalist, and terror in distant corridors of power.

Once he looked around the cabin, and wondered if he would miss it. The thought of the use to which the ship had once been put made his skin crawl, but that was shadowed by the quiet company of the weatherfinder and the bond of the wild flight. Ivana was awake again and watching him with her long jaw set, but she did not speak.

As they worked their way in over Poorfortune at last, Moon dropped a package overboard carefully labelled with Eliza Blancrose's name. The sprawling city had its own systems for such things—by the time the wounded *Hyssop* was in position to dock, the newsmongers of the *Poorfortune Exclamation* and the *High Harbour Times,* together with a bevy of Poorfortune police, were at the low docks crowding out a contingent of eager civil servants on the service of the Republic, and several alarmed gentlemen in dark suits whom Moon judged to be in Their Imperial Majesties' employ. Somewhere beyond them, customs officers gesticulated, disregarded.

Eliza was there with the linesmen, and first across to the *Hyssop*, helped willingly by an appreciative Tomasch. She held her hat on with one gloved hand.

"Who are the police here for?" asked Moon by way of greeting.

"Whoever has the best story," said Eliza. "They're relentlessly incorruptible, so now that they've seen you with me you'd better get off this tub. Does Cally have the Port Fury forms, and ship's papers? Then you'd better clear out. Come see me at the Palm Rooms—I owe you for this story and I've a lead who can put you in a likely game for a real antique—"

"I'm off old ships," said Moon. "I need a yacht. Something white and sleek, with no skeletons in its cupboards."

"Less piratical, but you never know what your luck will hold."

"Or for how long," said Moon. "Eliza, can you get Ivana to a doctor, quietly?"

"Who?" said Eliza.

Moon looked around for Ivana, but she had slipped between the eddies of people as easily as if they had been wind-currents, and was already on the dock. "I have to catch her," he said to Eliza.

He swung across the gap to the dock, but his path was harder. He dodged a Poorfortune policeman, was nearly collared by a hungry-looking man with a notebook and shining eyes and caught up with Ivana at the first turn of the stairs. Her shabby coat was only slung over her injured shoulder, and came away in Moon's hand. He said the first thing to come into his head.

"Where's the jacket?"

"I left it on the storeroom door," she answered.

"Don't you want it?"

"You think I want a souvenir? What's left of it is yours—you bought that fairly, at least."

Moon drew breath. *The game of squares had been even,* he intended to say, *and just because it was chance doesn't mean it wasn't fair.* "I don't know your name," he said.

She didn't answer him. Above, the police were engaged with Fuille, the ship and the cargo. Eliza had drawn the attention of the journalists away from Moon and Ivana where they stood hidden from the higher platform. Half a minute might pass before they must be recognised, or vanish into the streets below.

"That needs to be seen to by a doctor," said Moon, nodding at her shoulder, clumsily but effectively bandaged.

"It already has been," said Ivana with a wan smile, and touched the sleeve of her shirt. If that was meant as any sort of compliment, it struck Moon as half-hearted. His work had been brief and ugly, and throughout the short operation in the heart of the storm he had been of the impression that Ivana was careful to give her instructions in very small words.

She turned with her hand on the railing and Moon said, "Wait. I've got a bit laid by, and there's always a game in this town. We—we flew well together, you and I. Fly with me again?" He remembered that the *Hyssop*, unmasked as *The Ravens*, was as good as lost. "I'm sure to have a ship again, soon. My luck will come back, it always does. Like the wind."

"You have to catch luck!" said Ivana, then shook her head and laughed weakly. "You have to hold on to it, Moon."

"You can't hold on to the wind," said Moon. "But who knows? We survived that storm—maybe you are my luck. Come, Ivana! I'm sure Eliza will put you up until I find a ship and more of a crew. She knows how to keep secrets."

Ivana looked up to where the torn sailcloth and trailing lines of the *Hyssop* were visible, sagging in the breeze below the platform. "I'm going home. By sea. I'd rather mend people who've been foolish than hurt myself through folly."

Moon, standing still, felt that he was ducking and weaving again, in pursuit of Ivana vanishing, only this time he could not see his way. "I'll get you a real weatherfinder tattoo, if you want one. I don't want to fly guideless again, Ivana."

But something he had said was wrong, or not enough. Ivana was descending again, faster than he could follow.

"Please!" he called down. "I'll pay you better than your doctor!"

She looked up. Her face was still too pale, drawn out long like that of the lost figurehead, and Moon felt a pain of double loss.

"You couldn't pay me enough," she said, disappeared around the next turning of the stairs and was lost in the human rivers of Poorfortune.

*A ship*, Moon told himself. *First find a ship, then a weatherfinder.*

"You haven't any caution," said Eliza merrily, arriving beside him with the expression of a well-fed cat. "Thank you," she said, releasing Alban, who shouldered his own duffel bag and hurried away, head down. Eliza tucked her arm through Moon's. "Poor lad, anyone can see he's not meant for a breezy. Well, there's sufficient variety of employment here. Now, come with me. I have a deadline and therefore am expected to be in a hurry. You must tell me everything. And then buy dinner, for I did beat you to Poorfortune."

As he helped her up into a high-sprung cab she said, "Did your Ivana get away, then?"

"Yes," said Moon.

"Was she pretty?"

Moon looked up at his sister. Her face was sympathetic, amused but unsurprised.

"No," he said, suddenly. "Damn it, Eliza, don't look at me like that. I'll tell you everything later. I have to go."

"I'm a journalist, Moon!" said Eliza, but he had stepped back and waved the cab driver on. She had to lean out and call the last words back. "Later isn't good enough!"

"And congratulations!" he shouted, but he did not wait to see if Eliza heard. He was already longing for clear sky, and pressing through the brown and crowded streets which led down to the old harbour, and the sea.

## *Ella and the Flame*

The people went out of town on foot, horseback and cart, to where the trees grew scraggy on the dusty hills. The house they sought should have been difficult to find. It lay beyond the hard ground of the rutted road, hidden by grey screens of trees, in as unfriendly a valley as any in that hungry country. No clearer path led to it than the faint tangled traces made by cattle or goats or the feet of a solitary child going to school. But many of the townspeople had been there before, on private errands, and the small crowd found its way unerringly.

At the rear of the procession rode the Governor himself. He had known the town when he was a young man gaining experience of the world, but now he returned in all his dignity. He had heard the grumblings and complaints of the dry-spirited people. It had been a long time since rain had fallen. They struggled to live on soil grown thin and shallow creeks run low and rank, while cattle and children sickened and starved. The inhabitants of the house that lay beyond the town had once promised health and cures, but their abilities had been stretched. The merciless drought seemed a punishment for relying on such frail assistance. Each disease, each misfortune assumed an air of malevolence. The Governor had assured the people that he would see justice done, and his presence lent an undeniable distinction to the proceedings.

The Governor was not surprised when the scrubby wilderness split to reveal the small house neat and grey in its unnaturally green garden. It had been a familiar destination in that youth he had put severely behind him. He was glad to set both memories and rumours to rest at last, like old letters cast into a fire.

Those who had gone ahead had already surrounded the cottage. The doors and shutters were closed.

"They are all inside, sir," said the Mayor to the Governor. "They will not come out and beg. They will not admit their wickedness."

The Governor nodded and then a slight frown troubled his serene brow. "There is a child?" he asked, and the faint hesitation in that hitherto resolute voice troubled the Mayor, for promises of governments had proved hollow before now. The fatherless child was grown undeniably like the women who lived in the cottage, and the Mayor did not think it necessary to trouble needlessly the conscience of one who would not have to live with the consequences of this day's activities.

"It goes to the school," he answered. "Your Honour may recall the teacher said that she would keep the children in. Though," he added, regretful, "some poison can only be burned out."

The Governor nodded. Unpleasant thoughts occurred to him of a girl he had known too well and castles he built in the air when he was young and foolish, but he put those images out of his mind and looked sternly at the cottage and the crowd ready and eager to perpetrate justice.

"You heard the evidence," said the Mayor. The Governor inclined his head regally, and replied,

"Let justice be done."

Planks and timbers fell against the door like the beating of a deep drum. The sisters held each others' hands and sat on the floor, heads touching. The beams fell like doom against the shutters, and the women closed their eyes.

"We will die," said Anne, the eldest, simply. When she said "we," it sounded so small. Just the four of them: three siblings and the child, so slight and brittle a number.

"We have died before," said the youngest sister, Sable. When she spoke, she meant all who had ever lived and died like them: sisters and aunts and brothers and uncles and parents.

"We are the only ones left to die," said the middle one, Mary, holding the child on her lap, although Ella had long grown too tall for such a seat. "We are the last of all."

"People have hated us too fiercely," said Anne. "Even those we once thought loved us."

"That man has hated us too fiercely," said Sable. "And I cannot believe I ever thought . . ." She fell silent and frowned at Ella, for neither Sable's pride nor her idea of family had ever let it seem necessary to her to tell Ella of the past. "Will you forgive me that folly?"

Anne smiled and shook her head "What is there to forgive, Sable? Youth is always foolish"—here she touched Ella's hand—"and yours gave us perhaps more joy than we had a right to. But death has always loved our family too well."

"What is it like, death?" asked Ella, still enough of a child to be sure the others knew the answer. Anne and Mary and Sable were silent, and the sounds outside were like the knocking of bones and the scattering of stones on a grave. To them death had taken on the features of a face once welcome, before it had grown great and regretted them. None of them wished to say that to the child.

"Dying is like going to sleep after a long day," said Anne gently, "when you cannot keep your eyes open however much you want to. You can struggle or go quietly, but darkness falls and all your limbs go loose and easy."

"Dying is like waking to a bright morning," said Sable, "when everything is so fresh and new, you are sure no-one has ever seen it before."

"Dying is like fire," said Mary dully. "All flash and flame and at the end there is nothing but ashes and cinders."

Ella frowned over this, for they had raised her to look for truth in stories. With no more questions to answer or tales to tell, they all fell silent again. It was quieter outside. They heard voices of friends and neighbours, harsh laughter of customers and schoolmates, the distant clatter of bundles of sticks and sheaves of dry grass.

"I do not wish to die cowering," said Anne at last.

"What does it matter?" said Mary. "No-one will know."

"We will," said Sable. "Here and now and for a moment, we will know."

"No-one will tell stories of it," said Mary.

"Do you think that because we only tell it to ourselves, it will be any less of a story? Whomever else have we ever told them to?" said Anne.

"To me," said Ella.

"There," said Sable. "You see? We must make a story for her to tell, for we have told our tales and now we must live them through to the end, but Ella has never told a great tale, and that would be a poor way for one of our family to die."

"Very well," said Mary. "We shall not die like cowards, but telling a grand tale."

"A nighttime tale," said Anne, "To make the sleeping sweet, and the sleeper wake new-made."

"Like caterpillars out of their cases, and embers fanned back to flame," said Sable. Then she remembered and said brightly, "There are pinecones which only grow into trees after fire."

They stood together, still clasping hands. The house was dark now that the cracks at the edges of shutters and doors were hidden from the sun. Only the light of the hurricane lamp fell golden and bronze on their hair and skin until they seemed creatures of metal and flame. It lit upon the pots and ladles, on the ends of the nails that came through the door, and on the fragments of glass that had fallen from the windows before the shutters were closed upon them.

They put on their finest clothes: Anne's gown, yellowed and pressed with age; Mary's go-to-meeting best with buttons at wrist and neck; Sable's red dress. Ella, who had not yet owned a fine dress, the sisters dressed in the prettiest things they could find. They made her a cloak of the lace veil Sable had sewn before Ella was born (which Sable had never worn and Ella would now never have a chance to wear), and clasped it with a colourful tin brooch.

The sisters put on all the jewellery that had been too good or gaudy, bright or dull to wear every day: their mother's rings and their grandmothers' pearls, cheap necklaces bright as beetle-cases wound around their heads like crowns, earrings hooked one to the other. They looped pearls and beads about Ella's throat and brow and arms. They pinned up their hair. From the vase of flowers (taken from the garden that would soon be crushed and trampled and salted), they took roses and pale jasmine to put behind their ears. Sashes and scarves hung at their shoulders and elbows like wings, and they clipped papery yellow daisies and soft lavender and fluttering ribbons to their shoes. Ella wore Anne's old dancing shoes, wrapped tight around her small feet with glittering glass beads until the shoes shone like light through windows.

"We look like princesses," said Ella.

"Like queens!" said Anne, and Mary smiled, and Sable held out her arms and spun.

"Be careful! The lamp!" said Mary, then put her hands over her mouth. Anne laughed in horror, and Sable snatched the lamp up in one hand and caught Ella to her side with the other, and danced on.

Outside, there was a murmuring, the sound of shouting heard through the thick wood.

"He can hear us laugh," whispered Mary. "He is driving them on to bay for our blood."

"Let them have it," said Anne. "They shall not have Ella's story." She turned up the light so that it threw their shadows crazily onto the walls. "Now, this is to be your story, dear-heart," said Anne to Ella. "So you must begin it."

"But let it have no Governors or Mayors or declarations or judgments," said Mary.

"How do I begin?" said Ella.

"Why, the way all tellers of tales begin, little goose!" said Sable.

Mary closed her eyes and, as if remembering something long lost, said, "Once upon a time . . ."

Ella began. "Once upon a time there was a girl. She was kind—"

"And good—" said Mary.

"And clever—" said Anne.

"And lovely," sighed Sable.

"Yes," said Ella. "All of those. But she was very unfortunate, for a—a . . ."

"Not a Governor," said Sable.

"An evil prince!" said Ella.

Anne nodded approvingly, and Ella raced on:

"An evil prince had taken away everything she loved and a great dragon had settled upon the land."

Sable jumped to her feet. "Let me be the dragon!" she cried. "Look!" And she cast great shadows with her arms so that they looked like jaws.

"It looks like a dog!" exclaimed Ella, scornful.

"It's a wolf-dragon," said Sable. "Go on!"

Outside, there was a roar of voices, and then a hissing, a whispering.

"Go on!" said Anne urgently. "A great dragon?"

"No, three dragons!" revised Ella, suddenly gleeful. "Because the evil prince hated the girl's aunts . . . no, her sisters. He hated them because they were good and wise and he was not, and so he changed them into dragons."

So Anne cast a demure dragon upon the wall, and Mary a reluctant one, and Sable moved her sleeves against the light like beating wings, and outside the whispering was broken by sharp crackling sounds and a faint acrid smell seeped between the boards of the door and shutters.

"And the girl wanted to rescue her sisters," said Ella.

"Of course she did!" said Sable.

"So she went looking for a brave knight," said Ella. "But all the knights in the land were afraid of the prince, and could only see dragons when they looked at the three sisters. And no-one else would help her because they were afraid of the dragons too, and of the prince, and they put their hands over their ears and teased her and threw things at her and chased her out of school and out of the town and wouldn't listen to her when she told them that the dragons weren't dragons at all, but really her family."

"Thus people ever were," said Mary.

"How did she save her sisters?" asked Anne.

"She . . . she didn't know what to do." Ella faltered. "Because people started to say she was too fond of dragons altogether, even though they weren't really dragons. She started to think perhaps dragons were better than people after all, for they were still beautiful and bold." She lapsed into a troubled silence.

"But she thought of all the stories her sisters had told her," prompted Anne.

"And made a few up herself," said Sable, "because she herself was such a bold, bright girl."

"And she thought that the problem was that everyone had forgotten," said Ella. She caught at Sable's flapping sleeve and said, "Because the people had forgotten the dragons were girls who had been their friends, and the wicked prince even made her sisters forget they had ever been anything but dragons."

"Were they terribly fierce dragons?" whispered Sable.

"Oh, very," said Ella. "The best sort of dragons, if they really had been dragons. They had great red wings and spiky spines, and breathed fire and ate knights and everything." Sable laughed hoarsely and put her arms around Ella and kissed the top of her head.

"Go on," said Anne, and coughed at the pale smoke that curled its way under the door. The crackling was louder than her cough.

"So," said Ella, "she gathered everything she thought might make people remember who the dragons really were. She found, um, hair in the sisters' combs—"

"And necklaces they had worn," said Sable, jangling hers.

"And threads from lace collars," said Mary.

"And strings from their violins," said Anne.

"And paper from their books," said Ella. It was growing warmer in the house. "And feathers from pens they had written with."

"And branches from their rosebushes," said Mary.

"And nettles that had stung them," said Sable.

"And all sorts of things from the stories they had told," said Anne.

"She knotted them into a great big shining net," said Ella. "And because she knew the dragons had burned all the hillsides about them and the embers would be very hot, she made shoes out of metal and glass that would not burn, and lined them with old dancing shoes because she knew that glass would hurt to walk on almost as much as coals, and she set off to the hills to find the dragons."

"She was a very clever girl," said Anne.

Mary wiped her eyes, for the smell of burning wood and the thickening air was making them water. "Did she have to walk far?"

"No," said Ella, "but she had to run. The prince and all the people were there when she arrived. The prince was trying to kill the dragons, because then everyone would think he was wonderful, but they were very large—bigger than he expected. And then he saw the girl and thought maybe they would eat her and be distracted while he killed them."

"What a wicked man," said Sable. It sounded like a wind was roaring outside the house, and the flame of the lamp flickered.

Mary sat down and leaned against Anne's legs. She coughed, and when she stopped she said, "Go on, Ella. I want to know how it ends." Sable and Anne sat down beside her. Ella stood before them, small but magnificent in lace and beads.

"The girl did not want to talk to the prince in case he made her forget too, but she showed him the net and pointed to the dragons. He didn't know who she was, but he could see the net was remarkable. So he helped her fling it up and over the heads of the dragons, and it fell down about them, and all the people saw that they were the three sisters, and the sisters remembered that they ought really to be people again. They turned into women and the girl ran to them and wrapped her coat and her cape and the net around them, and gave them the shoes she had made for them."

"What did the prince do?" asked Mary.

"He was very surprised," said Ella. "But he wasn't at all happy." Her breath caught, hot in her chest, and she coughed and gasped and made herself go on, though her voice sounded strange. "He picked up his sword, which wasn't fair at all for the only weapon they had was the net and that was made of things that were good against dragons, not against wicked princes. But the three sisters opened their mouths and breathed out fire, just as if they were still dragons, and then they picked up their sister in the net and flew, just as if they still had great red wings, over the burnt hills and the trees and far away until they came home."

She stood, looking down at them, and Sable took her hands and drew her down into their arms. "And did they live happily?" asked Sable.

Although it was so very hot, Ella curled up against her and watched the lamplight die behind a veil of choking smoke. She felt Anne's hand on hers and Mary's hand on her hair. Their breathing was slow, as if they were falling asleep. "Of course they did," said Ella as the sound of hungry flames moved around and above them. "For ever and ever, and everyone was happy because the wicked prince was gone, and the sisters lived very quietly in a beautiful house in a garden full of roses. But they never, ever, ever forgot they had been dragons."

The fire roared outside, and inside the sisters fell asleep one by one in each others' arms. Ella struggled to stay awake as long as she could, and through burning eyes and thick smoke she saw Death come through the wall and touch the sisters, one at a time—Anne, then Mary, and Sable last of all, so that they shone brighter than candles, brighter than dragons, before they vanished away. Then Death came right up to Ella and bent down and looked her in the eyes.

"Get away from me, wicked old prince," murmured Ella. "For I am the last of my kind, and I have told a great story, and my mother and my aunts are turned to dragons, and I am not afraid of you."

And perhaps Death believed her, for it backed away, and Ella sat up. The beams and burning shingles fell about her like leaves and curling bark, and the smoke billowed up and away and peeled back to show the midnight sky, with its stars bright as sparks, but cold.

The crowd around the house fell silent. For all the heat of the fire in front of them, the clear night was ice at their backs. For long years the memory of the chill of it lay like a curse on the town. The Governor returned to the city a broken man—some said it was because of what he had done, but others that it was because of what he had seen: a daughter who burned bright as the moon—bright as white-hot iron. She walked out of the burning ruins and through the fearful crowd and strode away, in her dress of smouldering lace and her shoes that shone like glass. She disappeared into the dry hills, and though for days afterwards fire raged through the trees and farms, Ella was never seen again.

# Not to Be Taken

Lucinda collected poison bottles. Great knobbly hobnailed clear bottles and fine sleep-blue slim ones, coffin-shaped flasks and flagons with a death's-head moulded into their sides. She admired them for their shades, their emptiness, the ways they fluted her breath and fractured the light from the coloured windows of her apartment above the grocery store.

When she was old enough to dissolve the trust that contained her past and smart enough to pack up her degrees and her curiosity, she moved back to the fringe of a town she had told counsellors and psychologists that she barely remembered. The apartment was clean except for the smell of flour and stale olive oil, a sparkling of dust disturbed when boxes of stored canned goods had been hastily removed by the grocer. The linoleum was faded around the footings of furniture that had been sold more than a decade before.

Lucinda pulled up the flooring, washed out marks in the walls (incautious storage, measurements made, perhaps, by a detective, the stains of small hands) and painted the rooms sunny yellow, the colour of soap and beginnings. She hung mirrors all along one wall, put shelves of bricks and beams in front of them and set up her collection (it was very small, then)—a miniature vitreous city, milky-old and new-glinting.

"Who shall I be?" she asked the self on the other side of it.

"Care, care!" cried a crow from the rain-blossomed tree outside. Lucinda, smiling, turned from her handiwork and swung open the window, shifting the street through its mulberry-and-amber panes.

"Do I know you, or just your song?" she asked the crow. The day was blue as cyanide on its glossy back. Between them, below the sill and over the footpath, was the iron awning of the grocery store: just the height for a child to crawl onto, to hide, or escape, or retrieve poisoned meat that had been dropped for birds.

"Care!" said the crow. It was not young. Lucinda wondered what else it had seen through those panes, and put a plate of fruit on the ledge.

"Never say I don't listen," she told it. "Now, crow. No-one else here knows me anymore, so tell me—what should I become?"

She decided to be beautiful, and busy, like the pictures in the news of vanished girls—loved, missed, desired. She cut and curled and brightened her hair until it was the colour of foxes. She bought dresses from the markets: unlikely flowers on old linen, the weave cool and heavy. She made up her eyes until they gleamed like wind-stripped leaves. She went to lectures on antiques and field mushrooms, paged through books on glass in the library, and expanded her bottle collection: ribbed and latticed, square and oval, corked and capped and stoppered.

Every morning, the old crow called by for breakfast. Sometimes it brought a young crow with it. "Care," said the old one. The younger ruffled the feathers over its shoulders, cocked its head and craked uncertainly. Lucinda unwrapped a parcel that had been left for her in the grocery store, withdrew a fine amber ampoule and held it up to her eye. The crows looked back at her through it.

"You're quite right," she answered them. "I should have someone fall in love with me, at least for the novelty of it, and see if I can't get a young carrion-eater of my own—someone to teach the real ways of the world." She lowered the ampoule. "Sepia doesn't suit you."

She made a list of men in town who had *noticed* her, and who ought to fall for a girl like the one she had made herself into.

She decided, for convenience, on the deliveryman who most often brought her parcels. She learned his schedule, followed his route through town (streets of tall beautiful houses, lanes where MISSING posters fluttered on telephone poles, roads that frayed into countryside, with scraggly trees and rusted cars, and sheds which might hold anything). She spaced her purchases; she wore vintage sundresses when she waited for him on the spine of wooden stairs that clung to the side of the grocery store. He was, objectively, good-looking in a quiet way: brown-eyed and brown-haired, unobtrusive. Slim but strong.

"What's in all these, love?" he asked one day, and his sudden smile had a charm Lucinda wasn't prepared for—she realised he was practised at not being noticed, ordinarily. He smelled faintly of almonds and sweet alcohols. "Shoes?"

"Glass," said Lucinda, and although she had never been able to blush, she kept her green eyes and her white smile wide.

She was sure he imagined leadlight lampshades or ornamental butterflies spinning in windows. She could tell from his nod and his smile. When it was too late to matter, he could find out the truth.

"Care, care," called the old crow, when Lucinda went back upstairs. Summer was hot outside: bitumen and small suburban roadkill and melting sugar. The air in the apartment was the colour of sunflowers.

"Care?" said the young crow.

Lucinda, who was not easily moved, remembered the deliveryman's unexpectedly forceful charm. "I will," she said, thoughtfully.

She increased her collection. She stopped going to lectures, she coloured her own hair, she bought only the types of dresses he complimented—dresses with flowers like the ones tattooed on his arms. The rest of her money she spent on auctions of damp decaying boxes of bottles retrieved from landfills, on bids for strange precious containers: nostrums and patent remedies and little clinking graves that still breathed out ancient deaths. Serviceable things from an age when what now could be found by any enterprising girl under sinks and in medicine cabinets, in stained plastic or fraying cardboard, had been enduring as well as useful.

"Care!" shouted the crows through her window at dawn. The young crow didn't have enough experience of the world to put its heart into it.

"You haven't any savings at all!" Lucinda retorted. "Go find something gleaming!" But when they brought her bottle-caps, she relented and shared her lunch with them, perched on the windowsill.

When the deliveryman finally took her out, he said, "I heard there were murders in your apartment, once. A whole family. It was empty for years."

"Did you live around here then?" she asked.

"I don't live here now," he said. "I've been saving up for a place outside of town. Plants. Songbirds. Clean water." He never would drink water in town.

He saw her home, and went with her up into her apartment, where there were no ghosts, no sign of murders, although she saw him glance around. The little bulbs Lucinda had strung at the back of the mirrored shelves made the display of bottles glow like a rose window.

"See what you've brought me?" murmured Lucinda.

The lights played all colours across his tattooed arms and his evening-shaved face. Venom green and monkshood purple, white concentrated into needles, whisky-amber. They hollowed his cheeks and shadowed his eyes, and when he grimaced his teeth seemed too large for his face.

She realised that she wanted him to like them. The bottles were, of course, the price she had paid to lure him. But he reminded her of them: a hollow-boned buoyancy, a glancing boldness, a promise of power, each angle hinting at the skeleton inside.

"Are they all poison bottles?" he asked, bending to examine them.

"Yes," said Lucinda, happy she didn't have to explain. "Or at least, things that might be. It's a matter of dosage, you see—" She stopped herself before she began to talk of her own experiments in that regard, but he did not notice. *Care*, she thought.

"Some women collect books," he said. "Or frog figurines. Or jewellery."

"But look at them!" said Lucinda, and stepped close enough that he would feel the heat of her arm beside his. "Look at the stories, the information, the history. Who knows what tragedies these caused—or prevented. Even the design of the bottles themselves, the attempts to communicate, to be read without literacy—see the skull? And feel this pattern—that is so you can find what you're looking for even in the dark."

He glanced at her sidelong.

"And look—" She lifted out a bottle and held it to the lamp so that it lanced out in all the shades of a trapped garden. "Prettier than emeralds."

"It's dangerous," said the deliveryman. "Here on display, where anyone could—If there were children . . ."

"There aren't," said Lucinda, sharply, and then corrected herself with a wistful sigh. It was late, she reminded herself, and success was a dangerous drug. What would the crows say? She smiled to herself, for she knew the answer.

"I could get you a cabinet with a lock," he said.

To Lucinda's knowledge, neither lock nor lid had ever stopped a clever child getting what she wanted. "But these are empty," she said. Most of them.

She set the green bottle down regretfully and looked up at the deliveryman with a slight pout. Lucinda had practiced the nuances of that expression in the bathroom mirror. She had let him think for months that she was buying vintage tumblers, or wineglasses, or hand-blown ornaments, after all, but it would have been nice if he could have been impressed by the truth.

He slung an arm around her, and Lucinda, who found she did not like the strength of it, wondered how to need comforting, to be comforted. She had learned, generally, to correct circumstances before that point. She leaned her head experimentally on his shoulder. "Don't you collect anything?" she asked.

"Life," he said.

"Oh," said Lucinda, and traced the tattooed plants on his arms. Some she knew the names of. Poppies. Foxgloves. Hemlock.

"What did you think I was doing with you?" he asked. He said it lightly, but as if he meant it, and tucked a curl behind her ear.

They were wary with each other, Lucinda and her deliveryman. Lucinda, after foster-families and facilities, colleges and counsellors, was at least used to that. But she was not used to being the one to tread most carefully (after all, a lover who is fascinated by mortality is as much to be watched out for as one who wishes to possess life). But they fell into the habit of each other, as much as they kept watchful.

Perhaps Lucinda had meant to stay living in her room above the grocery store, with its coloured windows and small records of a hundred deaths. Perhaps the deliveryman had never intended to take her home, vital and gleaming. Plans change.

They married at the courthouse in the crisp warm winter, him in brown corduroy and her in sunflower linen, and bought the house the same day—with Lucinda's name on the title, as a wedding gift. She had cleaned out her apartment, and when she went in to say goodbye to the grocer, Lucinda let her deliveryman assume she left the key there, just as she had let the grocers assume she was, like them, a tenant. A lady has a right to her mysteries.

The deliveryman had rented—and they now owned—a handful of acres outside of town, untidy with olive-grey trees. But near the house, the lawns were well kept, bright with flower beds, gleaming with greenhouses, sheds, a tidy fire-drum away from the buildings—new-dug, new-built, glowing with flowers, raucous with birds.

The house, however, was as rambling and shaggy as the trees. Three floors, broad low verandas and a few high wood-laced balconies. A water tank, its paint chipped away, on a timber stand. So many doors, too many windows. More, perhaps, than were needed for the rooms Lucinda walked in—more, perhaps (behind a false wall in the attic, behind a shelf under the stairs) than Lucinda knew. A gentleman, too, may know how to keep secrets.

But they repaired it together, and painted the rooms airy; they filled it with flowers cut from the gardens (pale trumpets and dim hoods and fierce berries), with shelves of bottles and with glass boxes of trapped plants, their roots pressed bloodlessly against the surfaces like ghastly hair, or fingers.

"Our house," he told her, with a smile that might have been pride. Lucinda decided to become the sort of woman who was pleased by that. She cooked—that amused her. She sewed plausibly. She studied magazines about country houses, and ordered a tall bird feeder, which the deliveryman, grumbling, delivered. But she rarely saw crows, and was often not sure whether they were hers, although once she found a gift of a rusted earring on the kitchen windowsill, and a locket in the grass below the bird feeder.

The first time Lucinda was sick (after wine), the deliveryman's lips also blistered. The second time, she felt ill after dinner, while he vomited blood. The doctor called the police, who went to the house. They looked at the poison bottles, the brilliant flowers. Whose were the bottles? Hers, of course. They did not ask about the flowers.

And accidents, after all, happen.

*Perhaps*, thought Lucinda, to whose guardians and classmates and counsellors accidents (nothing drastic, no pattern anyone would notice—Lucinda had learned moderation) had often happened.

It was summer again, and hot. The flower beds rippled and stank. A tree near the house died, turning bronze. The deliveryman said he would dig it up, cut it down, but he didn't.

The third time, only Lucinda was ill, and it had quite a different cause. She walked from the doctor's back past the grocery store to where she had parked, her fingers splayed on her stomach.

"Care!" cried the crows, from the tree outside her old apartment. Heat from the sidewalk pooled around her ankles.

"I am," she said. "I do." It was true, for she liked to have her way. She did not know whether the crows believed her. "If you visited more often, you would know."

The deliveryman was delighted. He treated her, now, as if she could shatter, as if a cold wind could wither her, as if she were a case around a rare seedling. She must not lift anything heavier than a broom, she should not go into town unless he drove her, or eat unless he knew the food was healthy. He asked needless questions about her family (surely something was known of them?), bought bottled water (she was glad of that) and vitamins (less so), and spent evenings reading advice to inflict on her. Outside, the tree withered.

Lucinda bore it smilingly, but one day when he was working she drove herself into town, to breathe, to plan. When she passed the grocery store, she saw the old crow on the awning, hunched and rumpled.

"Care?" said the young crow beside it. They rarely drew close enough to talk to her, at the house.

"Too much," answered Lucinda. Her smile had grown uncomfortable with so much use. She could imitate patience, but the months loomed very drearily ahead of her. She missed the noise and life of even this fringe of town, with its litter and unmown verges, its scandals and worries, markets and crows.

She lingered until late afternoon, although she knew her deliveryman would not like it (*What if you were caught after dark, or the car broke down? Women vanish*). When she returned, she pulled the shoes off her sore feet and stood inside the door for a while, wondering. A light had gone out of the house. It was not the deliveryman, for his mood was bright—and yet he seemed colourless, faded like a page in an old newspaper. Only his own colour, and none that she had lent him.

There were no flowers, she realised. Outside the window, in the fanning fingers of sunset, the garden beds had been dug under. The jugs and vases were empty of flowers, although the terrariums, contained, were grim in their marine shadows. The ceiling bulbs glinted off no bottles.

"Dear," she said, "where are they all?"

"They were too dangerous," he said. "I can't take any chances." She wondered, idly, if there were still knives in the kitchen, bleach in the laundry.

"I thought *you* collected life," she said.

He smiled, but without the charm she had thought she once called out of him. "A matter of dosage. Babies are small."

"And where are my bottles?" she asked, feeling herself shrinking inside her smile.

"My darling," he said, his own friendliness unshaken. "While you were out, I cleaned the house, to make it safe."

"But where are they?" she asked. "My dear?"

"I've opened one of the old rooms, the storerooms, and painted it. Come upstairs."

"When have you been painting it?" she asked from the bottom of the stairs.

"Now and then," he said. "As a surprise." He beckoned to her from above.

At the landing, she said, "How strange. I never smelled paint."

He looked at her from the upper hallway, and smiled. "You think you're the only one who can keep a secret?"

She ascended. He had, after all, once promised her a cabinet for the bottles. Perhaps he had gifted her a room. And if not—the future could always be brought forward, could it not? She was free to change her plans.

The door was half-concealed as a hall table, a mirror on it reflecting back the sunset outside. It opened silently.

The room inside was yellow and white, and all the things Lucinda had not yet thought to buy for a baby were there: crouched new and waiting. There was a crib and a cot-bed, a tiny side-room with a toilet and sink, an enamel basin, and a wide window seat.

Lucinda, leaning on the seat, looked down through the white bars—over the steep narrow roof of the high porch and the wide curved one of the low verandas, and across the garden, with its dug-over flower beds neat as graves. In the blades of sun she could see quite clearly other regular shapes in the lawn, as if there had been other flower beds there, too, dug over long before.

She had after all, she realised with falling shoulders, a few things to learn from the world. Against the world. Beyond the low greenhouses, the shade-cloths over disturbed earth, she could see a glint of light around the incinerator, as if glass had been broken and spilled around it. Deliberately careless.

"But where are my bottles?" she asked his reflection in the window.

"Put away."

"Where?"

"Where they can do no harm."

"Where?" asked Lucinda, and could not keep the edge from her voice—a child's threat, and less effectual.

"You shouldn't think so much about death," he said. "Think about what you're growing. What you will become."

"*I*," said Lucinda, "am not a terrarium. I am not a garden bed or a secret nursery. They were *my* things."

"You wanted this, beloved. Me. My name. My house. My child."

A child, yes, she thought. It was not meant to be this much trouble. He had been just a deliveryman with a ready smile, and flowers tattooed on his arms. There had been a new flower there, lately, on a day she thought he was working. He had said, when she asked, it was just something he had seen and liked.

"Can't you be happy?" he asked now—not pleading, just a weightless, pleasant question.

He should have been as angry as she was. She had been rude, after all his efforts. She turned and looked at him curiously. His arm was still red from the tattoo and, under that, scratches from some—so he had said—boxes. *He's amused,* she thought. *He thinks he knows I know something I haven't even bothered to suspect.*

"Aren't you happy?"

"I was!" said Lucinda.

He shrugged, left the room and locked the door behind him.

Lucinda stared at it. She considered who she was. Then, although it shattered that version of Lucinda, she shook the door and shouted, kicked it with her bare feet.

"I am going downstairs, now," he said through the wall. "When I come back, you will see sense."

Under the new paint of the window bars, the screws were rusted in place. Lucinda could not move them. She opened the empty closet, pulled back the rugs and the mattresses, traced the skirting boards with her fingers. She found nothing to use to free herself, no other exit without violence. She did find sanded-back scratches in the paint-under-the-paint, hatched like a calendar of days. There were stains between the floorboards.

Lucinda sat on the window seat and thought of the gardens below the garden, grassed over; the unused storage rooms. All the absences inherent in the life of a deliveryman. She was coolly certain that Lucinda—Lucinda with the fox-coloured hair and the vintage linen dresses, Lucinda with the aprons and the furnishing fabric—must die here. Had never, perhaps, really lived here.

She thought, too, of how the deliveryman had changed toward her that first night above the grocery store, when he saw her collection. Of how he had tolerated the bottles until now, displayed them when the police investigated their accidental poisonings. She thought of her name on the title to this place, and the flowers on his arm, and his researching, and of girls on missing posters and how only the crows, perhaps, would notice that she was gone.

*If I escape,* she thought, *and tell the police, he will tell them he is afraid of me. He will point out that I own this house, and have lived here since it was bought, and since he is often away and I am left here, how could I not know what is hidden in it or buried in the lawns? He will tell them I tried to poison him, those times we were sick. He will tell them, perhaps, who I have been, and what I collect now, and the trail of small illnesses that joins the two. And then other people will decide who I must be.*

Birds were fluting in the golden evening, sweet and mellifluous and . . . harsh. Lucinda reached through the bars and pushed the window open.

"Care! Care!" she called. Nobody would. The crows were the only friendship she'd fostered, and no doubt they were in town, outside the apartment.

But she waited, and they arrived: the young crow—glossy and assured—and, staggering a little on its wings, the old crow.

On the roof below her window, they cocked their heads at her.

She held out her empty hands. The crows, hoping for fruit or meat, picked and pecked at her palms, looked at her quizzically, then flew away.

Lucinda never cried, unless there were grounds to. She did not think that, until the baby could survive without her, the deliveryman would do anything to hurt her. Perhaps.

"You are reckless," he said to her through the door the next day. "It would be best for you if you stay in there and rest."

Morning floated in the room, as if lecture-and-linen Lucinda was there with her.

"I will be reasonable," she said soothingly.

He laughed, and his charm jangled like shards. "The way you were with the bottles?"

"I will tear your throat out with my own teeth!" said Lucinda.

"This will be good for us," he said.

That day, picking over salad and bottled water, Lucinda wondered about the snarl in her own voice. She could be that, perhaps—dredge whatever that had been to the surface, and wear it in place of her other self.

She heard crows in the trees, but they did not come near the house.

The next morning, Lucinda was woken by them. "Care! Care!" they shouted in the open window. They were gone by the time she was upright. But on the window was a flower, a dead mouse, a curved fragment of thick glass.

"Oh, well *done*!" said Lucinda.

When the deliveryman brought food for her, she put some out for the crows. Then she pressed her face against the bars and peered through to find what she could see. Little to speak of. The roofline was higher than she expected, for the height of the ceiling. She did not think they had an attic. There was a little window where there should not have been one: quite dark, except for what might have been the print of a hand on the pane. There was the bloody stain of rust on a sheet of roof tin, running down to the gutter.

The gutter which ran to the water tank.

Lucinda tossed the flower out. It fluttered against the roof and lay wilting on the corrugations. She picked the mouse up by its tail and flung it, awkwardly, calculating the arc. It went over the edge of the veranda, into the grass.

Lucinda considered swearing, but there was no-one to hear, and surely there had been more dangerous things than dead mice in any number of water tanks, and no-one the worse for wear.

The piece of glass, when she threw it, sprang and clattered down the roof, and landed in the gutter.

Lucinda did not like waiting, but she was good at it.

The day eased past. The crows returned for their share of her dinner. She heard them eating and muttering to themselves, but she did not stand up until they were gone.

When she did, she found, again, a flower—nothing very deadly—and another shard. Curved, this time, as if it were from the shoulder of a bottle. She looked at the shadows cast down the roof and saw there the shifting silhouettes of the crows. Watching her.

She turned it, catching the sun. "Care!" she said, to make her point. Then she pushed it down the roof, to drop and sparkle into the gutter. The flower she propped in a corner of the window frame.

The next day, there was a brown lustre to the blue sky. The crows brought her only pieces of bottles. She gave them more of her food than she wished to. She praised them—she hoped—with crow-sounds. Then she flung their gifts into the gutter.

Each day, the crows brought her more. A chunk of hobnailed surface here, a rippled coin of milk glass there. Lucinda held each piece to the light, hoping to see some trace of residue—she had never washed out the bottles, and some had never been empty. If she could find a way to poison herself—a little—so that he had to take her to a doctor . . . But that wouldn't solve enough of her problems.

And with each fragment of beauty, fragile as a life, but carefully chosen, freighted with meaning, she felt her blood thicken with anger.

"All of them," she told the crows. "Every bottle you can find."

They had been watching her. They brought her all they could fly with: broken bottles, unshattered phials, and dropped them onto the roof to roll into the gutter.

The deliveryman opened the door.

"What's that racket?" he said, idly.

Lucinda sat, innocent, in the window seat. "Perhaps it's hail." The heat pressed down like a hand.

"It isn't."

"Ghosts?" suggested Lucinda.

He laughed, easily. "I've made sure there are no ghosts in this house."

"Not even in the garden?"

He smiled, but he himself was somewhere far behind those eyes, busy in a hidden room.

He stepped inside the room, locking the door behind him. If he looked out, he might see the poison bottles in the gutters.

"It's birds," she said. "Shaking nuts from the trees."

"Ah," he said. "I can deal with birds."

Lucinda had never been afraid for anyone else, but the crows were useful to her. "Take care!" she whispered to the them, after the deliveryman was gone. "Don't eat anything but what I give you. Do you understand?"

They did not. But before they died, they brought some of the poisoned meat to share with her—their strange elder, their odd huge nestling—and Lucinda watched them convulse and fall, fluttering, from the roof.

Dry-eyed, she tossed the poisoned meat down to the gutter—she had no doubt the deliveryman had not been moderate in the dose. Above, the sky bellied low.

That afternoon, at last, it rained.

The curtaining clouds broke. Water sluiced the roof, washed the shards, dragged the poisoned meat downward, foamed the gutters, flooded the tank. *Good clean water.*

She had the few bottles he'd brought her, and before the rain began she'd filled the little yellow basin in the bathroom.

Lucinda waited.

The storm passed, cloudy grey to amber, then bottle-green, then indigo-glass night. The deliveryman did not climb the stairs, but perhaps he was repairing storm damage.

Morning was thick with steam rising from the wet earth. He did not knock on her door. But perhaps he had deliveries to make. Women to find—perhaps even to keep. He would want someone to raise her child.

A clear blue day, and clouds behind the rim of the sky. Lucinda drank sparingly, but she was hungry.

The sun set, and the sun rose, and set again. She hammered on the door. No indoor lamps streamed from the windows onto the lawn.

Lucinda switched her own light off and on, over and over. She did not know their neighbours, on the other side of the trees.

No-one came.

What, she wondered, if the water from the tap was perfectly drinkable, and something else had delayed him, and she died in the midst of plenty? Or if someone realised she had *not* been drinking from the taps, and asked other questions.

But no-one rang to find out why the deliveryman was missing (unless he was not), or to check on him (unless he had abandoned her here, moved on to another life), or to find her (but who would think to look for her, now that the crows were gone?).

Her head hurt, her spit was thick, and the tap in the little yellow bathroom dripped slowly. The earth exhaled, all its water being drawn back to the sky. The grass that nosed green from the garden beds was already yellowing.

By the next day, it might never have rained. The dead tree rattled. Lucinda lay on the window seat and stared at the ceiling. Behind her eyes, she was in the apartment above the grocery store, a college, a dozen foster-homes, the apartment again—in each of them, beneath whoever-she-was-then, had been the thin thread of herself, and in each place, power had been easy to find. Bottles and boxes and pills . . .

"*Care*," said a voice above her. Thin and ragged and raw as Lucinda's bones. The old crow, one eye milky, feathers askew, but alive.

"What have you been eating all these years, that let you live through that?" murmured Lucinda. "I haven't got anything for you now. But wait a little."

Old Crow dropped a bottle onto the sill. Lucinda pulled herself upright. The bottle tilted there a moment, then rolled out over the ledge.

Lucinda darted her arm through the bars and caught it.

Just a tiny one, old-fashioned and rounded. Still sealed. Or re-sealed. There was liquid inside it. Lucinda couldn't remember what it had held, or what her deliveryman might have put into it. She tilted it, blinding as a diamond in the morning, the last of her treasures, and watched it spangle across the roof.

"Oh," she said. "Well done, old crow."

Lucinda bundled together toilet paper, the net from the crib, strips of her own limp dress. She pushed them between the window bars. The old crow watched, dispassionately.

Lucinda played the bottle through the sun, coaxing it, until a point of fire fixed on the cloth, and the presentiment of smoke curled from it. *I could burn it all down*, thought Lucinda, who was used to being subtler. And there was an infant flame.

She brought the tinder inside, put it in the enamel basin, and blew it into life. She fed it strips of dampened cloth until the smoke darkened. Too little smoke, too much flame.

She tried to billow smoke from the window. Not enough. The wind spread it thin, the trees combed it invisible. And what would the neighbours, even if they noticed it, care for a trickle of smoke, where rubbish had been burned only days before?

*Who shall I be?* thought Lucinda again. She'd known children who burned things—she'd preferred to keep her skills unnoticed. There was, she supposed, a glory in not being secret.

She let the flame sink, and tended it all day, banked and glowing like a marigold as the sun slid over the house and the tree-shadows turned.

The old crow left and returned with a dead mouse. A leaf. Something that might have been a finger, once.

"Someone will have to explain *that*," she said to the crow. She threw it out again.

At sunset, she brought the fire to life again. She wound a tight ball of cloth, lit it, flung it over the edge of the roof. The flames blackened as it flew.

The next flared and died in the gutter. She was tired, so tired. It was hard to throw through the bars. She had broken apart the crib, but it did not burn well, and the slats of the bed were a poor catapult.

The old crow huddled in a corner of the windowsill, unperturbed. Lucinda looked at it speculatively. She could catch it, get her arms around that broad-shouldered, sharp-breasted little body. It was nearly dead anyway; a crow carrying fire . . .

It was too tired, she decided, brusquely, and picked up that last bottle. She opened it. A sharp smell. A spirit. Just a little weight. She spilled the slightest drop onto the smouldering cloth. There was an evil flame, a cough of smoke. What was it the arson-children in the clinics and institutions had told her?

She stoppered the bottle with a strip of cloth, held the end of the strip to the smoking basin, and when it was smouldering she flung it out over the roof, into the nearest trees. The dead ones. If it fell into the tangle of leaves and bark at their base . . .

"Burn," commanded Lucinda, and felt a shiver take hold high in her spine.

A wisp of smoke, violet in the dusk. A small, sharp pop as the bottle burst. A sunset glow up the tree's trunk, licking and brightening the bark. Banners streaming up from the dead leaves.

"You couldn't have done better," she told the crow.

"Care," it said, and limped along the sill as if to admire the flames.

"Someone must be able to see it now," said Lucinda. The wind blew fire snapping back towards the house, all talons and claws.

She turned and sank to sit on the floor, back against the side of the window seat. Red light flowed through the window like liquid, and it was some time before she realised the ringing in her ears was sirens.

She had no interest in returning to the deliveryman's house, after axes and ambulances, hospitals and detectives, evidence and interrogations. The walls, she understood, had been peeled open, the floorboards cracked like ribs, the flowerless gardens dug up again. Questions about the house, the deliveryman, vanished girls, had been answered—other people's questions. Lucinda had none.

"Do you have anyone to look after you?" people asked. "You must be due soon."

"Yes," said Lucinda calmly, at each door she passed through. She wore borrowed clothes, stiff and sombre as a burned tree, or as the detectives in all the confidence of their authority.

She went back to her own small apartment over the grocery store. It smelled of spices and floor cleaner. There was dust, but no insects, no mice. She'd taken care that wouldn't happen.

She did not ask if any of her collection had remained. No-one had asked her about them—not as if they were of interest, or might be hers—and she would not make them do so. The Lucinda they had belonged to, the Lucinda of fox-coloured curls and cheerful dresses, antiques lectures and auctions, seemed childish now. Besides, there were cabinets set subtly into these walls too, with the best of her collection: ones with mottled labels and unbroken seals, and others in plastic and legal warnings, any of which might come in handy one day.

She let her hair grow out again, and admired the new silver threads in it. She bought long dark dresses and an antique cradle, candelabra and polished wooden furniture. But the only bottle on display was a large ornamental jar of alcohol with a mouth wide enough to swallow the folded body of an old crow, to fly on in darkening amber.

# A Hedge of Yellow Roses

Vagabonds leave signs in the road for those who know how to read them. Royalists also have their secret language of warnings and betrayals. This story, too, in its fashion, is a sign to mark the way I went.

As with all the lessons of my life, no human voice told it to me. I gathered the threads from spindle-grass and crow-black clouds, from amber autumn roses and the thorns that tore my sleeves.

*Once, there was a prince . . .*

Having given myself, body and soul, to the service of my prince, I, Vermeille, found myself fleeing armed rebellion. This, at an age when one of my career and ambitions might have hoped to be settled in a fine house, with a garden and even children at my knee. But that carefully husbanded future had been rent asunder, and now I was homeless, far from the city where I'd dwelt for more years than I cared to admit to those who would scoff at my true age. My lord was said to be exiled, yet I still hoped, then, to meet him in a land far beyond the hills.

Certainly I could not stay in the beautiful city, for that cloud-kingdom to which I had struggled so long to ascend had already been torn apart. No matter how humble my birth, I had allied myself with the royal house and in doing so had marked myself out as surely as if I'd worn a traitor's brand. No concession would be made for me by revolutionaries or otherwise.

I rode disguised as a common soldier; not so common that I could not afford a horse, but I took good care to make both the beast (a grey, shabbily caparisoned) and myself appear sufficiently disreputable as to make neither halt nor hindrance worth a vigilante's trouble. I shall let you imagine how that abraded my sensibilities, for I had become accustomed to damask and carriages, satin and featherbeds.

I bore three messages, none conveyed by ink: news of the murder of a king, a sword wrapped in a cape and tied to my saddle, and a secret so close to my own heart that even I did not then suspect it. Beyond these I had only my wits, and few enough of those.

Anxious and fearful, riding hard and sleeping rough, I sickened. My thoughts strayed to happier times past and those I hoped would come—moonspinnings, all. The horse, too, wandered. When at last I roused it was to find that we stood on a hillside gold with clattering spindle-grass, and the lowering clouds too close.

Spindle-grass is no better for horses than storms are for benighted travellers, and there was no more food on that slope than there was hint of shelter. I had resigned myself to pressing on, when the last escaping light of the sun struck fire from what had seemed only a nearer cloud. It was instead, I realised, a stand of trees, with something radiant within.

We crossed the grey stones of a cold hill stream. My horse made a good deal of fuss, and perhaps the water was deeper than I'd thought, for by the far side I was splashed to my thighs.

As we drew closer it became apparent our goal was not a forest, but a low large thicket. A few late birds still settled to its branches, and beyond its highest reach was the unmistakable haze of moss-grown roofs. The beckoning gleam glanced once more then faded with the sunset. Whoever had built and tended this place had long since abandoned it. To my way of thinking and given my current circumstances, this was all to the good.

"We may spend the night dry, or at least in the lee of a wall," I said to the horse, and urged him onward.

The wind sank, gathered itself again, and tore at the sparse grass and me in equal measure. The air grew grey with dusk. The hillside was poor, stony and ridged, with but a few starved weeds, which my horse snatched at greedily. If ever there'd been fields, they were long worn away, stone walls disassembled by winters and the slow shifting of the earth. We found the faint hollow of a ditch, which became rough with tilted stones and resolved at last into the remnant of a path. This brought us to the entrance of the compound.

Vintners grow roses beside their vines to warn of pestilence; royal gardeners raise them (costly stock!) as a boast and glory. Whether the bushes surrounding this house had been planted for service or beauty I made no guess. They now stood guard for a place that needed none. Thick and unnaturally thorned, spikes as long as stilettos and bright as needles, the woody branches had woven themselves into a thick wattle fence, daubed with leaf-mould. I could hear birds settling in the upper branches, but the net was too dense to see them.

From afar, I'd thought a shattered windowpane had thrown a reflection to draw us here, but now I realised otherwise. The hedge was heavy with roses, blown and blossoming, and all rich as amber, bronze, butter, parchment. At the hedge's crest, twice as high as I sat on horseback, some few still gleamed the dull gold of lanterns.

Their perfume was sickly sweet.

Though the path bade fair to be overgrown, I urged my horse on and soon discerned the deeper shadows of what had once been a gate. I ducked my head and shrank from the barbs, while the grey horse pressed slowly forward. Once, twice and again I felt a tearing on arm or cheek, and bethought myself to back out of the leafy tunnel. But finally stone overarched us, purple light opened ahead, and I sighed in relief as I straightened.

We were in a walled courtyard. Weeds grew through cracked stones, and the several doors that faced us all hung ajar. Grey-green roofs of the towered house, outbuildings and a vacant dovecote angled down to us. Tall cold chimneys were topped with bristles of twigs and the broken wheel of a stork's nest. Dry leaves, like the shadows of birds, rustled past my horse's hooves.

I slid to earth, clinging to the saddle. As I steadied myself I looked back the way we had come. The tunnel must have turned sharply for it now seemed blocked with blossoms and briars. Where the hedge overtopped the wall, the roses were reddening.

"*And so they came to the Tower Perilous*," I murmured. Ah! So recently surrounded by salons of poets and there I was addressing a horse.

When I faced the courtyard once more, it was to find we were not alone.

The woman appeared terribly young, frail as an ivory fan. Her antique dress was frayed to threads that, like the strands of her hair, lifted in the breeze. I could discern little of her features in the half-light. Yet for all the poverty which clearly beset us both, for a heart's beat I felt as if we were players in a romance on a courtly stage: I no shabby soldier but a knight; she no starveling peasant but a lady waiting to greet a noble guest.

"Good den, my lord," said she, with quaint formality.

I swept as theatrical a bow as I knew, but with the movement, the overgrown courtyard bucked beneath my feet, my empty stomach revolted and my hand lost hold of the shifting saddle. I fell.

She caught at me and for a breath I thought her hands crabbed and clawed. Her fluttering sleeves struck at my face like feathers.

"Hush, hush," said the girl, steadying me. "I cannot carry you, good Sir Knight. Hush, you are come very far to sleep on stone or in hedge." Her cool hand—human, untaloned—touched my face briefly.

I blinked and stared. Her face was near, her eyes wide and luminous as the roses. Her expression was unguarded, and I was disconcerted. It had been very long since I'd seen someone who had not learned to wear a mask of subservience, civility, or war. The first flecks of rain fell, and they stung like ice.

She stepped away. "You should not bow to me," she said, lowering her gaze. "No wealth or title belongs to this land. I am only Enna."

"You are the mistress of this house?"

She looked up again and smiled. "As much as any can make such claim," she replied. I marvelled at how much beauty could appear, where there was no cold jewelled facade to hide it. I wondered if that was how I had appeared to my lord, when first he took up with me.

"Then I am Miles," I said. "I am but a masterless knight." She seemed to accept this answer though it would never have satisfied anyone from the city I had so recently fled. The girl was not worldly-wise.

"Come. There is still room for guests. Your skin is hot as a flame."

Once within the shadowy ruination of the great house, she produced a shaded taper, then led me up bowed stairs and along a dust-hung hall to a chamber which must have once been a large salon or gallery. There were no furnishings. The candlelight, though dazzling in the dark, was small—I could only tell that the space was airy and broad, filled with what I first thought drifts of gold, then of straw, then as I looked longer, piles of leaves.

"The beds have been long since burned for winter kindling, but you may sleep here. At least you are beneath a roof," said Enna. She gave a quick, hopeful smile and left.

I'd barely wrapped myself in my greatcoat before falling asleep. I did not expect to dream.

The first time, rain hissed outside, the frail roof groaned, and darkness spread like moss and water stains down the walls. I told my dream-self the house had stood too many years to fall in one night. I told myself the night-fancy merely echoed the sudden decay of our bright kingdom.

I slitted my eyes and peered out, and found the room full of light. It hung like golden tapestries, and painted the sackcloth of my hostess' dress like damask. She stood at the threshold of the gallery, and another figure—something like a woman—stood beside her, in a robe soft with plumes.

"Do you think he will be the one?" asked the girl.

"If he were, he would wake and see you for what you are," answered the other. "Resign yourself to disappointment, goddaughter."

"Perhaps he wakes and merely pretends to sleep."

"Then he is still not the one we require, for he is no gentleman," said the other. "It is only tricksters and common soldiers who feign sleep to gain an end, and such are not for you."

She crossed the room with a rustling swoop of wings as if to shake me—and I woke to the sound of pigeons rummaging in the rafters, the wind like voices in ruined towers.

I slept again, and thought myself surrounded by many mirrors. They doubled back a crowd of folk in velvet finery, masked with glass-and-ivory visages of birds: I was in a ballroom. Their clothes were wonderful, fantasies for a masquerade and yet with silhouettes long-lost to fashion, sleeves with a queer cut, full skirts falling short of soft-heeled, square-toed shoes. The beaks of their masks were sharp, ground like razors, and the eyes that peered out were very beautiful, and wild.

Yet they were all faintly transparent, as if the mirrors in reflecting them had drawn out their reality, their substance. Through sleeve and epaulet, peplum and bodice, ribbon and lace, I could see at the epicentre a single, solemn figure. It was the girl, Enna, but much younger, in primrose silk, with saffron ribbons in her hair and a crow (glossy blue and stars of candlelight dancing from its back and brows) perched on her shoulder. "Not a true prince among them," rasped the crow, and again with a sound of nails on glass, "Not a one!"

I awoke in the tangle of my coat, breathing in crushed leaves. Lightning leaked briefly through shrunken shutters. The walls were still bare, no mirrors in evidence, no revellers, no crows. Rolling onto my back I stared blindly at the ceiling. (Had it been painted with stars?) In more innocent days I might have counted this a nightmare, but since then I had stood before a palace and been spattered with blood from the throat of a king.

When I wept, I rather fear it was for lost festivals such as that in my dream. All the cruel beauty I had made my own was shattered like porcelain. All the gilt and satin were gone, leaving nothing save dried leaves.

Yet a third time I dreamt. This time Enna lay a little distance from me. Her dress was all the colours of night and dawn; pearls and feathers were tangled in her hair with a disorder that would have cost time and care to achieve, had it been brought to existence in the waking world.

"You have a gentle face," she said, and reached towards my lips with one finger—but her hand was crabbed and clawed.

I flinched and opened my eyes.

I was cold in my sweat-soaked clothes, half-buried in dead rose leaves. Morning light, the colour of milk-and-water, seeped through the slats of the shutters but brought no warmth. There was a lingering stench of bile and my mouth was as foul as if birds had nested there.

In all my dreams the threshold had been hung with a door carved of interlocking branches, but in the daylight the hinges were rusted and unburdened. In the empty space stood the girl, a basin in her hands.

"I trust you slept well," she said, eyes downcast, and brought me the dish of water. Her fingers were roughened by no more than ordinary work—if there was ordinary work for one who dwelt in such a place. The fine dress of my dreams was replaced by the same drab rag of my arrival.

"I thought I would have slept as the dead," I answered. "But nightmares troubled me."

She looked up. I could see the amber ring about her irises and her wide pupils cast back the reflection of my face hawk-sharp with fever and hunger.

"You will sleep better far from here," she said. "I let you in because of the storm, but it has passed and ordinary decency will not permit that you stay."

"You fear for your safety?" I asked, amused. Even disguised as I was, she was clearly far healthier and stronger than I. And who was there here to be affronted by my presence?

"I am protected," she said coolly. "I fear for yours. You dreamed of flying. Travellers before you have leaped from the tower, or tried to soar across the river. Others . . ."

"I did not dream of flying."

She had no ready words.

"I dreamed of birds," I confessed. "But they were revellers at a masque."

Enna left the dish of water by me, and walked quickly away.

After I had washed as well as I might, I wandered to the courtyard and found her combing the grey horse's tangled mane with fierce intensity. The beast bore it well enough, but in the overhanging branches of the hedge an ill assortment of birds swung and shouted at me, before they beat their way up into the sky.

"This is a fine animal, beneath the mud," she said.

"We have that in common, though both of us suffer from hunger."

She turned, eyes dark with contrition. "Forgive me," she said. "I forgot."

"That men must eat?" It was a jest, but she looked at me in reproach.

I sketched a bow, cautiously, and this time the ground stayed where it should. "It is I who must crave forgiveness, fair Enna. I impose on your hospitality. But if you would have me leave, and not simply become bones whitening in the hedge, then I must beg alms of you."

She was not the sort to long hold a grudge. Though there remained no table in the kitchen, she laid a cloth upon the floor and served what seemed a slurry of chaff and water.

"Can this sustain life?" I asked.

"It has sustained yours these three days past. What you did not cast up again."

I mused on this while I ate. Three days of dreams, while I thought but one had passed. The dish was more substantial than it appeared and the emptiness in my belly and the weakness in my bones eased. Though my stomach was still unsettled, I did not shame myself by vomiting.

"Are you a nobleman?" she asked.

I thought before I answered. "Times are bad for noblemen, child. A wise person will answer they've never held a drop of such blood in their veins. That, if you had, you would have spilled it yourself. Tell anyone who asks that you tore this house to ruins with your own hands for liberty and loyalty."

"That would not be true."

"Yet sometimes lies may be the only thing to save us."

She regarded me solemnly until I spoke again. "Why are you alone, Enna? Where is your family? Have you no . . ." I regarded her, but could not guess her age. "No husband?"

Enna glanced out the doorway. A little whipbird strutted proudly along the horse's back. "May I tell you a story, Sir Miles?"

"What else do our kind do?" I asked lightly, but she had not the self-deprecating humour of a self-made courtier and looked blankly at me. "Yes," I added, and leaned my head against the wall, much wearier than I felt I had cause to be.

~

"Once upon a time, a very long time ago," she began, a child telling a tale using the rules of the stories she had heard, "there was a green valley and in that valley was a wealthy farmholding. The couple who lived there lived well. They were happy and proud, but they had no children.

"'Will you wish for a child?' their friends and relatives asked. 'Will you summon the old powers of the hills? Will you pray?'

"'We may as well call to the birds,' said the farmer and his wife. But in time they had a daughter.

"'Who will stand at her naming?' their friends and relatives asked. 'And who will you choose as her godparents?'

"Now, the parents had no wish to give offence to those who were not chosen. 'As well ask the birds,' they said.

"Their daughter grew, and seasons were rich. The valley flourished, the house was made larger. Dances were held there, minor noblemen journeyed to visit, and rode and hunted in the hills.

"'Who will marry your daughter?' asked the friends and relations.

"'A prince, and no one less,' laughed her parents. There were many princes in those days.

"But before her parents could see her of an age to be wed or betrothed, death came to the valley and took them away.

"Among those friends and relatives who survived, there were many who wanted the rich farmland. They planned to marry the girl to their sons and brothers—but who was to decide which suitor would do?

"Now," said Enna, "you must see it was only in jest that my parents made the birds my godparents. But birds take their responsibilities seriously."

"I did not know that."

"Well, they have so few." Enna shrugged. We sat in silence while, outside, roses wept soft petals, tawny as velvet, into the courtyard.

"I did not even know that crows could speak," I offered.

She made a small noise, as if it were a matter of no great note. As if everyone knew it.

"What happened next?

"The rival suitors came upon an idea. They did not know how, whether it was whispered at their windows as they fell asleep, or murmured in the trees when they went riding. But it was decided a ball should be held so that the girl herself might choose from any suitable admirer who met all appropriate requirements. This was still a rich valley, this farmholding the lock and I the key. There were those who hoped to grasp it—me—not for my own sake, but for the land's. There were, I understand, rather many such men."

"You understand?" I echoed.

"I was young. It was a very long time ago." She pulled her knees to her chest, folded her arms about and rested her chin on them.

"None proved worthy, for although there were noblemen among them, there were no princes—and birds, who listen at windows, knew what my parents had required. When none of their suits were acceptable, the gentlemen grew irate and insulting. The birds said none should have me until I found someone who valued my heart above my land. When the suitors threatened to take what would not be given, the birds turned all their minds to madness, and every man who has reached this place since has gone mad. With the years, the land grew untended and sour, the road was slowly lost and I have waited ever since."

"How long has that been?"

"I don't know. I cannot even remember the name of the Queen who ruled. I was very young, and birds take little notice of such things."

I thought of the unprincely candidates. "Didn't your godparents think the punishment a little extreme?"

She shrugged. "They are birds."

"And the roses?" I asked, considering the only plant that thrived in this desolation.

"I planted them on the graves, and there were so many graves . . . They grew into the hedge you see now. But the suitors didn't all die. Some only thought they had turned into birds. A few really did, and flew away. Some soared and sang in the branches for a long time."

"And you've seen no-one since?"

"Only from afar. But they tell me stories, my godparents. They listen at windows, and bring me word of the world. Only—only I think it is not the same as being in it."

I had no answer to this. Her recounting was no more fantastic than any I could spin. Who would believe that in a rose-hung city—the most civilised in the world!—street-sweepers would drag a king from his palace of white and gold, out into a common square, and cut off his head? Who would believe that peasants would grow to hate the beauty of the realm so much they would set it to burn?

Though I did not believe in nursery tales, anyone would be forgiven for thinking that my own fortunate rise and meteoric fall were no more than the substance of a fable.

I stood, swaying a little, and returned to the courtyard. The birds, on roof and hedge and wall (different feathers flocked together), watched me with unnerving steadiness. Their eyes—orange, black and blue—followed my progress. I reached the arch by which I had entered and found the way matted with roses blooming, here a bloody orange. My little strength could not shift them.

"They will only part for princely blood," said Enna. "But for them to do so, you must take me with you."

"You are welcome to come, though I do not know where I ride. I can take you to a town, find a place where you will be comfortable." As if I knew where I myself could go.

"You must take me with you as your bride," said she.

"I cannot marry you, Enna." I laughed, though I meant it kindly.

"It is the only way we may leave!" she cried. "I do not want your bones to whiten here!"

"I passed through once," I said, and touched the scabbed lines where thorns had scored my arm. "Though I am no prince."

In the outbuilding where my horse had been stabled there was no straw, only the dry golden petals which lay like grass, matted with feathers. Through the unshuttered windows winged shadows drifted.

I saddled the grey, wondering where I might find sanctuary, if indeed there was sanctuary to be had anywhere. I closed my eyes and saw the head of the king as a great golden rose, snipped away and rolling along bloodied cobbles. After so many years of schooling my emotions, it felt as if a dam had burst within me, and I had not the strength to hold it back.

And Enna followed, still talking.

"You were courteous to me. I nursed you and watched over your sleep. You passed through the hedge of thorns. You woke in dreams and saw not madness, but truth. You believed my story! It proves you are a true prince!"

"Your head is filled with fairy tales, child!" I said, and bent to pull the sword from its wrappings. How heavy it was, and how weary was I, my tiredness born of something deeper than travel, my illness of more than heartsickness. "I did not seek this valley, nor you. I am only fleeing death."

I carried the blade to the gateway in the wall, swung it with what remained of my might. The branches shook birds into the air, petals fell like sleep and the rents in my flesh stung anew. Yet there was not a mark on the twisted limbs.

"I love you!" said Enna.

"I am not even a false prince," I said. "And I do not love you."

"You were kind!" she almost wailed. "You are *here*!" She stretched out her hand and—may I be forgiven—I took it and held it in my own.

I felt the weight of flesh and the lightness of her bones, the quick-pulsing blood in her palm. I was not tempted by the land, or the ruined house, or even the dreams of what they had once been and might be again. I was not tempted even by the unkempt beauty of the girl. But her cry for kindness, for companionship, for love—oh, I heard that in the chord of my own being.

"Sir Miles!" she began again.

"That is not my name," I said, returning to the stable. As I rewrapped the blade, I saw a scar in the watered steel, a mark in the shape of a rose-barb.

"You travel in disguise, but you are a prince! What other knight is masterless? What other blood may pass the roses—did you not see how their colour changed?"

I did not answer. There must be a way, another door, a farm gate. Fire—fire would burn a passage through. I would be ready to leave with the grey horse if I could, else over the hedge if I had strength to climb. I could stand on the horse's back. Perhaps from outside I could open the hedge again. I ignored my shaking hands as they made the bridle ring.

"Look at me!"

Enna had pulled her shabby dress over her head and her fine hair blew like silk in the light through the stable door.

Her body was thin and dirty, a maze of gooseflesh, ribbed with scars and welted with scabs. Some had lifted, and from beneath the stubs of young feathers sprouted. She stepped forward, grasped one of my hands and held it to her stomach, where the bones of her ribs began. Her skin, there unbroken, was already raised and rough with the pressure of feathers thrusting from below.

"What is this?" I asked, numb.

"This is what shall become of me, or what I shall become." She released my hands, then pulled me to her and kissed me with uncertain lips. She was still a child, no matter how long she'd lived, and fumbled inexpertly with the collar of my shirt. I caught at her trembling fingers while she begged, "It is the only other way out of this place."

"Then I am sorry for you."

"You do not want me?" she pleaded.

"No, Enna."

"But I am yours for the having! You must! You are a prince, and I have waited so very, very long. I have lost count of the generations of my godparents, of how many have watched for you. Please, you must—have you no heart?"

"It is given to another, child."

"As desperate as I?"

"Desperation is not love, Enna, and don't believe anyone who tells you otherwise!"

"But you're a prince—"

I cried out, though it broke more hearts than hers, though I shouted the words at myself as much as her. "Do you not understand, foolish child? There are no princes left! If your fate hangs upon one then you are truly doomed!"

"No, that is not true! You are here!"

"I *loved* a prince, Enna. I still do. But I fear he must be dead. He has not turned to a bird, he shall not fly over borders and meet me in some foreign court no matter how much I yearn and pray. He loved me, but he is dead, and he shall never know his son. The blood of the child I now know I carry is the only princely blood left in this land. How else could I have passed the roses?"

"A child?" echoed Enna.

"I am no secret prince, girl, but base-born, a prince's mistress." I tried to speak harshly, but we both wept. I gathered her to me, wrapped her in my long coat, and we sank down into the leaves. "Hush," I said, through my own sobs. "Let us think. There must be some escape."

"There is only one," said Enna to my collarbone, where her hands were knotted into fists. Her nails felt sharp against the hollow of my throat. A crow in the window-embrasure clacked its beak impatiently. I believed I felt my own fingers twisting into claws.

"Perhaps my godparents never meant to give me up," said Enna quietly. "Maybe it is not love that will free me, but having my heart broken."

"I have found," I ventured, "that birds and princes break hearts very well. They both live such short lives."

Enna cried herself to sleep. I extracted myself and stood, looked down at her, half-hidden by my wretched soldier's coat. She was—must be—so much older than I. Yet I had lived far more, been made and unmade by the world, bereft and unwidowed, nearly a mother. There had been no godmother, avian or otherwise, to guide me, and perhaps that was as well.

As quietly as I could I went back into the courtyard. The grey horse dozed in the pale sunlight, and the watchful birds had settled again: crows in the branches, whipbirds on my mount's shoulders, pigeons, long-wild housedoves, and little quarrelling sparrows on the cracked pavement. On the roofs, light elegant egrets waited like sentinels, and owls shifted irritably in the shadows.

In the centre of the enclosure, I turned a full circle and cleared my throat.

"Oh, most gracious watchers and guardians," I said, for I had been used to treat with similarly vain and status-conscious creatures. "Most venerable and honourable birds, wise avians, Strigidae, Corvidae, Passeridae . . ." I reached the limit of my scholarship and felt my folly; then I rallied. I had weathered the scoffing of the greatest, most glittering of courts—why should I blush for these feather dusters?

I conjured my best memory of a true courtly bow, swept off my non-existent hat, flung out one arm and bent deeply, until the nettles and the incursions of spindle-grass nearly pricked my face.

The birds strutted and shuffled, swayed on their perches, tilted their heads. I glanced at them from under my brows, drew breath and balance, then straightened.

"Through your wisdom and keen observation, you will by now understand that I am no prince. I do, however, carry within me the blood of the royal line. As such I, Vermeille, am the only and last claimant ever likely to cross the hedge. I beg that you hear my words, and let the girl Enna go free."

"What would you give us?" demanded a crow. Its voice startled me, but I had heard such harsh and avaricious mockery before and steeled myself to wait.

"Gold?" asked a magpie.

"The light of your eyes?" A raven.

A whipbird piped, "Your first-born child?"

They were knowing ones, and I imagined it was not the breeze but their wild untidy magic which swirled the leaves about my feet. I kept my arms at my sides, palms open.

"No doubt such gold, light, and children as I carry will all fall to your kind in the fullness of time. I owe nothing, I do not seek to buy your charge, and I request no favour beyond this: that you release the child.

"But you have discharged your duty as godparents admirably and in reward I will offer a word of advice. I have travelled from the plainlands where cattle-birds tag at the heels of oxen; over gentle lands where wrens sing; across the crane-stalked river that leads to the sea of gulls and flows about the island city where pigeons and sparrows strut at their ease between the houses of men. And each of their kind could tell you, wise lords and ladies of the air, these two truths:

"The first is that while birds cling to their nature, mankind are changeable, and must be so, else they die. If you hold Enna here any longer you cease to protect her, you will render her unable to change. Even your own kind must fly or fall from the nest, but cannot stay there forever.

"The second is that war and rebellion turn rich pickings up to the light just as a plough's blade does worms. You may stay here in this untilled country and leave the bloody spoils to your gentler rivals. Or you may free yourselves from your own spells, and those of your forefathers, and leave this stagnant land to seek your fortune."

The creatures shifted and conferred among themselves in their own languages. A feathered parliament of nobles who had forgotten why they'd been elevated, who remembered only the power of their position, not its responsibilities. Such revolutionary thoughts made me sink my nails into my palms. *I'm sorry, my love.*

But they were blunt and artless birds for all their self-importance, and wielded no court airs or subtleties. In their thirst for princes they had almost forgotten their charge.

"What—what will become of the child? Without us?" asked a mottled, fan-tailed dove.

"Is she a child?" I asked. "You have held her here so long, waiting, that she is barely able to grow. So long, that there are no princes left in the land. This I swear to you."

"Save one," said the low voice of an owl beneath the eaves.

I rested my hand on my own stomach. "And he shall have neither crown nor country," I said.

I sensed a presence at my elbow, and with my free hand reached for Enna's.

The birds spoke among themselves once more until at last an old crow dropped from the hedge and landed on the hand I'd raised to shield my eyes. There were grey feathers among the black, and its gnarled claws bit into my skin.

"If what you say is true—and we have no reason to disbelieve—then you have done us a favour, servant-of-the-dead-princes. All our lives, and our mothers', for a hundred nestings, have been devoted to raising and protecting this one. We are agreed, now that we think on it, that assuredly, she is more than of age.

"But let her leave with you, that we may not have failed the trust we were given. And we will serve you likewise."

Before I could ask what that meant, they lifted up from hand, roof, courtyard, branch and chimney, a dappled whirlwind, a mottled cloud that cleared the wall and beat away across the fields. I caught myself wondering what manner of power

Enna's folk had possessed, to tie that mismatched flock so casually, so tightly, to such an obligation.

"Come," I said to her. "We must seek our own fortunes." She was dressed again. Her eyes had already lost their inhuman light, and she seemed more present, too, than when she'd first met me in the courtyard. As if she had matured in the minute it took the birds to pass.

Before we left, I bade Enna wrap up in strips of wet cloth such cuttings as I could take from the hedge, which yielded at last to the blade of my sword. I filled, too, the secret pockets of my coat, and weighted my saddlebags with heavy yellow petals, their fragrance now rich and rare with the promise of freedom.

I remembered the roses grown by vineyards and in kings' gardens. These must be such as had rarely, if ever, been seen elsewhere in the world. I said, "We may yet turn them to gold. We shall have need of it."

We mounted the grey horse and the hedge gave way before us. Enna's arms wrapped around me and her cheek pressed to my back as we rode out down the ditch of a path and up through the rattling spindle-grass. A whipbird darted behind us, a solitary escort.

I did not look back at hedge, valley or kingdom and, though I cannot speak with certainty, I suspect Enna's thoughts were fixed on the horizon of the future as firmly as mine.

# The Tangled Streets

"Ariadne Winter?"

The woman standing over Aria was narrow and dark, yet the bulky vest, numerous belts, and the square and mysterious holsters that police everywhere seemed to find necessary made her loom in the hospital corridor. She was carrying Aria's shoulder bag, her silhouette shadowed in front of the empty windows, which the flickering fluorescent tubes turned into mirrors. Beyond them, Aria was dimly aware, the city spread out under the night.

The policewoman's uniform was not quite the right shade of blue, and the embroidered state logo with its wreath of green leaves rising like wings around it was unfamiliar. Little differences from home, but enough to have been discomforting even if there had not been a glint of knowledge in the woman's eyes. The badge on her right sleeve read "Gray."

"You shouldn't have shot him," said Aria, her voice fraying. She picked nervously at the edge of the bandage a paramedic had fastened around her forearm.

"He followed you through the . . . perimeter," said the policewoman coolly. "And he had a knife." The latter, Aria thought, was more of an excuse than anything else. The woman returned the shoulder bag to Aria, whose fingers clenched around the straps. Officer Gray then perched on the lip of the orange plastic bucket seat opposite hers. Any natural ease the policewoman might have had was obstructed by the belts and vest of her uniform. Aria, powerless and embarrassed, looked down at her own arm. The edge of the bandage was already unravelling.

"Do you want to know what the surgeon said, seeing what we'd brought in with you?"

Aria waited.

"'Tell those bloody northerners I'm not a necromancer.'"

Aria, to hide her surprise and weariness, looked down at her own hands, still filthy with dirt and blood and ink.

"Neither am I," she said in a low voice.

Officer Gray's black eyebrows drew together. "What, exactly, *are* you?"

Aria raised her palms up, helpless. She saw the policewoman's shoulders tense at the movement, and let her hands fall back to her lap. "I'm not anything—I'm just Ariadne Winter." She had another, a proper name, but there was no call to give it. "This was meant to be a holiday. I want to go home." To her shame, she burst into tears.

Officer Gray waited, unmoved. When Aria's tears resolved into hiccoughs, the police officer said, "There are borders in cities. Boundaries some of the authorities know about, and walk, and watch, as far as we can. Old crimes still under investigation, old punishments. Old budgetary constraints. Most people don't know about them; never find them. But you aren't a regular tourist. You walked right out of the middle of them."

"I am a tourist," said Aria. "At least, I was trying to be."

The officer waited in silence and Aria, anxious to fill it, hoping to trade the facts for an explanation, began to tell her story.

Ariadne Winter liked to spend her holidays wandering. In consequence, that afternoon she had lost herself. That, of course, was the charm and purpose of walking alone through an unfamiliar city, between quaint crowded terraces built for colder winters, under trees where there was no guilt in not knowing their names, beneath birds whose accents had changed.

She was not alarmed. She was, however, aware of an enchantment in these streets stronger than the mere play of light on brown leaves and power lines. It was not like the weighty glamour of the city centre below, where the earliest buildings stood small and proud between mirrored towers, and where something marvellous always seemed on the verge of happening, but long ago and to someone else—the recurring dream of momentous events that haunts old architecture and steep stone stairs.

What Aria felt here was immediate and alive. It was not entirely welcoming, but she let the streets lead her past sweet decaying terrace houses and sun-spangled alleys, nameless garden-plants and tiny cafe-galleries. She was a visitor here, this city's magic could have no greater interest in her than she did in it, and evening was still a long way off.

With her small shoulder bag striking her hip, she trotted happily around an unsigned corner, following only her own inclination or a whim of the wind, and found herself in the unexpected broad turn of a lane. It was wider than the street off which it branched, but utterly quiet. There were no cars crouched waiting along its kerbs. Fallen leaves lay curled motionless, golden as glass in the unshifting sun; no birds sang.

One side of the lane was formed by the brick walls of back gardens. The other side had a stone wall, stained moss-grey. At the point where the lane curved back to the street perched a set of solid, high metal gates. They were patterned with dull-pointed crowns and heavy-headed lions, plated with coppery light. A sign beside them stated they were Private Property, and warned against trespassing.

"Curious," said Aria. It was not the sudden antiqued splendour that intrigued her so much as the lack of any magical overlay. Whatever enchantment she had felt shifting in the streets beyond had fallen still here. Her palms itched with her desire to look for a crack in the gate and peer through. She glanced furtively around and realised she was not alone.

A man was standing on the narrow sidewalk opposite. He wore a slim silver suit, and held a phone to his ear, listening. He did not face her directly, but he wore dark glasses. Aria could not tell whether he was watching her. There was a nervous, bitter twist to his mouth. He shut his phone without speaking into it, and Aria felt his attention alight on her.

"Hello," she said, reminding herself that she had nothing to feel guilty about yet, that intention was not a crime and that she had only wanted to look, which was not trespassing. Then, because he was dressed as if he belonged in a many-windowed office tower, she asked, "Are you lost, too?"

"Telephones don't work inside," he said, his voice soured with dissatisfaction. His hair was very pale and spiked, although it was feathered with late afternoon light. If he had spoken with a hint of arrogance, Aria wouldn't have liked him at all—as it was, she reserved judgment.

"Do you work here?" She gestured at the gate, although it looked like the sort of place that might have security guards, or a maid, gardeners, maybe even caterers; people who wore uniforms, not suits. "What do you do?"

"Lull people into a false sense of security," said the man. Aria decided he must be a lawyer. He tilted his head back towards the sky. "You should get back to wherever you're from. Before dark."

"Oh, I will," said Aria, cheerfully. She had a healthy respect for the night-side of cities, even those which weren't her own. "I'm never *permanently* lost. And night's hours away—I know where I'm staying."

He took off his glasses and cleaned them with the lining of his jacket. He had pale eyebrows and bleached-blue, worried eyes. He put his glasses back on. "It falls faster than you'd think."

Aria shifted her shoulder bag, then smiled. He was so brittle and stylish, yet there was no sarcasm in his tone.

"Are you . . . warning me?"

He hesitated—and she wished she could see his eyes again—then said, "Eventually, everyone stays lost."

Aria held up her hands. "Peace!" she laughed. "I'm just sight-seeing. I didn't mean to step on any toes, so I'll wander out again."

"It's not as simple as that, Ariadne Winter," he said. "The streets are a web."

"Oh," said Aria. A great deal now made sense: The silent building perched behind the gates like a fat spider crouching at the centre of its silk. This man, watching out for her. Not a lawyer, then, but someone who knew a little of the patterns of the world.

"What is the web strung to catch?" she asked, since she could as easily leave a question unasked as she could leave a street unexplored. "And how did you know my name?"

But she could see from the set of his jaw that the second query answered the first and a thrill—not quite of fear, not yet—ran across her shoulders.

"I'm on holidays," she said, as if that should be a talisman. "And I'm just me. Why catch me?"

The man shrugged. "Maybe they were starved for a Winter. Maybe you're worth something. Maybe you can do something clever. You found your way to this lane, after all. You shouldn't have been able to do that. The *others* have gone out into the streets looking for you. I have to go back inside, I've been away too long. You could come in with me, if you like, and ask."

For the first time there was mockery in his voice, and that was more of a warning to Aria, who suspected she did not know enough to be properly afraid.

"You come with me," she shot back. "You know the way."

"I've done what I can," he said. "I don't dislike you; I don't know you. Whatever you are, I don't think it would be good for you to enter. And if you are something . . . different"—again, that sour twist of his mouth—"it might not be good for anyone else either."

Aria hated to run scared, or be thought gullible. Maybe this was something they did to tourists here. Or perhaps her cousins, who were remarkable, and who teased her kindly, had arranged this as a prank, although their tricks were not usually distinguished by subtlety. What decided her, in the end, was that if this was a joke, the man did not seem to be enjoying it.

"Walk away, Ariadne Winter," he said.

"Just like that?"

His glasses reflected the sky darkly. "No," he sighed. "Probably not."

Aria nodded. She gripped the strap of her shoulder bag and walked around the bow of the lane—past the gates with their soft-edged lions, features blurred by time or art. She kicked through the coins of leaves (chestnut? box? the freedom of not knowing had lost some of its appeal) out into the blue shadow of the terrace on the corner.

And arrived back at the other end of the lane.

"Oh! That's not fair!"

The man had crossed to the gate and lifted one silver-sleeved arm to open it, but stopped with his hand still raised.

"You're in a loop," he said. Aria had not noticed the spark of hope in his voice before, but she could tell now that it had gone.

"Then I'll just have to run at it," she said. She sprinted back to the corner, and leaped as she reached the road. For a moment, she saw the red darkness of her eyelids closed against the sun, and then she was out on the street in the bright afternoon. She stopped just before two women with Pekingese dogs walked by, and realised the man had not said what *sort* of people were combing the streets for her. She lingered for a moment on the street corner, feeling obviously from out of town, then turned and ran back into the lane, up to the gates. The man had opened a smaller door set into the large ones. Through it, Aria glimpsed cool green trees.

"Come with me!" she said.

He spun around. "I saw you get out," he said, and then his voice dropped to a whisper. "Why did you come back?"

"You said—" began Aria excitedly, and he put his hand abruptly over her mouth. His skin was dry, and scratched slightly against her lips. He shut the little gate, bringing out of it a last gust of breeze that smelled like air-conditioning, all ice and pines. He took off his glasses again, his pale eyes tired and the lines in his face too deep.

"Sound carries," he said.

"So does fear," whispered Aria, moving his hand away. The bones of his long fingers felt frail. "You warned me because you're afraid, and not just for me—you said yourself you don't know me. So you're afraid for yourself. Why do you stay?"

"It's too late for me. I can't leave."

"Why not?"

"I can't travel in and out at will. We who live here do not have an entirely uncomfortable life, Ariadne Winter. There are ways to survive, even to thrive after a fashion, but I cannot believe you would choose it."

"You can't know that. The only reason you would think so is because *you* wouldn't choose it."

"I cannot leave."

"I can," said Aria. She held out her hand.

"I would slow you, and we will not go unnoticed."

"Then we'll run," she suggested. She reached down and took his cool, papery hand. She hoped he was alive; it would make this difficult if he was not. She knew of paper-men and straw-men, but they were never weary like him, and rarely kind.

"What's your name?" she asked.

"Jeremy Lantern," he said, as if it were of little importance. She could tell it was not truly his name, but if he had another it crouched tiny and distant and unreachable to her.

She nodded, then ran, towing Jeremy through the blinding light to the end of the lane, and there they jumped.

It was as if they were drowning in treacle, in black molasses that let no light through, only a warm brown darkness. *We'll be trapped here,* thought Aria, her panic slow as syrup. *We'll be vanished, or become a trick of the light, or be suspended, and people will think we are living statues and throw coins at us forever.* Gradually she extended her free hand, and felt the darkness toughen beneath her fingers, like a membrane.

*It's a wall,* she thought, and then, *No, it's a border.* She pushed weakly at it with her fingernails. Behind her, Jeremy was slipping away. She tightened her grip on his hand, and tore out into the world.

The light was like a knife. They tumbled, stunned and reeling, into the crisp afternoon, fell against a street sign, and each other, and gasped at the sharp air. Jeremy had grown even paler.

There was no sign of the barrier. Light and a breeze winked in the lane. Aria put her forehead against the shoulder of Jeremy's suit—the fabric still clean and unwrinkled—and took a steadying breath.

"You should not have been able to do that." Jeremy's voice shook. "I didn't expect . . ."

"I told you we'd be fine," said Aria, her brightness brittle in her own ears. She straightened and stepped away from him. "Coming?"

Aria saw her reflection in his dark glasses. "I think . . ." He stumbled to a stop. "I think I will."

He sounded surprised, and Aria wondered if there had just been a test, and what it had been, and who had passed it.

"You can always go back," she suggested.

"Don't tempt me," said Jeremy tightly. He let go of her hand. "We'd best hurry."

Aria recalled the gradual climb to this street. She looked at Jeremy for guidance, but he shook his head, so she led them down the footpath. Aria was good at retracing her steps—an advantage for someone who liked to wander—and she did so now, glimpsing a familiar terrace-garden here, unpainted shutters romantic in the slanting light there. Across that way was a building she had noted because it was grown over with a profusion of leafless vines (she had wondered if it was ivy, and if ivy lost its foliage).

Jeremy walked a little closer than necessary, as if to keep her within arm's reach. She did not mind. The air was pleasantly cool. Nothing threatened them. Few people passed nearby, and the traffic was desultory.

"We've been walking downhill since we left the lane," said Jeremy.

"Yes. Not steeply, though."

"Try and point uphill," said Jeremy. He sounded tired.

Aria turned. They were only a few metres below a crest in the road.

"It's another loop," he said. "Like the lane."

"No," said Aria. "It's something else. We haven't been here yet. I'd have remembered that red door."

"Doors change."

"Oh, shut up," said Aria, with forced cheerfulness, and saw Jeremy's shoulders relax slightly. "This isn't like the lane."

Yet it was undeniable that, however far they had walked, they were no nearer the bottom of the hill. She tried to guess where to go next, and felt what familiarity had been there lurch and evaporate.

"The lane was still, closed," she said. "Here, things are shifting to keep us inside. And once we know what's happening, we can fix it. Look—did they have maps there, inside? Or paintings of these streets or the hills? Any sort of picture of the place?"

"Maps of the world," said Jeremy. "And big inlaid globes." He showed the height of them with his hand.

*Aspirational,* thought Aria with an inward shudder. "No street directories?"

"Not that I ever saw," said Jeremy. "They had spoken direction in the cars."

Aria wondered if any voice could talk them out of this. She tried to bring up a map on her phone. It stuttered and failed. Jeremy's was no better.

"I need paper and a pen."

Jeremy produced a sleek silver pen and a slender pocketknife from inside his jacket. After an investigation of his remaining pockets he replaced the knife and said, "I only have this. No paper."

Aria hunted in her shoulder bag and found a narrow receipt from a cafe, too small for her sprawling handwriting. "It looks like we're staying in one spot," she said. "But we aren't, we know that. We keep moving—it's just that we aren't getting anywhere." She drew a line across the paper and folded it tightly. "Maybe it's like—this is the map, and this"—she unfolded it in concertina steps—"is what is happening. The street unfolds into more lanes and terraces and walls. Does that make any sense?"

"Yes," said Jeremy. He took the tiny piece of folded paper and held it so that they were looking at the stacked layers end-on. "You're saying the closed map is the map on your phone, and the navigation system, but we don't have access to them. We've been sent deeper. But wouldn't someone notice the suburb is so much larger than it should be?"

"Maybe it has reflections," said Aria. "Or variations, or shadows. Or maybe it's exactly what you said: deeper, and if we'd scratched the paint on a blue door back when we started we would have found the mark had gone through to the red paint on this red door, here."

"An endlessly refracting prison," said Jeremy slowly.

"Prism," Aria corrected.

"You're implying there's a way out."

"Damn it, Jeremy!" She ran her hands through her hair and glared at him. "I'm making this up as I go, okay?"

Jeremy blinked, a rapid movement of his almost translucent eyelids. "Really?"

Aria felt a flush of shame. "Yes, really. I've never been lost-lost before. It's the only sort of talent I have—not being lost—and I don't like not being able to use it."

"Ariadne Winter," he said sadly, changing the topic. "Why take that name? Doesn't Winter stand for despair?"

"That's Summer," said Aria, surprised in her turn. "Decadence and despair. Autumn's resignation and Spring is carelessness. People always get them wrong." Most of her cousins went by the name of Spring, outside family circles. "Winter is baseless optimism. Where there's life, there's hope." She wanted to ask him in return why he went by Lantern, but she had an idea. "Are you certain you haven't got any more paper?"

A further search revealed no more paper, the gutters were inconveniently litter-free, and Aria was growing uncomfortable about the thought of who and what might be in the silent houses. The sunlight shifted and sank. Dogs barked on other streets, or on this street in other times.

Aria pushed one sleeve up above her elbow. "It's about maps, I think," she said. "I hope. If you've got a map, you've got some sort of power over the land, or power to get over it. You get into its head, or it gets into yours. So we'll draw our own map and follow it out."

"And that will work?"

*I'm losing him again,* she thought. *He'll slip back to that lane, and I won't let him. Not unless he wants to, and he doesn't, I'm sure.*

"Absolutely!" she said, inventing. "Think about who makes maps, and why. They're all about ownership or escape." She opened the pen and made a mark on her forearm. "This is where we are. This is the street with the red door, and we turned here, and here . . ." She closed her eyes and thought back to the lane, and to the shape of the streets she had walked before then.

She was used to proceeding based on recognition rather than actual reconstruction. She marked the map out hastily while the ink dried cold on her arm.

"They've realised I'm gone," said Jeremy. "Listen."

"I'm listening," said Aria, but she was trying to remember how the streets had bent and turned, wondering if she was crazy and why her heart was beating so fast.

There was a low grinding sound under the earth, growing into a directionless panic. She looked up at Jeremy's frightened eyes.

"I thought we'd be out before now," he said. "They must have come back from searching and found the lane open and—"

"And you gone?"

"If I go back, I could delay them. You've got a chance."

"More than I had to begin with? Jeremy, how much of a chance do you think I have?"

"Not much."

"Do you think I'll have more chance without help?"

"What help?" asked Jeremy listlessly. "I just didn't want your blood on my hands. What's behind those gates, it will suck you dry."

Aria thought of his paper-dry fingers, his colourless face. "Vampires?" she hazarded.

"No. A power. A hunger. A large and formless beast." He closed his eyes for a moment. "Like a cat, but dropping blood like roses. It collects what it needs or thinks it can use. Power and strength and hope." He opened his eyes again. "Telling you to run was the only thing I could think of."

"Then let's go," said Aria, holding up her arm. The map was drawn poorly and in haste, but it would have to do. "We have our map, the sun's going down and I'd rather not run alone."

They ran, and the dogs of the folded streets were barking. The sky flickered, and as they followed the path she'd drawn, Aria finally worked out what caused the loop. When they ran through the long shadows, she could see the towers of the city centre below, and beyond them, the tiled roofs and chimneys. When they ran into sunlight, there was no city. They were travelling in and out of times.

"Jeremy!" she gasped, caught between alarm and discovery, for she had guessed correctly. The streets and years were nested in upon themselves.

"I see it," answered Jeremy grimly. "I just hope you get us out on the right side of things."

The evening's shadows gathered, coiling blue out of gardens and side streets. Aria saw them from the corner of her eye, but paid little attention until one brushed her sleeve, and the fabric jerked and tore. She felt a scratch like a thorn against her upper arm and discovered new speed, but Jeremy was already outpacing her.

"Where to?" he managed.

She held up her arm, trying to look at the map without stumbling. "Turn right. There's a little laneway . . ." Even as she said it, she knew she had not remembered a lane here. The pen must have skipped as she drew her map, yet as she looked ahead she saw that the houses did not meet along the street.

Jeremy, who did not know there was not meant to be a laneway, plunged into the gap between two terrace houses. It was barely wider than his shoulders. Aria dived after, and ran into him. They stumbled to a halt and both looked back in time to see a sleek black car slide past the entrance. The stinging shadows lifted like leaves in its wake. Aria did not ask Jeremy whether it was one of *their* cars.

The laneway rose steep and cold between windowless walls, then tipped them down again, spilling them from between the houses. Now they were amid trees, thickly overgrown gardens and a spear-headed fence which staggered identically on each side, as if it had been split to let the pathway through.

"Do you know where this comes out?" gasped Jeremy.

"No, but I don't think *they'll* know either." He kept running, and Aria held up a hand. "Stop, let me breathe."

"There'll be time for that."

"Stop!"

Jeremy stumbled to a walk and Aria doubled over to catch her breath, then sank down to sit on the path, uncapping the pen. She examined her arm.

"Your shoulder is bleeding," said Jeremy, squatting next to her.

"I think—*think*—we should come out onto a street with cafes, and then there's a church, so there must be a churchyard—we can cut through that."

She could not really remember a churchyard, but she had not remembered the lane either. She did not want to think, just now, that she might be able to create these things. It was enough to be able to open a way through.

"A graveyard?" said Jeremy uncomfortably.

"No," said Aria, who had been about to add little crosses to mark the headstones. "Just a gate and some grass and stairs down to a street below." She was sure she had climbed a hill before she became aware of the brooding tension over these streets. If they could only get down again, they might be safe.

She held up her hand and Jeremy pulled her to her feet. He touched her shoulder and she winced. "Shadows can get into your blood," he said. "You don't know where they've been."

Aria didn't reply. She already felt light-headed from running. There were sparks in her mind, falling dots of light. "Then you have to stay with me. I'll probably need you to carry me to a doctor, once we're out. And then I want you to explain all this." Jeremy frowned at her as if she had hurt herself deliberately, to trap him into an escape he wasn't sure he wanted.

At the end of the pathway they paused to check the street was clear, before darting across to the old stone church. Where trees broke the light, the building was solid enough, but in the patches of unshadowed, afternoon sun the golden-grey stone was barely visible. There was, at least, a yard next to the church, just as she had drawn it, even the two gravestones she had marked before she changed her mind.

"They've found the lane," said Jeremy. Behind them, shadow was filling it, spilling slowly down. It oozed between the half-fences and out, to pool in the gutter before rising to flow over the road. It was the same colour as the dark windows on that smooth, silent car.

"We're almost out," said Aria. "See, there over the trees? The city is solid. The city is now." She felt sick, her legs ached and she didn't think she could run any farther, let alone invent new paths to run on.

Gripping Jeremy's hand, she limped determinedly through the churchyard towards the wall, which should have topped a fall to the street below, with its busy evening traffic and pedestrians shouting or slouching along the footpath.

She had been right, at least, about this being the edge of the domain, but although she kept a brave face for Jeremy's sake, she knew they had reached it too late. Shadows were seeping through the trees, creeping between the headstones, and they called to her, to the heaviness that was spreading through her arm and neck and shoulder, slowing her down until all she wanted was to sink into cool dreams.

One way or the other, it would soon be sunset. The light was red-golden. It caught and dazzled on the leaves. She would have sat down, save that Jeremy had an arm around her ribs and wouldn't let her.

"You're stronger than you look," she murmured. That seemed important. Something about lulling. Reluctant, brittle Jeremy Lantern—she did not want to trust her weight to him, yet she rested her head on his chest, feeling the feather-thin angle of his collarbone even through his jacket, and yawned. "This has been a very strange holiday."

The shadows coalesced. They ran together like ink and rose into a form. When Aria blinked, she saw the afterimage of a crowd, but when she opened her eyes again there was only a single figure, a woman shaped of indigo and delft china.

"Who is that?" whispered Aria.

"That is them," said Jeremy calmly. "And also it, the creature bleeding roses."

"I thought you said it was a beast."

"Why?" asked Jeremy, in mild surprise. "What do you see?"

"Come," said the woman (or beast, or multitude) and held out something like hands. She moved no faster than the creeping of night.

Aria turned her head slowly. She saw the wall at the end of the churchyard, just behind them, but when she tried to remember what was beyond it, she could only think of an eternity of ocean, sighing like stars.

Jeremy was speaking to the woman. "I'll come back with you. But you don't need her. She isn't what you think she is," he said.

"No," said the woman. Her voice—if it was a woman, if it was a voice—was deep and liquid, rippling like oil. "She is more, and shall be ours, even as you are, Lantern. The shadows already have her."

"Even as I am," echoed Jeremy. His hand tightened on Aria's waist, and then he turned and kissed her. She parted her lips in surprise. His other hand on her hurt shoulder felt almost warm, although it shook a little, and for the first time since she had climbed to these tangled streets, she felt safe.

Then a thin thread of pain lanced out from her shoulder, striking through the fog of her thoughts, sharp as a wire, brittle as a shard of glass. *He belongs to the creature*, she told herself. *This is his job. He told me. Lulling into a false sense of security. He's trying to kill me, or send me to sleep, and I not sure it isn't the same thing in the end.*

"I want to go home," she murmured.

"This is home," said the figure. "Ask Jeremy. He is full of the shadows of this place, and neither knows nor needs another refuge."

The light through the trees turned Aria's world into wheeling suns, and leaning against Jeremy's thin shoulder, she felt quite certain that the figure was both utterly right and terribly mistaken. Or perhaps, she mused, she was confusing the figure for herself. Jeremy had said the shadows would get into her blood.

"We had not expected him to be taken in by the lies of a Winter," the woman went on.

"You know me better than that," said Jeremy humbly, but Aria could feel his words and his heartbeat shake in his chest. "I wanted to test her to see if she could do what you—what *we*—hoped. She has a good memory, but that is all. The Winter blood is thin in her. She's nothing."

"That's harsh," murmured Aria. But her memories were shifting. The ocean of night was receding, even as she felt Jeremy grow cold, as if he had drawn the shadows out of her with that kiss. But her head was clearing too slowly. Each thought she tried to pull free clung stickily to the next.

"Look at her," said Jeremy. There was a blue tinge to his neck and jaw.

"We have, carefully," said the figure. "Did you really think you could seduce us into believing your lies, or that she could help you leave us? That you could live without us, hollow boy? These are my streets, Jeremy Lantern. My walls."

"But they aren't, are they?" said Aria, muzzily. "There's nothing of you in them. You have to travel along the roads, and stay between the walls."

"Hush," whispered Jeremy, but Aria was still too sleepy to feel afraid, and while there was some light she would struggle to survive.

"It's a trap, isn't it?" she said conversationally.

"No!" said Jeremy.

"I'm not talking to you," said Aria, straightening. She looked down at the map on her arm and said to the woman, "It's a maze, all these streets. A prison-labyrinth. You're stuck here digging deeper and deeper, running in circles years-thick and never getting away. And you don't have a red thread, or even a map you can follow out of it."

"We need no map!" snapped the woman.

Aria rubbed at the ink on her arm. It didn't smudge. "It's permanent," she said to Jeremy, accusingly. She could feel him growing cold as evening, and leaned closer, not grudging him what warmth she could offer.

The figure advanced, shadows roiling around it like skirts, licking forward across the thin grass as if sniffing out the echo of the line Aria had drawn. "We shall have our red thread soon enough, map-reader," it said. "And it will lead us to all the world."

"She's not a map-reader," said Jeremy, although there was little point left in denying it or in defending Aria now.

"She's a world-reader," said the woman, scornful of Jeremy even as her shadows stretched forward like hunger.

"But I'm neither," said Aria, wonderingly. She took hold of Jeremy's sleeve. "I didn't have a map at all, so I must be a map-maker, a world-maker." It occurred to her this would give her cousins pause, but the thought and the cousins seemed dim and far away. "I drew a path for us from the heart of your rat's-nest, all the way to the wall that keeps you in."

"It keeps us all in," said the woman, amused.

Aria took Jeremy's pen out of her pocket. They had retreated and the wall pressed against the back of her legs, its stone rough and clammy. Carefully, for her hand shook, she finished drawing on her arm: a gate in the wall, and tiny lines for the stairs leading out into freedom. She did not look up until she had finished drawing.

Then she glanced to the side and saw that there in the wall, camouflaged by the angle of the stones and the blood-red light of sunset, was a rusted metal gate, set a little ajar, and the top of a set of stairs worn concave with age and use.

"Come on, Jeremy," she said, trying to keep her voice steady.

"Run," said Jeremy, but Aria dragged him after her through the gate and into the shadows between the wall and the stone balustrade.

"No!" cried Jeremy. "Let me go. Someone must stop it getting out!"

"How?" panted Aria. "You? How can you lull her asleep when you're so afraid? You had lost that battle before I came."

*And you must be half-afraid of me*, she realised sadly, *or else you would have lulled me to sleep and I would be dreaming now.* "Who has kept her in this long, Jeremy? Who was strong enough to trap her?"

Jeremy did not answer. Aria towed him down the stairs, and they were not simply stairs she had invented, but stairs that existed on their own and had been used by others—cracked and patched with cement, old and mossy and stinking of urine, cigarette-ends, and freedom.

Darkness spilled after them, with a viscous, probing swiftness. It bellied and grew, swelling above the walls as if still confined by them, forcing its way through the gate, darkening the edges of Aria's sight.

Aria and Jeremy scrambled down to the street, and fled out of the shadows of the stairs, into the sunset light. Straight into the arms of two police, who pushed them aside, eyes and weapons trained on the gate.

"After all this time?" said the woman—the multitude, the beast—from the shadows at the top of the wall. "After all these years, you are all that are sent to stop me?" Laughter shook the mortar between the stones and inky tendrils leaked down. "Have they forgotten me and left the door so poorly guarded?"

"The gate," shouted Jeremy. "Close the gate!"

Aria scrubbed uselessly at the indelible lines on her arm.

"The red thread," she murmured. "Jeremy, give me your knife!" The paths were only ink, after all. Surely blood was more powerful.

Jeremy pulled out his knife. He held Aria's wrist and she closed her eyes, bracing against the swift cold blade, as he sliced across her arm through the path they had followed, or made. Through the stairs, and her skin.

A man shouted, "Stop!"

She realised, later, it must have been one of the police. It was followed by a noise like falling stones. When she opened her eyes, there was far too much blood for the thin throbbing pain in her arm. Jeremy was curled in it. Night poured out of his chest: a spreading darkness of shadows that faded like smoke, while blood spread and stayed.

"Back away," said the policeman.

"No, no, no!" whispered Aria. She had her hands on Jeremy's chest, and scarlet welled out between her fingers. Hands were trying to lift her away, but she had something more important to do.

"Stop the shadows," she told the owner of the arms. "That's what you're here for, isn't it? That's all he was trying to do."

But Jeremy had succeeded. The air was clearing, the shadows were simply the shades of evening, and her own blood running down her arm dissolved the streets and alleys she had drawn. Nothing extraordinary would come down the stairs now.

"Can you reroute death?" she asked the evening, the distant lights and sirens. Her own blood throbbed to the sounds.

"Don't try," whispered Jeremy. "You'll get us both lost." She felt him try to force her to acquiesce, but he was too weak. The desire to sit and watch him die faded with Jeremy's strength.

Whatever of himself he had saved and hidden from the creature in the maze had not withstood that single bullet. Brittle Jeremy Lantern.

"You're losing your touch," she told him. "And you're still alive, so all's not lost."

"It will be soon," murmured Jeremy. "There are larger mazes than those streets, and darker labyrinths." His heartbeat fluttered under her fingers like a bird's wings.

*A red thread through a maze*, thought Aria, and because it was all she had, she drew with their mingled blood on Jeremy's chest a new path: a tangled maze to keep life in for just a little longer.

The doctor, short and gingery, regarded Aria narrowly when Officer Gray brought her in to the theatre. It was late at night, but even so, very few people seemed to be on this floor. The doors were poorly signed. Not so much a secret wing as an unobtrusive one. Hidden by being unremarkable, like boundaries in a city, and families in the world.

"This is Doctor Payne," said Officer Gray.

"My own name," said the doctor, with a voice like sand, as if used to mockery and the hint of a smirk in the policewoman's voice. "Do you know who this is?"

Jeremy lay on the table, at once too pale and too bloodied under the unnatural light. His shirt had been cut away and his eyes were almost entirely closed.

"He told me his name is Jeremy Lantern," said Aria. "It isn't his real, own name. Whatever that is, I think it's been hidden for a long time."

"Do you now?" said the doctor dryly. "Frankly, it was a good shot, he should be dead, and I'm not a miracle-worker. But between your devilry, Miss Winter, and whatever your Mr Lantern did with his name, he hasn't quite died. Not that I'd say he's alive. Look at this." The doctor's hand, powdery in its translucent glove, touched Jeremy's shoulder and brought away a piece of him—a shard, like broken porcelain.

Aria wanted to hide her face against someone's shoulder, but the policewoman was the only candidate and she was not a comforting presence.

"Our friend here doesn't seem to be showing up on any records," continued the doctor, glancing once at Officer Gray for confirmation. "It happens. Stray bodies get dragged in more often than you'd think, although usually they aren't so well dressed." The remains of Jeremy's silvery suit were dark with drying blood.

"From what I understand," the doctor went on, "you're likely to be the only one who cares whether he lives or dies. And the only one to raise a stink about it, which is all you people seem to be good for. That's why you're here. Oh, don't look alarmed, I'm a doctor. Do no harm, and so on. Open the window, Claudia, just in case."

Officer Gray complied. There was a crisp wind, and to Aria the traffic sounded very heavy for so late. She sensed it moving through the night, up to starlit mountains or along the shore of a moonless sea.

The doctor opened Jeremy's chest, lifting the cold skin away as if it were dead leaves and snapping open the ribs like pale twigs. Aria, light-headed, leaned against the door. Officer Gray was watching the procedure with sardonic interest and folded arms. The doctor's gloved hands reached into the cavity of Jeremy's chest, lifted out something small and grey and set it on the bed. It sat on the blue sheets for a moment as if stunned, then shook itself—a tiny bird, bedraggled and forlorn.

Aria straightened. "Jeremy?" she whispered. But if it was Jeremy, it gave no sign that it knew her.

"I haven't seen this before," said the doctor, with professional interest. "Chances are, if this is him, it's been locked away so long it doesn't even know itself anymore."

The bird shook out its wings, hopped to the edge of the bed, and then flew. For a horrible moment it battered about the room, maddened by light and partial freedom. Then it found the open window and was gone.

The doctor turned away as if Aria was not there, and drew the sheet up over the empty body. It was already collapsing in on itself. "I wish more of them would have the decency to clean up after themselves. A logistical nightmare. Vampires, now, they're tidy. I like vampires."

The police officer put her hand comfortlessly on Aria's shoulder.

"Time for you to go home, Ariadne Winter, before someone with a bigger budget takes an interest in you."

"What about those tangled streets?" whispered Aria. "And the shadow woman, and all of it?"

"That's our problem," said Officer Gray. But Aria knew that was not true. She was growing too aware of the pulsing night beyond the windows, the shape of the city, the stark presence of those prison-streets. She could have pointed to them blindfolded. Her own warm, small northern city, her family, her quarrelling laughing cousins: those all felt very distant, compared to the near urgency of questions to be answered, trees to learn the names of, a grey bird to find.

Jeremy had been right, Aria had lost them both. For better or worse, she had knotted her own life to this city, and those streets. She had already, so carelessly, come home.

# *The Present Only Toucheth Thee*

You have been following me from almost the beginning.

Seed-black eyes, thread-fine whiskers, delicate claws that prickle and scrape. Darting and hiding, on your quest across the unswept concrete. I have found a rusted trap, and will welcome your company while I repair it, but you pay it no heed (does it puzzle you? amuse you?). Your course is set towards—not me, but my book.

That is how I know it is you.

Mortality was never my besetting weakness, but here are some creatures you have been:

A doe, milk-white, grazing near my cave one evening. Your hide would become the cover of this book.

A lamb, incautious, of whose skin I made the first parchment-page.

The pine (which fell before the doe was born) whose resin yielded soot for my ink.

Three lives, single-souled, to supply my pen. Although I have forgotten the language I wrote in, I can guess the meaning, for what does any man write, except *I am here*.

The coincidence that calls you back, life after life, to the book is also the power that makes its words true. The words shimmer and act, the letters ripple and *be*. But what do you want with it, little one?

❧

I have beaten you and killed you, one plague year when you were a rat. Much, much later, when the secrets of disease were unlocked, I amused myself by imagining you became after that a flea, and after that, a fleck of the plague itself. In another half-emptied city, you were a thief, fumbling from hunger, only your soul carrying you forward. Justice was swift, there: I had you hanged.

There were times when you were long absent, although I suspect you were once a convolvulus spiralling towards my many-paned window.

You have certainly been a spider, in a city of sun-baked brick that is lost now to time. A little long-legged peace-lover, webbing and winding the book when you thought I did not notice. You were too small to even lift the cover, and so I let you linger, unthreatening company, as concerned with the book as I. When you died, curled in your strands, I almost mourned.

Twenty years later, when you were a handsome youth with gold on your upper arms and wrists, and royal scarlet daringly woven through your robes, they bore you on a litter to my door and you entered with wide, acquisitive eyes. I imagined that you remembered the taste of mites and moths, that your scarlet lips were still powdery with their wings.

You offered me much for the book, when you saw it—you recognised rarity and power, I think. You certainly knew bloodshed.

I can only conjecture, you see, what it will mean for you if you take my book, or for me if I lose it. I have written my long life in those pages (on skins I suspect you have worn, and on others no doubt innocent), since first I guessed its tripled power. It has sustained me when I have been pursued and threatened, when lesser men would have surrendered.

(Were you also the rabbit I boiled into glue? What of the flax that became the thread that stitched the pages? The reed that formed my pen?)

I have tried to make another such book, but there are more souls in the world now. How am I to find anyone twice, except you, who are bound to me? You, who remain undiminished, one of the first.

When you were a general, razing villages, and I fled with the book strapped beneath my clothes, I was curious: Had you begun to remember the secret I whispered into the dying mouth of that arrogant lad? Or did you rage because you were crowded now by thin, diluted souls, you who had been almost solitary in the youth of the world?

Once, for a time, you recurred in the children of a new factory-town. Starved, or work-mutilated, or too richly dressed, always you found your way to my door, and always your eyes lit on that book. Each child—nine, or seven, or five—was of an age to have come into being on the death of the last whose body was buried under my floor.

Why that loop? Were children any cheaper, then, than they have ever been? Or had the pattern become familiar to you?

I, also, have a rare soul, and an old one. When the world grew over-full, I moved up among mountains, intending to watch them erode to their ancestral bones.

It took several lives for you to find me there, and I wondered if you were crossing the ocean to me on ships that plunged down to a darkness so undisturbed that it remembered you. Or were you ascending from the plains in a train that choked on its own smoke in a long tunnel, so that you died as peaceful as sleeping?

There was a young woman with a camera. Climbing high, she found my hut; it was seventy years before the retreating glacier released her body.

For some of that time you were an eagle, clear-eyed, but even when the great windstorms destroyed my shelter, I kept the book under a stone.

Would we ever have ended? If I had not written you into my life, would you have spread like dye through the clouded pool of history? Or if I had not bound my existence to yours, would I have died and lived as others do, diminishing, always seeking an immortality I surrendered in the first youth of the world?

(We loved each other, once, until you took the key I forbade you.)

If there are others like either of us, they are too knotted in their own stories, their own repeating secrets, for me to find them.

The Methuselah trees have fallen to storms or smoke, and the ancient sea-sponges are passing; there is a great lizard I have seen more than once, but perhaps it is merely old. Some sharks, I have heard, circulate in the currents for centuries—who knows what they have learned. And I am told the cockroaches will outlive everything else, take the lean, lost souls remaining into their number, and inherit the earth.

Even now, as I bait this trap with food from my own plate, I am certain of this: when the waters rise and the sun burns hot and close, I will ask myself whether I have seen the last of you. Yet what if we survive that, as well, and the world freezes like hate? Suppose, when you wade through ashen snow and find me, this book remains the only thing left to burn?

When ice brittles the water and the sky, and my breath is frost, you will come to me in your final body. You will curl at my foot, or alight at my elbow, or stand over me, and mean or even say, "*This time, set us both free. Let us warm our hands a little at the pyre of all that has ever been, the lives I had and the lives you refused, and rest.*"

## On Pepper Creek

The Gardiners brought a boggart with them to Pepper Creek.

It stowed away in the great tarred-and-corded chest they brought from the Old Country, bundled in with Mrs Gardiner's Irish linen and the silver coffeepot with its pattern of vines; hidden like Mr Gardiner's past.

Perhaps little Peggy Gardiner caught its tail as she wound a length of tatted lace to store away. Perhaps the boggart jumped in to retrieve something it considered particularly its own—the red spinning top, bright with lead paint, that belonged to Tobey Gardiner—and was shut in when the lid was closed.

Or perhaps it was simply sleeping inside when Mr Gardiner fetched the chest from the cottage's attic, high up under mossy slates, within honey-coloured walls, while outside the bees swayed heavy in the roses; in such a bed, and in such a bower, a boggart could rest, sustained by the dreams of its people below. Dreams and fears.

For it is possible the boggart only chose to remember the Old House and the Old Country so: as a place diamond-paned, pollen-dusted, from which one must be dragged unwillingly away. But like Mr Gardiner (who was not a neighbourly man, and who did not wish to wait for the Law to tap on his door), the boggart might have had its own reasons to leave.

It stayed in the chest all through their long sea voyage for, unlike Tobey Gardiner (who, with his mother, had a taste for danger), the boggart did not thrill to the smell of salt and tar, the creak of lines, the shrieks of gulls.

It did not emerge when the chest was swung and dragged ashore into a vicious young city, where the masts of ships were higher than the buildings and the shops full of traps and guns and goldminer's shovels, and where Peggy Gardiner (who, like her father, had a taste for plunder) looked about with delight.

If the boggart sneezed as fine dust sifted into the chest on the long, foundering journey by bullock dray and cart, no one heard over the swearing and lowing.

But when at last the Gardiners reached Pepper Creek, the boggart spidered out of the chest, peeked through the gaps in the wall of the slab hut and realised a terrible mistake had been made.

Mrs Gardiner had inherited the land and the hut from her brother. Her husband, for all her hopes and his adventures, had not made them rich, and this was the only fortune they had. One might ask from whom Mrs Gardiner's brother had acquired the land, for even such as the Gardiners like to imagine they are civilised, and rely upon contracts and leases and the arguments of gold, when it suits their purposes. Certainly someone had lived there before, for vegetables had been planted near Pepper Creek—although the Gardiners (who were not accustomed to tilling the earth) did not recognise the leaves and trod them underfoot.

But the Gardiners did not ask, and when the boggart climbed up to where, in a better-regulated land, its pleasant attic had been, it found itself on a bark roof. It looked around at a wilderness of stars, a galaxy of trees, and was afraid.

For in the Old Country, where one constantly risks treading on the hem of a neighbour's coat (or, as the case may be, the tassel of its tail), the boggart had made a luxury of solitude, and of stealing, souring and mocking. It had not suspected it could be lonely.

This new house, however, had no ghost-steadied foundations, no comfortable chimneys full of the voices of centuries, no ample cellars stocked with dry darkness and fine, aged horrors. It did not even have the taste of a family's history, no hint of Mrs Gardiner's brother's fate, save a smell like grit-scoured bone. Worse, the straggling pale trees outside the hut, the marshy hollow near Pepper Creek and the dream-dark water to which the Gardiners laid claim were already inhabited.

There were animals, of course, and birds, nonsensical chortlers and bounders. But other creatures lived there too, like none the boggart had known. And these were not spirits to be quarrelled with and cowed and banished to another place. Vast and wounded and bewildered, at twilight they keened and sang in the dry grass, and at night they howled shrill and guttural in the branches. By day they dragged twig-thin fingers over the bark of the hut. Like loose sand in the breezes they hissed, "This, *this* is what will happen if your people are beaten and killed and driven away, out of the good soil, away from the sweet water and the bones of their many-great-grandparents. This loss, this terrible sorrow, is what will become of you—soon. *Soon*."

Such behaviour was not polite. It was not done. In the Old Country, boggart-kind ignored each other as best they could and respected each place (marsh or house) as a castle, inviolate. Humans, too, took care not to see, always holding up lights and speaking in loud voices, so that one had time to get out of the way.

But in this whispering, shivering world of untrimmed, slender-leaved trees and walls through which the moon could peer, the boggart felt utterly visible, pinned—wriggling—down by the great blue glass of the sky.

For a little while, the boggart planned to get the Gardiners away, back to the distant cottage where things had, surely, been better. But there was hardly scope to play at its old tricks, or torment the Gardiners into leaving: so little food here to sour, so many noises already in the night.

Mrs Gardiner fidgeted and sighed, it's true, and Mr Gardiner (who was not born to be a farmer) scowled and went out with his gun, and Peggy and Tobey quarrelled. The Gardiners spoke of the Old Country—they dreamed of it; they feared the wide bush and the tight rations. They wanted gold and ease, and had been used to taking what they could. But home was too far away now; there was nothing there for the Gardiners but poverty and punishment. And the boggart's heart, to be honest, was not in its old tricks, for always outside They were watching, and there was a hunger there.

"Soon," they murmured, and the boggart did not ask how such beings, awful and vast, measured time.

The boggart fretted and worried. *Hush*, it willed at the Gardiners. *Be quiet*, it whispered against their dreams. *Tread lightly. There are things out there bigger and older and more watchful than you, and they are angry.*

Each axe-fall, each gunshot, each comfortable cat-spit of logs on the simple hearth made it jump, and always the air through the chinks in the walls sounded like breathing.

The boggart clung to the Gardiners. It was a breeze against an apron, a furring of burrs on a trouser leg, smoke from the fire winding against ankles.

When the Gardiners went down to Pepper Creek to fetch water or wash, the boggart whisked after them and bristled at the lean and low-bellied creatures below the water and in the branches above, which watched with a grim patience too vast for a boggart to contain or understand. At night, it patrolled the hut, meeting fiercely through the spaces in the walls the amused, aloof gazes of Them-Out-There.

Once or twice Mr Gardiner thought, absently, that he saw a child stagger across the earth floor clinging to his wife's skirts (had she not been prettier, once?), until he remembered Peggy and Tobey were grown taller than that. It was a trick of the light, and he did not like it. He missed high roads, rich and easy as they had been before the constabulary plagued them, and hard gambling before the players grew wise to his ways with the cards; he did not care for this hut and these trees and this honest family life.

Mrs Gardiner remembered a cat she had once had, in the old cottage. When she was half-asleep with weariness and boredom, she fancied it perched with a twitching tail on one of the spindly chairs Mr Gardiner (who was not a carpenter) had built. Once, when a twig snapped outside, she even thought she woke to needle-sharp claws pricking her shoulder.

Peggy and Tobey glimpsed the boggart, too, and blamed each other, and fought, for apart from anything else there were no fresh adventures to be had here, no neighbouring children to torment—no tin soldiers to steal, no marbles to annex, no noses to bloody.

They were all eating their hearts out for something more.

The boggart grew thin and mangy. How it wished it had slipped out of the chest in that young, stinking city, where there had at least been new milk and new stone houses, and where there must already have been a few of its own kind: decent, well-brought-up boggarts who minded their place.

If only it had slithered out of the chest and hidden in the belly of the ship. Yes, great sea spirits reeking of fish and blubber had pressed against the hull, humming rude remarks and working at the ship's seams with watery fingers. But the ship's rat-bogles had dashed and snapped and sneered at them. That might have been a fine life for a boggart, part of that bold crew.

Oh, best of all, if only it had stayed behind in that golden cottage hung with flowering vines and attended by fat bees, where oak and ivy and holly had grown glossy and green, and where fat, comfortable cows leaned against stones carved by ancestors of the Gardiners when the boggart's own greatest-grandmothers had been spry.

For in the memory of the boggart, as in the memory of the Gardiners, the steady grey rain of the Old Country had become soft as a woollen shawl, the bitter snows bright as sugar. Chilblains and close quarters, superiority and hunger, the workhouse and the prison and what-will-become-of-Tobey-if-he-grows-wilder and what-will-become-of-Peggy-if-she-speaks-her-mind had shrunk almost entirely into the distance.

As for what Those-Who-Were-There-First made of all this, you would have to speak to them. They might not have tried to drown Peggy when she went to swim, but they did not lift a talon to help when a sunken branch caught at her and she barely fought free. They did not, perhaps, spook the horse when Tobey tried to ride it, but there was laughter in the treetops when he fell. And in the weeds (if they were weeds) that choked the new garden and the branches (if they were branches) that clawed Mr Gardiner's face when he rode for supplies to the far-distant town (if that is where he went), the boggart suspected Their hand.

The boggart was not cut out for such a life. It was meant to make comfortable mischief, not to wear itself to the bone protecting a family as thankless as the Gardiners while fear soured its stomach and sent hot rashes of panic across its back. But the hut was crowded with fears and dreams, and at last the boggart took hold of them and began to spin itself a nest.

There was only one place to build. The great chest was now the base of the sole table in the hut. It had never been unpacked, for what call was there here for Irish linen, or silver, or tatted lace? The boggart wisped back in and began to weave together hopes and wishes, shadows and longings. It turned and rustled, heedless of the noise, for always outside it heard, "Soon, soon . . ." It did not wish to hear any more.

Mrs Gardiner noticed the sounds. "There's something in that chest," she murmured to herself. She cleared the table of its beaded fly netting, enamelled tin plates and clutter of spurs and playing cards and damper crumbs (for the Gardiners had never got around to building a shelf in the hut, and the boggart had given up stealing).

Odd to imagine that anything could be in that chest and alive after so many months, although there were stories of toads that lived for centuries trapped in stones. Her fingers were bloodied before she pried up the nails that held the chest closed, but Mrs Gardiner had learned not to mind a little blood: she had a neat way with a bullet hole, and could mend near-invisibly the tears left by a blade and clean gore from gold as tidily as picking the monogram off a silk handkerchief.

Oh, the smell that rose to meet her. The soft-cold sweetness of old linen with cracked wands of lavender nestled in its folds. A warmth like the memory of a cat on warm stone. The sugary decay of paper in which the yards of lace had been wrapped (for Peggy Gardiner's wedding, perhaps—even such as the Gardiners know how to hope).

Below that, a stem of silver, although surely the handle of a coffeepot could not put out buds. And lower still, where there should have been blankets and winter clothes, dark and dry against her raw hands was a drift of rose petals. She did not remember scattering those in the chest.

Mrs Gardiner leaned further in, until the petals covered her hands to the wrists. Beneath them she felt the cool, clasped blossoms of fresh flowers. She was elbow deep now, and then up to her shoulders. She heard the sweet, simple tune of a blackbird. Then she was over the side and gone entirely.

When Peggy and Tobey came indoors, they called for their mother, and for their father too. Mr Gardiner saw the open chest, the dead flowers drifting on the floor, the prints of bloodied hands. He knew of such things—vanishings and violence were the spice of his old wild life.

"Stay here. Don't let anyone in," he told the children. Then he rode off into the trees shouting Mrs Gardiner's name. He was not a man to go for help. The great creatures watched and murmured. The leaves shifted like a smile.

"Look," said Peggy, peering into the chest. "Your old spinning top." It was a baby's toy, but red as uniforms and banners and poppies. When Peggy spun it on the lid of the chest, it rattled like a recruiting drum.

"What else is there?" said Tobey, and bent over the side. The cloth and paper were rucked up like waves on the wide sea, and through the holes in the hut's roof a beam of sunlight struck foam-white, gold-bright from the silver pot. There was a smell of salt and tar, rum and kelp, as if something of the ship had got into the chest after all.

"I can hear the sea!" said Tobey.

"Let me!" cried Peggy, and shouldered him aside. Squabbling and shoving, they burrowed down, searching for adventure and treasure.

When Mr Gardiner returned, night was rising from the dry earth. The oil lamp burned, lighting his way home (for the boggart minded its duties), but the hut was empty.

Mr Gardiner searched for Peggy and Tobey, and called for them, but the silent air weighed down his cries, and the only answers were howls in the hills.

He sat inside all night, his gun across his knees. He thought of all he had done that might have come back to haunt him, and what he might yet do if he had no family to carry with him. Beside him, the chest sat like an open grave.

Out of it, the boggart wafted a breath of roses. To Mr Gardiner, that draught smelt like flowers at a funeral. The boggart sent him scents of smoke and thatch, of ancient stone—but to Mr Gardiner these were as chill as prison walls. A salt breeze made him think of impressment, the creak of oak sounded like gallows and the peculiar scarlet smell was like old blood and retribution.

When these lures failed, the boggart whispered to him in Mrs Gardiner's voice and ghosted up the laughter of children. All night it wheedled and promised. But a boggart is a creature of place and memory, dreams and history. It offered nothing Mr Gardiner wanted: only the past, which weighs a man down, and family, which after all is a habit that can be thrown off. And who can say whether the boggart truly wanted Mr Gardiner? He was not, after all, a restful man.

When the night turned grey, Mr Gardiner put out the lamp. He looked for a long time at the silver and the linen, but they were too heavy to carry for what they were worth here. He lifted the lid back onto the chest and hammered it in place. He took his gun and a swag, his horse and a new name, and rode away.

As for what happened to him next, I cannot say. Perhaps at last the voices in the branches breathed, "*Now*."

But the boggart had gathered three Gardiners safe into its nest, wrapped in wishes and old lace at the bottom of the great chest. It burrowed itself down and pulled paper and shadow over them all and closed its eyes very tightly. And a boggart can sleep a good while, if it chooses.

The slabs of the hut turned grey and splintered. Great cottony cobwebs clouded around it. The roof fell in, the trees leaned close. If bushfires came near, the creatures in the trees, entertained by the boggart's alarm, at least did not encourage the sparks to reach the hut. If at last other families returned to Pepper Creek and called it by an older name, perhaps the spirits told them the story as a joke. Perhaps not. You would have to ask them.

The Gardiners brought a boggart with them to Pepper Creek, and if no one has found it, it sleeps there still.

## *Annie Coal*

Annie Coal's grandmother stood at the low door of their cottage, beneath the great horseshoe set into the wooden crossbeam. She was spinning with her little bone drop-spindle, with the fine strong hands which never looked as old as the rest of her. The slanting sun cut shadows deep as caverns in her face.

The cottage was small, but it was high on its hillside, above any other cottage, and there was all the valley around them: the gathering silver threads of the streams, and the smooth green mound of Curdie Caperwit's own High Hill quite near its centre. Annie, sitting cross-legged in the grass and combing thistles out of wool, had been looking across the day, and dreaming of Angel Tal's tales of princesses and heroes.

"You are a princess! A princess of the house of Coal," Annie's grandmother scolded now, as she had ever since little motherless Annie had first *wished*. "That woman's tales do nothing to fill an empty stomach. I've always said so. To think she asked for the raising of you. Her! Angel Tal! She's foolish as thistledown and common as dirt."

Angel, who lived far below, almost at the gate of the valley, told wonderful stories of impossible things—fortresses and queens and ships with dragon-heads. Lowland tales of gods and littlefolk, of whom those strange people gossiped and by whom they swore, but in whom they didn't believe at all. In the valley, the world was held like a thread between Granny and Curdie, and the hills hung on it like laundry. No-one lived above them, and no-one except their own folk rested under the earth.

So once, when Annie was small, she might have believed her grandmother. But Annie was almost grown now—bigger than her slight grandmother, who was frailer these last years; nearly as tall as her father, Lewel, who had become stooped and grey from travelling too much when he was young. Now, *common as dirt* did not sound so dreadful. The earth was good here, in the valley where the Coals reigned—the grass was rich, the tall shaggy cattle were sturdy and fat and the broad humorous sheep leapt and blundered. And Angel Tal was kind, and her tales full of wonders: bridges that spidered across rivers, waters deep as death, buildings clustered together like stones piled in a cairn, and people bright as kingfishers, close-shouldering as sheep.

*I only want to see them*, Annie thought. *That isn't the same as wanting to leave forever.*

"Oh, hush, Mother," Annie's father said. "Our Annie is a Coal, and knows it. If that isn't good enough for her, all the gold and crowns in all the lands won't make a mite of difference."

Granny snorted. "So say you, Lewel!"

"And Angel's never said a word to cross you, Mother," said Lewel, firmly. "Annie, go and call the cattle home."

"I've never even seen gold," said Annie, bundling her work into its reed basket. "Not a coin of it. Father has. *Angel* has. All I have is wool and thistles."

Granny laughed. "Then you're richer than most, my Annie, for they grow on earth that's your own. Hear *my* tale: Gold shines like the sun when it pries between the shutters, and coins are like shards of flint that rattle and weigh you down. But as for being a Coal! That's pride and courage and wilfulness, and all our green valley and all the time in it—yours to hoard and yours to spend. This hill for a throne, and the sun for a crown." She rapped Annie's head lightly with the spindle.

"Get along, Annie," said her father, and winked at her. "The old woman's thoughts are straying."

Annie put her basket in the cottage and stomped, grumbling, down the hill. She had never minded being ordinary, and she had never doubted that the valley was extraordinary—her father had been into the wide world, after all, and returned anyway. She merely wanted to *see.*

But when Granny was in these moods, Annie *almost* wanted to believe that a Coal was something special to be, something that swung above the world like a heron. And as Annie tramped sturdily on, the annoyance prickled at her skin, like a burr in a coat, that it was *Granny* who made her wish this—Granny, of all people, who was sensible about so many things, like settling the fire for the night with stern words, and not leaving the entrance to their valley open to lowlanders, and never going into the dark beneath High Hill.

The tall red cattle had wandered a long way, down to sweet pasture, almost to the gates of the valley, where bramble-briars and thorn-bundles blocked the way above and around the swift silver stream.

"Hey up, hey all, and hi for home!" called Annie. The cows of their few neighbours—a scattering of lesser Coals, one or two quieter families—ambled out of her way. The Coal cows swung up their heavy heads one by one, and lumbered into a trot, full bellies swaying under the tented bones of their backs, and their horns tossing against the sinking light.

As she followed them back up the valley, Annie pretended she was a real lowland princess, tall and strong, with gold in her veins and law in her voice, which her red-cloaked subjects hastened to obey. She stood tall, and strode with what she supposed was a regal gait. She condescended to the cattle, and nodded graciously to the birds, and when they forded the stream she directed a distant bow—as to fellow-royalty—up towards High Hill, where Curdie Caperwit lived.

She could not, of course, condescend to Angel Tal, who came smiling out of her white house as the cattle ambled past. Angel bent to embrace her, as if she were merely Annie, and that was quite enough.

Angel Tal, although she had lived there since Annie remembered, was new to the valley, and her house had been built in a very different style to Granny's cottage, or the other earth-and-grass dwellings. It even had a hot stove with jewel-bright tiles. And although all the ladies in Angel's stories married adventuring knights, Angel never had, even though she was round and beautiful and Annie's father said she was the most patient woman he had met.

"Is Granny wandering in her mind?" asked Annie.

"She's sane as anyone in this valley," said Angel, and sighed. "If I'd told a single tale of that woman or this land to my own old people, little love, they wouldn't have believed me."

Annie knew better than to ask about Angel's people, for she would only ever say that was "long ago and far below," and instead tell tales of clever heroes, or lovers fleeing in ships before vengeful enemies, of goddesses who wound time on a distaff, or a First King sleeping under a hill. But today Annie looked at Angel, shining in the late sun, and said, "Why haven't you got any *new* people, Angel? Why haven't you married a prince like in all the stories?"

"Ask your Granny," said Angel, which was the reply she gave for questions that would get no answer. "Besides, I have you, and Lewel."

The cattle were straying. Annie called them again, reaching to slap their slow hindquarters with an open hand. She trailed them back up the valley, past High Hill.

Curdie Caperwit, sitting in the grass, shouted down, as he did whatever the hour, "Gracious morning, human child."

"Mister Caperwit, sir," Annie called up to him. "Is there a First King asleep under High Hill?"

"Not at this moment," replied Curdie. "But we all go under at last. Most already have—the morning's nearly done." The sun was setting, but he gestured broadly to where vines hid the carved stone lintel of the caverns beneath High Hill. Curdie's House, as they called it. Things that could not be explained were said to come from there—snow in summer, and voices on the wind—and things that were lost forever were said to have fallen in. "You may step beneath and see, if you wish."

"No thank you," said Annie, firmly. Between Granny's warnings and a confusion of stories from Angel about tombs and caves and ghosts, Annie knew better than that.

Curdie Caperwit unfolded. He shrugged his thin shoulders and stretched his long knotted arms. "Sober and sage grows merry with time!" he said. "Noon draws near. Look to your grandmother, Annie Coal," and although he was so brittle and bent that Annie imagined she could hear him creak in the wind, he danced off around the crest of the hill.

When Annie arrived home, the light was almost gone from the sky, but her grandmother was already in bed.

"Are you ill?" asked Annie.

"I'm old," snapped her grandmother.

"You've always been old," said Annie.

"Rude child," said Granny. "I was young once, and better-looking than you!"

Annie could not imagine that; it was like imagining the beginning of the world. So she patted her grandmother's long lovely hands, and worried.

The next day Granny didn't get up, and wouldn't eat.

"I'm old," said Granny, "and far too many winters have got into my bones. More than you could understand, my mayfly grandchild." She couldn't get warm, though Annie built up the fire and told it to blaze steadily.

The next day Granny was far worse. She was sinking in on herself like the end of autumn. "Shall I fetch Angel Tal?" asked Annie.

"That woman will never pass through this door while I live," said Granny, and sighed. "For better or worse, those are the terms on which she stays in this valley. No, child. Here is what we must do. Send to the old man of the sea. Tell him your grandmother has grown far older than is needed, and that he must come back and set me to rights."

Annie went outside. There her father sat, sitting and smoking.

"She is talking about old men in the sea," she said. "But she won't let me get Angel."

Lewel was silent a time, then he said, "She's right, of course, and will be until the end of days. If anyone can fix her, it's Bright Seabrown. But I've never heard that he travelled so far upland in all my time, and Granny wouldn't stand the journey even to the gate of the valley."

Lewel had not left since Annie was born, and she did not like to think of him plunging into the world outside, the loud low lands of tales, that whirled as fast as their seasons.

"Will you really go?" she asked.

Lewel frowned up at her. It made his heavy eyebrows shift like restless creatures.

"I've been too long out of the way of the world," he said. "And I mocked Seabrown, as a boy. He will remember. You'd have a better chance of convincing him than I, and of coming home again."

"But I don't know anything about the world!" exclaimed Annie.

"Nor the world of you," said her father, "and that might be for the best."

There was very little to prepare. Early the next morning, Annie wrapped bread and cheese in her kerchief, and put on her heavy cape and sturdy boots.

Granny grasped Annie's wrist. Her beautiful hand was weak. "Go straight on out of the valley until you get to the sea," she said. "Find that old rascal Bright Seabrown, if that's still his name. The best way to find him was always to annoy him, for he thinks himself very wise—try knitting the foam, or spinning skeins of gulls. Tell him Millie sent you, and that he may have his kiss again."

"Who is Millie?" asked Annie.

"I am!" snapped her grandmother, and sank back into her pillows.

Annie had simply never thought of her grandmother being a child, or having parents, or being called *Millie*, and kissed. How very long ago all that must have been. But it was too late to ask for those stories now—and if Granny had wished to tell them, she would have.

"Goodbye," said Annie, humbly.

"Remember you are a princess," murmured Granny. "Whatever Lewel and that woman say."

"Remember you are a Coal!" said Lewel. "Pride and courage and wilfulness—just like your grandmother."

He gave Annie a little leather bag, pressed with softened patterns of leaves. "Ignore the clamour and glamour. Be quick and be clever, and never pay more than half what they tell you the price is."

"Yes, Father," said Annie, but when she looked at the little brown coins in the bag, she saw they had the round, cheerful face of a young man stamped into their surface. He looked like someone nice to know, and she did not think she could bear to spend them, as Father said she must. They jingled like ice.

"Go," said her father, and pushed her forward.

The cattle lowed, curious, but Annie walked on away from them, downhill in the dewy dawn.

As she went by High Hill, she saw Curdie. "Gracious morning, human child," he said, and for once he was right that it was—barely—morning. "Where are you going?"

"To the sea, sir," said Annie.

"To count the strawberries?" he asked.

"To count the waves," answered Annie.

"Well, that's a sad thing," said Curdie Caperwit, "and not something you want to do over—be sure to get it right the first time. Now throw us a kiss, Annie Coal!"

Annie blew him a kiss, and he leaped high in the air, as if to catch it.

Then he waved once with a closed hand, and wandered out of sight. Annie walked on.

In front of the white house, in the blush of dawn, Angel was waiting for her.

"You shouldn't go," said Angel. Her broad fair face was worried. "Stay here where it's safe, my darling. Your grandmother will last a long while yet. The wide world will have changed since I left it, but I still fear it will not love you—or else it will love you too well."

"I must go," said Annie. "I'll remember all your stories, and come home as soon as ever I can."

Emotions in the valley were like the streams: they might run swift, but they were never deep or turbulent. Angel's kind face grew more serious, and that troubled Annie. "Annie," said Angel, "I vowed never to cross your grandmother—neither her will nor her threshold. But this morning I'm near to doing so, just to keep you here, even if she throws me out and breaks my heart and I crumble to dust at the gate of the valley."

"Don't," begged Annie. "For I must see the world, at least once, and you must take care of them, despite and around whatever Granny says."

"Do you doubt I will?" said Angel. "Haven't I always?" Then she bent and kissed Annie's forehead. "I've no travelling-gift to give you, save my love," she said. "After all, love's all I've ever travelled on. But time's a strange thing, Annie. If it should get away from you, remember this valley. Remember us."

The valley, with its gate of woven thorns, was a very long way from the sea, and it seemed all the world lay between.

Annie walked straight ahead. She followed the stream as it grew swifter and steeper, broader and slower, gathering threads from other valleys and widening into what she supposed must be a river, far too deep to wade.

She discovered that there were many people in the world, more even than she might have guessed from Angel's stories. She ducked past clusters of pale stone houses, and skirted villages, and slept in tangled thickets, and finally reached what must be towns, too large to go around without risk of losing the river, and so full of men and women—taller and wiser and busier than her, with their voices like a swift, lazy echo of Angel's—that Annie was able to slip through their crowds unnoticed.

But Annie noticed a good deal. She studied their garments, curiously stiffened and cut, and dyed such brilliant colours that Annie could not imagine what plants yielded them. Granny, she knew, would sniff and call them common. But Annie wished she could take back a fold of scarlet wool, a twist of pure white lace, to show Granny, and to gladden Angel.

Her own good cape and sturdy boots looked shabby among such glory, and although her little store of food was soon gone, her coins went swiftly, too, and she could not bear to trick these bright people, as she was sure Lewel would have. But the coins were old, and of little value, and she had nothing else to exchange. Though they spoke of hard seasons and complained of taxes and fallow fields, everyone had more than her of everything—except, perhaps, time.

*Pride and courage and wilfulness*, thought Annie. She could at least be proud, and walk like a princess, although she soon guessed they saw her as a beggar child. *No shame in that*, she told herself firmly. It was, after all, for love of Granny that she travelled.

"Such a quaint little thing!" said a lady with an enormous white apron, who gave Annie thin soup and hard bread, and turned away the last little brown coin with a quick smile of wonder. "Why, you might almost be one of the folk from under the hills, who used to carry off sheep and maidens."

"The dead live under the hills," said Annie, lifting her chin. "Besides, I'm not so small. I'm almost to your shoulder, and may grow taller still."

The lady laughed, briskly but kindly. "Likely you will, little one," she said. "If you stand still long enough to grow. You've rough hands—I'll give you work, if you can settle to it."

"I have to go to the sea," said Annie. "I have to find Bright Seabrown."

The lady shook her head. "I don't know that name. But I know a carter travelling that way in the morning. He'll carry you some of the distance, for love of me."

Annie did not like to wait, even for the promise of faster travel, but the day was already late. And it struck her that perhaps most folks in the wide world were so tall and strong that they did not have many people to be kind to. She told herself it would be gracious to accept, as well as wise. And besides, she wished for one night not to sleep under the stars.

So she accepted, which seemed to please the lady. Annie admired her house, wide-eyed at all the wonders in it, although she was surprised to find coloured tiles—which must have once been as precious as those in Angel's stove—broken as if they were no more than river pebbles, and set into the floor around the fire.

But even if she would not cheat, as Lewel told her, Annie did not like to accept the lady's kindness as if it were tribute—Annie was, after all, only pretending to be a princess. So she asked the lady for work to do, and sat by the hearth through the night, carding wool until it was as soft and fine as she could make it, and all was combed into fine clouds. When she was done, she warned the fire sternly to lie low and keep watch. Then she curled up and slept until she was awoken by the exclamations of her hostess.

The lady, whose eyes were round and respectful that morning, gave Annie good bread and eggs and milk for breakfast, and a pouch of fine food to share with the carter.

"No-one will believe me," she said. "All that work done, the wool fine as silk, and the fire burning steady as glass. You won't stay, little one?"

"I have to get to the sea, and home again," said Annie.

The carter was not going all the way to the sea, but for most of the day his cart followed the river.

Annie rode in the back of the cart, on sacks of wool he was taking to another market in an even larger town. The road was rough and Annie, who had never before travelled higher above the ground than the soles of her boots, was afraid the thin-ribbed oxen—slow and sleepy—might stumble and throw her right off the cart.

*Courage*, Annie reminded herself. *You wanted to soar over the earth like a heron.* So she sat up and pretended to be queen of all she surveyed.

When they stopped to take on more sacks and to let the oxen drink, Annie got down and patted their ridged sides and scolded some heart and courage into them, as she would with her own red cattle. Then she climbed up on the seat beside the carter, and shared the meal the lady in the town had given them.

It was good, but as they rode on and on, farther and lower, and the river grew broad and brown, Annie began to feel as if something had been cut out of her—home, and thin sweet air, and soft grass, and clear water. And the road was so long that she grew afraid of just how large the world was, and how far away the sea might be. It was difficult to feel as if she were even merely ordinary anymore, or as if she would ever get home.

"Is there a king of all this land, sir?" she asked, to think of something else.

The oxen, their coats glossy now, were high-spirited and jaunty. The carter was struggling to keep them in hand. "Are you daft?" he asked, not unkindly. "There's always been a king on that grey throne, ruling from the sea to the mountains—aye, and down the other side. He's sat there for years and years, growing gaunt on misery, till they might stamp a death's head on the coins, in place of the king's. Mad, he is. Sending armies up into the mountains where no-one lives—his councillors put a stop to that. Chasing rumours like foxes until no-one could sleep easy."

Annie thought of the smiling young man on the small brown coins. "Why?" she asked.

"They *say*—the old people say—he lost his daughter. Stolen away by a fairy-lad. Likely she just ran off, not knowing what she had was good. *What's got into these beasts, acting like they're calves again?* Have you lived under a stone all your short life, girl?" He snorted, but cheerfully. "This gossip was old when you were born. She'd be an old, old woman now, if she lived."

Annie flushed, but she wondered, and she thought of Granny's fine hands, and her opinions. "Was—is—the king's name Coal?" she asked.

The carter merely laughed. "That's no sort of name for a king, that I ever heard," he said. He shouted the oxen to a halt, where the road curved away from the river, and nodded to it. "That way follows the river, and the sea's at the end of it."

But when Annie had dropped down into the grass, he leaned down to her and said, "What did you do to my cattle, hill-girl? They look like they've lost the bad years and doubled the good ones. We could make a fortune at the markets, you with a trick like that. And even in a lean season, the great markets are a grand sight. Won't you travel on?"

"No," said Annie, who had still not seen gold, and could not imagine a fortune, although she was a little wistful about the markets. "Thank you. I have to help my grandmother."

So she firmly gave him her last coin, in payment, and he let her take the rest of the food, and left her standing in the dusty wind, with the grass whispering around her boots. The world felt unbearably colourless and wide, as if even a bird circling wouldn't find a stain of real green, or be able to glimpse high hills.

Annie sighed. For a moment she had thought Granny might be right, that Granny herself might have been a true princess, with a crown and an old father still living, who missed her, and a throne, and all the things from stories, and good reasons for scoffing at Angel's inventions.

But of course, there was nothing of Granny in the faces on the coins, and the world did not belong to the Coals. If the carter told the truth (and certainly he knew more than she did) then not only this drab countryside but her own little valley and Curdie's High Hill all belonged to a sad old king on a grey throne.

Annie squared her jaw. "Don't be silly," she scolded herself. "You're Annie Coal, and if that isn't good enough for you then all the crowns in all the lands won't make a mite of difference, or get you to the sea any sooner. Pride and courage and wilfulness—that's as good as being a princess, or will have to be."

❧

It was easy to say that, as she walked on. But when she lay down at night by the track, the stars felt very far away, and uninterested in one small person in this sprawling world. And when she walked on next day, the ground grew bare and stony, until it reminded Annie of Granny's skin stretched dry over her sharp old bones.

The river dropped down and down, until it rumbled through a deep chasm. *Deep as Curdie's secrets*, as they might have said in the valley. And, sudden as a knife, the path Annie was on ended. Or, rather, the ground ended, and the path crossed the river by a thin web of ropes and planks. The bridge swayed much higher above the water than the ox cart had been above the road. There were white birds flying deep in shadow, far below.

"Be brave and bold," Annie told herself. On this side were Granny and the valley. On the other *might* be the old man of the sea. But in between was a terrible plunge.

Annie did try to cross, but her knees would not bend properly. At the first step, the rushing wind and the water far below struck up into her limbs. At the second, the bridge swayed so that the sky slid around it. At the third, her hands froze around the thin ropes. She tried to call for help, but all the sound she could make was the keening cry of the birds—and there was no-one else to hear.

Finally, although she thought it would be the last time she saw daylight, she closed her eyes and stepped back once, twice, three times, and fell down on the hard earth, sobbing for breath.

She lay there and listened to the birds scream as if they were falling. As if they were the spirits of people who had slipped from the bridge, and only wanted her to join them.

*The valley is higher above that river than the bridge*, she told herself at last, and sat up. *The hills and the town, too.* She would have to cross. Surely people did, and survived, for there was, after all, a path, and the bridge existed.

*But I won't go quite yet.* Her legs felt weak. Instead, Annie opened her satchel to eat the last of the food the lady had given her, in case she never had the chance to eat again. The bread, like the land, was now dry.

A white bird soared up out of the chasm and landed near her, regarding her first from one yellow eye and then from the other.

Annie threw it a scrap of the dry bread for, after all, if it was the ghost of someone who had fallen, it must be very hungry by now. "Although it must be nice," she said, "knowing you won't fall *again*."

A second bird landed, and a third. "If there were more of you," said Annie, "you could carry me across. If I had the yarn Granny had spun, to make a net, and if I could ask you politely." She broke off more of the bread, and threw it to them.

Then a fourth arrived, and a fifth, and Annie had an idea.

"I don't have enough pride or courage to get me over that bridge," she told the squabbling crowd of birds. "But I am a Coal, and that means I'm wilful, and while that bridge and I are both here, I intend to cross it!"

She stood, and the birds lifted up expectantly, for they could see she still held the last of the bread in her hands. Annie drew a deep breath, broke off a handful of crumbs, and scattered them onto the first rungs of the bridge. Some fell through, and some landed on the wood, but Annie could not see where it all went, for the air filled with birds. They shrieked and swooped and jostled the bridge, but they hid the chasm, and Annie stepped out.

As she walked, she crumbled more of the bread and threw it ahead of her, and so she crossed the river in a cloud of wings, and she was almost laughing when the bread ran out. Annie closed her eyes and scrambled up the last few swaying yards to solid earth, and dropped onto her hands and knees.

When she had caught her breath, she turned and waved to the birds. "Thank you!" she called. "That's all I have. But if you ever fly all the way to my valley, you will be very welcome there!"

Then, although her legs still felt unsteady, she walked on and on. The ground sloped down and the air grew clammy and salty. She pushed through wiry grass, starred with strawy flowers, until she came to the top of another cliff and saw at last, spread out to the edge of the sky, the great and shifting sea.

The sea, here, was nothing like Angel had described. She had spoken of it as something glimpsed from many-paned windows, merry with silken sails, or seen spangled from the decks of tossing ships. What Annie saw was huger than despair, big enough to hold every lost thing. Purple and green, it wrinkled and shifted like a cow twitching its hide to shake off flies.

And somewhere in that she must find one old man.

But she did discover a narrow path. Annie worked her way down it, pressing close to the cliff, down and down through the roar of the waves, until she stumbled into thick sand. It sank whispering beneath her boots and slipped silkily in through the holes in the leather.

The shore was pitted with flat stones and scattered with wood worn smooth and pale, but it was empty of people, and there were no caves in the cliffs.

"Bright Seabrown!" Annie called. No-one answered, although she called again, "Bright Seabrown! Please, sir! I'm sent from the valley and High Hill to fetch you back!"

Granny had said, *If that's still his name.* What if he had changed with his name, and no longer answered to it? Annie struggled through the deep dry sand onto the hard wet sand, and then through tangles of brown-green weed until the foam of the waves folded around her toes. Wave after wave after wave, but they were all still the ocean, just as Granny was still Millie Coal, even if Annie hadn't known it. She wondered how long the waves had rolled here, while the remote stars swung dizzily, and things changed over and over, the way nothing did in the valley. She wondered how long she would have to wait and call for Bright Seabrown.

Annie was too weary to feel pride or courage or wilfulness. She had no food or coins left to travel home again, and she felt small as a fleck of sand.

"Bright Seabrown!" she called. "Old man! My father mocked you but my grandmother knew you, and must see you again! Please!"

Only the waves answered, growling and hushing, and Annie wanted to cry. "I did ask nicely!" she shouted. She kicked at the sand, and sent a soft clot of it into the waves. It dissolved and swirled back onto the beach. Then she remembered what Granny had said. *The best way to find him is to annoy him.*

Annie sat down on the hard damp sand. "Old man! Old man!" she said, sadly. "I am a Coal, and I will throw the whole shore into the waves, grain by grain, until you come out and speak to me. And I will count every one."

She sat there as the daylight swelled and sank and brightened. She only shuffled down the beach when the water shifted too far away to throw the sand into, or scrambled back when the waves threatened to get into her boots. She counted every fleck of sand, and every shell, and whenever she ran out of numbers she started again. She began to feel that this was all she had ever done, and that she might do it for all time, and that the sound of the waves had hollowed her out entirely.

When a voice said, "Stop that, girl! Can't you see the waves are flinging it all back?" Annie could hardly remember what the words meant.

She turned, stiffly, and looked up at the man who was standing beside her. She should have seen him come along the shore, and of course he ought to have descended from the cliffs. But she looked at his footprints, soft-edged in the sand, and saw that they walked up out of the long lace-edged waves.

Bright Seabrown did not look old at all, but the strong smooth angles of his face reminded Annie of her grandmother's beautiful hands. And those, she had learned now, reminded her of the broken shells and driftwood that lay polished on the sand. Slowly, she stood up.

"Look up there," said the man, pointing to the cliff. Annie did, and saw the last light catching on the starry grass at its top. When she turned back to him, the man said, "I see it—there's a trace of that old high valley in your face, for all that you carry the dust of the lands between. I heard a rumour—aha, I have it! You're Millie Coal's foundling."

"I'm her granddaughter," said Annie.

The man shrugged as if it were the same thing. "What news of that bold lass?"

"She's old," said Annie, grim. "And she's sick."

"You needn't worry about Millie Coal," said Seabrown easily. "Coals are born to that valley, as I've taken to the ocean, although there's only one of me and they must share that little patch between them. Still, time treads cautiously around them—and around Millie more than most." His gaze had already turned back to the sea, which was softening into the same colour as the sky.

"She sent me to find you," said Annie, "and to say you might have your kiss again." But she was thinking *Millie Coal's foundling! What if I'm not even a Coal at all? What if Lewel only discovered me on his travels, or someone left me at the valley gate? What if I'm only a little knot of tiredness and fear, swaying in the middle of nothing*?

And she bent to pick up a handful of sand, and to throw it grain by grain into the waves. The stars were out.

Bright Seabrown put a hand, cold as it was lovely, on her arm. "You've been too long away from your valley, child," he said. "And too long here. Soon you won't move when the sea rises. Millie knows I've taken pity on drowners, but I'll not have a Coal haunting my halls, and counting for all of time. I met her son, did you know? A callow youth in a stolen boat, shouting insults into the waves—well, I called up a storm and ran him swiftly aground, and he learned his lesson."

That reminded Annie, very distantly, of a story of Angel's—the sea throwing out a long wild wave that let the heroine and her love escape pursuit. And thinking of Angel made Annie remember the valley, and warmth, and food.

"I want to go *home*," said Annie.

"Well, when Millie calls the tune, we all dance to it," said Bright Seabrown, resignedly. "Come away, child."

Bright Seabrown called, with a voice like a gull, and a grey horse galloped up the beach. It, too, must have run up out of the waves.

He put Annie up before him, and she clutched at a mane that was insubstantial as sea-foam. The horse was more restive than the ox cart, and felt even less certain than the rope bridge, which had at least been tied at each end.

At a word from Seabrown, it surged forward. It carried them inexorably up the dark cliff, and tore with a rushing thunder through the dry grass. When it reached the chasm it soared over as if on wings, and all the white birds roosting along the river rose up in a cloud below.

Seabrown laughed at Annie's alarm. "Old King Curdie kept a string of fine horses," he said, as they galloped on. "All strung about with silver. Has he given that tradition over?"

"Curdie *Caperwit*?" said Annie. "There isn't a horse in all our valley."

"Ah, is that the way of it?" said Seabrown. "Curdie in his dotage. He should have gone back into the world, like me."

But Annie was remembering the silvery horseshoe above Granny's door, and for the first time she wondered what had become of the horse that had worn it. Perhaps it had fallen to foam, and rushed away down the skeining silvery streams, and all the way out to sea.

*Perhaps that will happen to me*, she thought wearily, as the untiring horse tumbled them up the carter's track in the dawn. *I might not even be a Coal—I could just let go of the valley, and float away like sea-foam.*

She felt very light, there on the horse with only the knotted grip of Seabrown's arm to stop her drifting away. He was speaking, constant as the waves, of grand rides and firelight and starlight and dancing in the hills, or under them, or *up* them, or perhaps all three, as if the footfalls had raised the mountains as surely as the horse's hoofbeats hauled Seabrown and Annie up them. They galloped past a startled carter with a new-painted cart and proudly trotting oxen.

*Pride and courage and wilfulness*, she remembered, faintly, and then more keenly, she remembered Angel who had said, *Love's all I've ever travelled on.* And she had said, too, *Remember us.*

*They're still mine*, thought Annie. *Granny said I'm her granddaughter, and so I am, and I travelled all this way for love of them, and I will go home, I will.* And her heart lifted.

They passed through the town, and the people they passed bowed, and nodded. They did not laugh at Annie, or note her rough cape and worn-out boots. And although she did not see Bright Seabrown fling any coins, she saw children scramble after them in the street for spangles of silver, and she saw the kind lady—very well-dressed, now—raise a wondering hand as they passed.

Seabrown spoke on, waiting for no answer, and not troubling whether Annie understood. He spoke of the first throne, and the naming of the lands, and a gamble with the bones of the world and a sweet bargain struck with the lady of the valley, of the first ships and—with pride—of the great shipwrecks, of famous storms and monsters in the deep. But Annie found she missed the gossip of the carter, the hearth-kindnesses of strangers, the teasing wonder of the people she had met.

Nor did anyone greet them as she had greeted Curdie—*King Curdie!*—every day until she left the valley. The people in the villages and the hamlets and the far-flung farmsteads looked at them in awe. This, thought Annie, must be how kings in stories travelled: fast and high, while the world sped below them.

The road that had stretched so long under Annie's sturdy boots grew short, and the high hills sank around them. When she looked back, a veil of rain hid the hard low country between them and the sea. It swept after them as they rode on—up into the mountains where her own green valley lay, unchanging:

Granny and Lewel and Angel where she had left them, and Curdie capering eternally on High Hill.

When Annie pushed aside the knotted thorns to let Bright Seabrown ride his horse through the gate, she found it was autumn in the valley, and evening. There was a chill in the hollows, and the leaves on the few trees that crowned High Hill glittered like coins.

*If time should get away from you*, Angel had said. But everyone knew the seasons shifted differently in the lowlands.

Still, Curdie did not step out to call, "Gracious morning, human child!" as they rode by.

"Curdie!" shouted Annie. But only crows flew up in answer.

"Has he been awake all your life?" said Bright Seabrown. "There's an honour. He'll be safely under his hill, now. I daresay he'll wake when he chooses."

Up they climbed to Granny's cottage.

Angel was sitting at the door. She looked tired, and that made her seem older and smaller, but she held up her arms to Annie. "Oh my dearest!" she said. "You've grown!"

Bright Seabrown glanced at her, and laughed. "I know you," he said, and Angel looked puzzled. Then he ducked beneath the low door of Granny's house.

"Go in," said Angel. "She's poorly. And worse, since Curdie . . ."

"Went under the hill?" asked Annie.

"He said dawn was done and morning over," said Angel. "But go inside, my darling."

Bright Seabrown looked much too tall and alive in the smoky firelight, and the cottage far smaller than Annie remembered.

"You should come to the sea, Millie," said Seabrown, bending over the bed. "It would suit you."

Annie could see that her grandmother's eyes were bright, but she could not hear her answer. Lewel, who had been hidden by shadows, rested his hand briefly on Annie's shoulder, then went outside.

"Look at me," said the old man of the sea. "Handsome as ever. The change—any change—would do you good."

Granny murmured again—Annie thought she heard the word *singing*—and Seabrown laughed. "Yes, but they're difficult to catch," he said. "Have it your way, Millie Coal. As ever."

He bent, and kissed Granny, as if he were a prince in one of Angel's stories, and she a sleeping princess.

Granny smiled. She looked rested, younger even than Angel, and startlingly pretty. The folds softened from her face, until she might have been no older than Annie, and a stranger. Then she held out a hand—a beautiful hand, Granny's hand—and clasped not Seabrown's fingers but Annie's.

"It's spring again," she said, quite clearly. "Perhaps I *will* live forever, after all." Then she closed her eyes.

She did not open them again.

Seabrown stayed, but he kept apart—Annie thought he slept by the little laughing well from which the first stream flowed.

The next day, he watched as Annie helped Lewel and Angel carry Granny, wrapped in the blankets she had woven, down to High Hill. She was a very light burden.

At the carved stone doorway, at the curtain of vines, Angel stopped. She held a light and a twist of thread which was tied to Lewel and Annie so that they could find their way out again.

"It isn't my place to go in," she said to Annie. "Your grandmother wouldn't approve."

Into the darkness they carried Millie Coal.

"Bright Seabrown told me so many stories," said Annie, into the velvet silence. "Granny hardly told me any."

"She was stubborn," said Lewel. "And it was her valley."

But when they had laid her in a hollow in the heart of the hill, and found their way back to the leaves that tangled around the door, glowing red from the autumn daylight, Lewel took a leather bag out of his coat, and gave it to Annie.

"What is it?" she asked.

"Curdie would never let her have it, until the end," he said. "She wanted it given to you."

"To do what with?" asked Annie. She was not sure she could carry out another errand, not just yet.

"To look at and decide," said Lewel. "I made my choice before you were born—but whatever Granny said of Angel, you were raised a Coal. And you've braved the world, and returned."

He took Angel's hand, and they walked away, down towards the white house with the tiled stove. Annie watched them.

"What now, Annie Coal?" asked Bright Seabrown.

"I think you should leave," said Annie. "You were meant to fix her, but you killed her, although she was mad and wise and beautiful. You shouldn't have done that."

"You're a child," said Seabrown. "You think you will be so forever, but that is not granted even to a Coal. You think stories are only stories, and won't trouble you. Millie was happy to see me, and I took nothing she did not wish to give. You might remember that, little Annie. I could give you the gift I gave her—a long, long life, until everyone living forgets a time you didn't rule your valley. Until not a soul remembers you were once a child."

Annie remembered her father's hand on her shoulder, and Angel's embrace. She did not want to forget them, or be forgotten. She was glad Millie was her grandmother, but she did not want to be Millie.

"Thank you, then," said Annie gruffly. "But no."

Seabrown smiled, and looked calmly around. There was a good view from Curdie Caperwit's hill. Annie could see the flush of autumn change shade at the brambly gate, and mists rising beyond.

"I had forgotten what a pleasant country this is," he said. "It's been too long since I left. Perhaps I should claim it after all, or send the sea up the rivers."

Annie was afraid of his words, and of the memory of the waves and the sand and nothing to do but count them forever. But she thought she should not say that—Seabrown might grow angry, or smile and offer to gamble with her for it, or dazzle her with silver.

"If you forgot what this valley was like, you cannot have cared for it very much," she said. "Besides, you would have to live beside my father and me, and we would irritate you."

Seabrown laughed. "Very well, Annie Coal," he said, and gestured at the bag Lewel had given her. "I will leave. For now. I might even succeed in forgetting you, until someone else calls me by that old name. But remember"—and he tapped her forehead with a cold finger—"noon doesn't last as long as morning."

He called his horse from the stream, and rode away down the valley. Annie was not quite sure whether he vanished in the distance or dissolved into the swift water.

When he was gone, she felt the bag. Whatever was inside was hard, round as the rim of a plate, and heavy for its size. She opened the stiffening leather and saw a yellow gleam. Bright as the sun between shutters.

*Stories and stories and stories*, thought Annie. The word tasted bitter. *Princess of the House of Coal, and that no sort of name of a King.*

Millie Coal, and Bright Seabrown, and Curdie Caperwit were gone. But Annie still had the red cattle lowing, and the green valley. She had, for as long as she could hold onto them, Angel Tal and Lewel. Lewel who had loved Angel in spite of Granny, Lewel who had stolen Angel away and tricked the old man of the sea into speeding their ship. Angel who, Annie understood now, had the round face of the king on the coins, and who loved Annie as if she were her own. They had each thrown away a kingdom, thought Annie. For the sake of each other, and—in a way—for her.

Annie didn't need a crown to be wilful and courageous and proud. She didn't need a crown to love. She could dance like Curdie on High Hill, if she wished, or banish Bright Seabrown well enough without one. Nothing good ever came of crowns in stories.

She took the bag back to the door beneath the hill: Curdie's house, where the dead rested and where she supposed the First King really did sleep now.

The doorway was dark beneath the curling leaves, but Angel had left the candle and tinderbox sitting on a stone. Annie lit it and walked in. She did not go very far, but neither did the light.

Although the air had been still before, now it was full of whisperings, like people speaking in their sleep. The bag with its burden of gold grew heavy in her hands, and Annie felt as if she stood in a pit at the centre of all the lands, and the world and the stars and the seasons were coming loose and spinning around her.

"Thank you, Millie Coal," she said into the darkness. Her words fell like pebbles into swift water. "Thank you Curdie Caperwit. I am grateful, but the world was kind to me. I think—I think it isn't good for the lands below, to be cut off from us, or waiting on Seabrown's whim for it to rain or the seas to rise. We might be good neighbours to them, for a time."

She set the leather bag into a crevice in the floor, and pushed loose dirt over it. "I know you will all keep this safe, until I have need of it."

The rustling grew louder, like a rush of wind, or wings, or time. It snatched at the candle flame, and flared it up, and the candle burned down to a stump.

*Time!* thought Annie. That had been Granny's bargain, and the valley's gift, like dry leaves weighted down by Curdie's crown—and she had just given it up.

The flame guttered, and as darkness surged after her Annie fled to the thin light of the door. It no longer glowed like autumn. For a moment, a smell of snow freshened the stale air of the tunnel. Then Annie fought her way out between vines which were thick-grown over the stones. Flowers fell as she struggled free. The young grass was high, the day warm, and the air taut with humming. She had lost half a year already, and for a moment she felt again her heart in her throat as it had been above the chasm. *Let it be no more than that.*

But she was still young. It was spring, and white birds were winging above the valley.

"Remember me?" cried Annie, waving to them, and they screamed in welcome.

She laughed, and seeing smoke rising merrily from where the chimney of the little white house was hidden by the trees of her valley, Annie ran home.

# *Undine Love*

I stood on the front step of Apple Orchard Cottage and watched the worn white sedan pull up the drive under the jacaranda trees. When Jack Albury got out of it, I was surprised. He was near my age, but sleek and urbane. He looked like he ought to have arrived in something finned and red, in a shower of gravel with a slim, sunglassed beauty in the seat beside him. He seemed apologetic, until I recognised the expression in his eyes as tiredness.

"Welcome to Apple Orchard Cottage, Mr Albury," I said brightly. "I'm Tori Damson, your landlady, and I hope you enjoy your stay." I held out the key and, when he took it, proffered the gift basket. This was part of the Apple Orchard Cottage experience but Jack Albury was very much alone, and I wondered if the champagne had been a good idea. Since I took over the cottage, most of the guests had been couples celebrating anniversaries—but perhaps he was still expecting someone.

"Thank you," said Jack, and hesitated. He looked, if anything, a little lost.

"I've set the cottage in order," I said, beginning to flounder, "And if you need anything at all, my house is at the top of the hill."

"Thank you, Ms Damson," he said gravely, and I smiled and left. When I glanced back, he was fiddling with the keys and seemed to be studying the doorstep. When I looked back again, from halfway up the path between the apple trees, he had gone inside and closed the door.

Apple Orchard Cottage stood on the crest of a very small hill above a bend in the narrow river. The gnarled and neglected apple orchard ran up a larger hill behind the cottage. At the crest of that hill, farther from the water but with a fine view of the blue haze of eucalypt forests beyond, was the homestead.

When I bought the isolated farm the bed-and-breakfast had been the only profitable aspect. I kept the cottage operating for my own pleasure, although it wasn't a part of my family business. The cottage had far more charm than my rambling warren of a homestead. I liked prettying it up and arranging the leaflets from local attractions (water-skiing on the dam, a winery, the local fruit festival) and filling vases with wildflowers, but I was glad the guests kept to themselves. I wasn't very gifted with people.

Jack Albury surprised me again by coming to my house that afternoon. I was about to go on my rounds, and then drive up to the dam—my father had made a suggestion about the peculiar tracks I had seen there last time and I wanted to try it out. I suspected the tracks were connected to the regular disappearances of watches and spare change left on picnic blankets. Jack found me sitting on the lowest step, haversack slung over my shoulder, pulling my boots on.

"Hello," he said.

"Hello," I answered, and stood up. He looked me up and down, and at first I thought it was because I had changed from my floral sundress into work clothes and a hat.

He took a breath, paused, then said, "Are those bagpipes?"

I looked down at the pipes sticking out of the haversack. "Yes," I said, because sometimes honesty is the best policy, and because I was mesmerised by his perfect hair.

"Oh," said Jack. "And that, I take it, is a dog?"

Bartok, who looks like a cross between a pig and an armchair, sat looking at Jack with an approximation of keen intelligence. "More or less," I said, and then remembered that Jack was a paying guest and I was the landlady. I put down the bagpipes and pulled my hat off. "What can I do for you, Mr Albury?"

"Eggs," he said. "Mrs—the last owner—used to sell me eggs. I didn't realise, or I would have . . ." His voice trailed off. "And sugar."

"Oh," I said. "Yes, of course. Absolutely." I kicked my boots off again and ran upstairs.

"But if you're busy . . ." said Jack.

"No, no," I called over my shoulder. "Just—um—chores! Come inside and take what you need."

Jack followed me up the stairs, carefully picking his way between the pots of geraniums that had come with the farm.

I backed out of the refrigerator with eggs in one hand and the sugar bowl in the other. I kept the sugar in the refrigerator because of ants, but Jack didn't comment on that.

"Chores with bagpipes?" he said, inevitably, from the kitchen door.

"Yes," I said. "The, um, cows find it very soothing. And don't worry—I'll be far enough away that the sound won't bother you."

I put the eggs and sugar bowl in his hands. Jack was looking around at the books on the kitchen table and in the cabinets. I'd forgotten about them—I'm supposed to keep work secret but I have no gift for subtlety.

"Do you want a container?" I asked, to distract him.

"Yes please," he said, and frowned at the tattered paperback on the stovetop. It was titled, in lurid, dripping fonts, *A SCREAM AT MIDNIGHT: Legends of the Valley.*

"Cryptozoology," I reassured him. "Local legends. Just a hobby. I'm still unpacking."

"Oh," said Jack, and then, after I gave him an ice-cream container to put everything in, "Any ghost stories?"

I looked closely at him to see if he was joking, but mostly he just looked tired and earnest. "Not in the kitchen," I said, shepherding him out and into the living room, "but there are a few shelves of Gothic stuff out here. You're welcome to borrow some, if you want?"

He did—apparently stylish hair and a silk tie can belong to a melancholy reader. The ghost stories were between the cookbooks and the self-sufficiency handbooks, and since he didn't volunteer a preference I selected two with a high ratio of spine-chill to garish cover art. "Enjoy," I said. As we went down the stairs to where Bartok sat, still grinning resolutely at the air, I asked, with a determined effort at normal conversation, "So, what do you do?"

"I work," he said, and lifted the hand with the books in a wave before going back through the orchard. As I set out with Bartok I revised my opinion of Jack Albury again: good-looking, privileged and standoffish.

I concentrated on the boundaries and tracks, looking for telltale markings of unwanted pests and generally making my presence felt, which my parents always said was half the work.

It occurred to me that Jack's parting comment might not have been dismissive. It had sounded, if I considered the tone of his voice, bleakly true—as if life was just work, and this week was the one time he got to be Jack Albury.

Bartok found a newly uninhabited anthill and as he recovered from his hysteria I realised that Jack had, from what he said, been to Apple Orchard Cottage before, and that his was one of the few bookings that had come with the property. I wondered if the reason he worked was just to get away to the cottage. I was spinning a little story in my head of the hermitic tendencies of a young professional and how my gentle domesticity would draw him out of himself, when Bartok and I came to the top of a ridge and saw a distant glimpse of the dam wall. I swore as strongly as I could.

"Crap!" I said. "Oh, crap! Bartok!" Bartok sat and scratched himself and looked at me. "Jack Albury, Bartok!" I said. "What have I done?" I turned and ran back, the bagpipes rattling across my back, and Bartok lolloping around my legs. Once he stopped dead in front of me, staring at a piece of bark, but I leapt over him and kept running. I burned with humiliation. I was terrible with people—that was why my family had been happy for me to set up my district in the middle of nowhere. Introduced species were one thing—I could wrangle them like no-one's business, mostly—but actual humans with feelings shouldn't be let near me.

When we came to a view of Apple Orchard Cottage, I stopped to catch my breath. A trickle of blue smoke drifted from the chimney, and Jack Albury was walking in the reeds along the bank of the river. "Crap," I said again to myself and the stitch in my side. He hadn't driven off, but I didn't know if that was a relief. I limped back to the house.

The box of papers that came with the property contained a visitor's book heavily ornamented with teddy bears. I flipped through the pages until I found a large, angular signature that might be "J Albury." It was quite stark, just a signature between the gushing comments of the too-happy couples on either side. I looked at the date: almost exactly a year ago. I flipped further back. Another year. "J Albury." I groaned and closed the book and put my head on my knees.

Downstairs, Bartok barked at his tail. I pulled the scrapbook over. It was an obsessive collection of all newspaper and newsletter clippings which mentioned Apple Orchard Cottage, however indirectly. I flipped back through limp, folded pages and shoddy photographs until I found a collection of related articles. There was even some police correspondence—it must have been an exciting occasion for the valley. Honeymooners at local landmark, Apple Orchard Cottage, went picnicking at the dam. The bride went in for a swim, and was never seen again. There was an investigation, searches—nothing. The groom had been on the shore, joking with others near the barbeque at the time. My heart leapt at that—Jack Albury really didn't seem to be a comedian. I turned the page. This article was from a city newspaper. *Promising accountant J Albury* . . . I read beneath the photo. It was Jack. Much younger, and smiling broadly, but Jack, with his arm around a girl in white, with too many flowers in her hair. How young had they been married? I wondered. They looked like beautiful children. *On their honeymoon . . . two days after the wedding . . . tragedy . . . ordeal . . . investigations continue.* I stared at the scrapbook. "I really am a horrible person," I said out loud. The phone rang.

I scrambled across to where the phone sat, snatched up the receiver and lay on my stomach on the floor. "Mum, Mum!" I shouted.

"It's your father," said my dad. "Any luck with the bagpipes?"

"Dad!" I said. "I've done a terrible, terrible thing."

"Oh?" said my father. My parents are very calm, but my mother would have at least sounded concerned.

"There's a man at the cottage," I said, and rushed on before my dad's silence could grow ominous, "They warned me about him, they said years ago his wife drowned in the dam and he comes back for a week at the same time every year and wants to be alone and I left LEAFLETS in his room about WATER-SKIING ON THE DAM, and I joked with him and I lent him GHOST stories!"

I put my forehead on the carpet and then banged my head down once or twice, experimentally.

"Don't hit your head on the floor, Tori," said my father. "Here's your mother."

I repeated the story while my dad chuckled in the background. My mother's silence was the one she used when she was wondering whether there was anything to do but laugh.

"It's. Not. Funny," I said through gritted teeth.

"Ah," said my mother. "No, no you're right. It isn't. Is he still there?"

"Yes," I said miserably. "How am I meant to take his breakfast down tomorrow? I can't show my face. Maybe I'll leave the food on the doorstep and run." I brightened. "I'll go up to the dam early and look at those tracks."

"Tori," said my mother. "You need to face up to life, even the bits that are your own fault. Now, he's still there, so he wasn't too offended—and anyway, he knows you're new. Maybe he assumes you don't know. He might even be glad to have the opportunity to start over, after a fashion."

"Or he realised you're socially challenged," called my brother George in the background.

"Take me off speaker," I said.

"Alright, dear," said my mother patiently, "but if I cut you off, don't take it personally."

She did, and they didn't call back. It was only the regular call to make sure I was functioning as an independent adult and not burning the house down or accidentally encouraging a troupe of something that offered *wishes* to settle in the neighbourhood. Either they were satisfied on that point, or they were laughing too hard at my expense.

I rolled onto my back and stared at the light lengthening across the ceiling.

I was lying there when Jack came to the door and knocked.

"Hello?" he said, peering in. "Tori? I saw the dog . . ."

"Hello," I said from the floor, and then realised that probably didn't enhance the few shreds of dignity I had left. I sat up.

"Is everything alright?" he asked.

"Yes, fine," I said. "Thank you. And you?"

He looked quickly behind him at the sunlit orchard and said, "May I ask you a question?"

"Yes," I said, levering myself to my feet. "Of course. What is it?"

He sidled in, slightly embarrassed. He had taken his tie off and his expensive shoes and the hems of his trousers were sodden.

"I don't have a dryer," I said in advance.

"What?" He looked down. "Oh, no, I'll put them in front of the fireplace. I was wondering. Those books. Do you believe in ghosts?"

There's no right answer to this, I thought, and wished I could read him. My mother could read people. She'd know what he was really asking, or what he wanted to hear, and then would just go ahead and tell him what she thought anyway, but at least she wouldn't have to wonder if she was being an idiot.

"Why?" I asked. I didn't, of course, but there are ghosts and there are ghosts.

"Or—or other things," said Jack. "Those books in there—the crypto . . ."

"Cryptozoology?" I said, and lied again. "It's a hobby."

"So you don't believe it?"

I pulled a face. My parents, as far as I am aware, have gone through their whole lives without even being asked any awkward questions. Most people rarely see less ordinary creatures unless the creatures want to be noticed and I entertained a faint hope that Jack Albury might have an undiscovered talent, but reasoned that he probably saw a white cow through the trees.

"Do you want a cup of tea?" I asked.

Jack had coffee. I cleared off the table and when I had poured the water I put the enamel kettle down on top of a badly misspelled article my brother had sent me headed *Mysteries Of the Shalows: Damp Encounters with Mud- and shore-Dweling Myths,* which had proven spectacularly unenlightening. Jack stared at my kettle as if it had come out of a museum.

"So, ghosts," I said. "What brought this on?"

"I don't know—how much you know. About me," said Jack. And that was my answer to what brought it on. I hoped he wasn't in a mood to try communicating with the other side.

"A little," I admitted, and wanted to gasp out, *But I didn't when I put the leaflets in your room!* I restrained myself.

He bit his lip. "I've been coming here every year for years. Sometimes I pretend I can see her—Stefanie—my wife. I've never actually, well, seen things. I want to let someone know in case . . . just in case."

Maybe he thought he had a brain tumour. "Do you want to use the telephone?" I asked.

He shook his head. "Do you mind me telling you? I'll leave you alone afterwards."

It seemed a shame to waste the instant coffee. "No," I said.

"I'm afraid it will all sound like, well, like something out of one of those books," he said with a nervous laugh. "I can only describe what I saw, though." Then he didn't say anything.

"Why don't you try telling it as if you're telling a story," I suggested. "I promise not to laugh or—or be incredulous."

"Thank you," said Jack. "Because I don't believe it myself."

He had been coming to Apple Orchard Cottage for years—ever since Stefanie died. He could never quite bring himself to drive up to the dam, but he would wander along the bank of the river, through the reeds and under the trees, indulging his misery just this one week a year. He had done this today, and he saw something floating in the river. "My eyes were blurry," he said, staring past me at the wall, "and at first I thought—I thought it was a body, bloated and floating."

"A cow?" I suggested.

He shook his head. "A human body."

But it had shifted in the water and Jack rubbed his eyes and saw that it was not a dead person at all, but a creature—alive and slimy-green and nubbled all over. Something like a toad, but much larger, and with very blue eyes, which he thought was an unusual colour for a toad.

I agreed, but kept silent.

That was the first peculiar thing. The second was that it spoke to him. I raised my eyebrows politely, and Jack looked embarrassed and studied his hands.

"It's just nonsense," he mumbled.

"No," I said. "No, it's not. I mean, it might not be. Who's to say what's nonsense? It might be a sign." Signs were good.

Signs were mystical and noncommittal. In the back of my head I started cataloguing the unusual tracks and burrows I had seen recently—great warty blue-eyed toads were out of my immediate experience. "Go on. What did it say?"

"It spoke very old-fashioned English," said Jack. "That's what threw me. If it had hopped out on shore and said 'G'day, mate!' I would have known I was dreaming."

What the toad-thing said was "Greetings, faithful Jack Albury, why do you weep?" This made sense: some of the immigrant creatures were pretentiously archaic, to the point it would rub off on anyone who spent too much time talking to them.

"My wife," Jack had replied, startled into answering.

"There's many would not weep at that," said the toad-thing.

"She drowned," said Jack, harshly.

"Would you have her again at your side?" the creature asked.

"Heaven knows I would," said Jack.

"It is not heaven that can grant her to you," countered the creature.

"I won't believe she's gone anywhere else," said Jack.

The creature shook its head. "Neither heaven nor hell holds your Stefanie. She lives yet, after a fashion, and may yet be returned to you."

"How?" asked Jack. "I saw her go into the dam. She drowned."

"Drowning is not death," said the creature. "Have you not heard of the undines, the race of river-folk who love all treasure, cold or breathing? They have gathered many fair creatures to their chambers beneath the waves. Yet they, like death, may still be bargained with, if you have true coin and an unwavering heart."

"I haven't wavered yet," said Jack. "But why are you telling me this? What are you? What do you want?"

"What I am is yet to be determined," said the toad, "but the undines will require gold, and I too have my price."

"Name it," Jack challenged it.

The creature laughed. "You must let me spend one night eating from your plate and sleeping beside you on your pillow."

Jack stepped back. "Bugger that," he said. "Are you having me on, or is that how you test an unwavering heart? No-one's 'shared my pillow' since Stefanie died."

"Be it as you say," said the creature, but when Jack turned to fight his way back through the reeds, it said, "But consider, faithful Jack. Your Stefanie has spent these seven years wrapped in the arms of the undines—is it such a great sacrifice that I ask only to sleep upon your pillow, and that the once?"

Jack was silent, and at last he said, "I don't have any gold, and I don't suppose you take credit."

"You have gold," said the creature.

Jack stopped telling the story. "After that I came up here," he said. He shifted in his seat and gazed into his coffee. I looked at his hands. There was a pale mark on his left ring finger. "Maybe I was asleep," he said. "Maybe it was a sort of trance. It freaked me out." He shuddered. "The . . . *thing* wasn't the right colour, and it smelled like something rotting. Have you—" He paused and forced a laugh. "Are there any unusual neighbours?"

"A few," I said, without thinking. "Look, Jack. Mr Albury."

"Jack," he said.

"Jack," I said. "Even if it was a dream, it's the sort you should take seriously. Always be careful of bargains with strange creatures. You have to keep your word scrupulously, and even then, who knows?"

"But you don't think I'm mad," he said, with a level gaze.

I tipped my head to one side and considered. "I'm not good at reading people," I said, "so I might be wrong. You're obsessive, and probably desperate, but I don't think you're mad."

Jack gave another laugh—sharper, but not false. "You aren't exactly sensitive," he said, "but I think you can read just fine."

He stood up.

"Thank you for the coffee," he said, although he hadn't drunk any of it. "It's getting dark and I should go back."

He put one hand in his pocket, and I thought, *His wedding ring is in there, he hasn't bargained it away.*

"Have a good night," I said, as he went down the stairs. "And be careful."

I should have drugged his coffee and kept him out of trouble, but I do not have either foresight or common sense. I woke up in the morning thinking, *Undines! That's what made those tracks at the dam—something dragging itself over the mud with its hands.* Undines consider themselves to have delicate artistic appreciation, so naturally bagpipes would drive them away. I knew it had been a shot in the dark, but Dad's suggestion was right. I decided to head upstream early.

"Like lapsang souchong tea bags and possums," I told Bartok, beating out a good-morning tattoo on his ribs with the heels of my hands. He opened his mouth and let his tongue hang out. "Good old folk remedy," I assured him. "Keeps them right out of the roof." I washed my hands and put together the breakfast tray and carried it down to the cottage.

There was only Jack's car there, and I would have heard if anyone had driven in or out during the night, but when I set down the tray outside the door, I heard voices. There was no TV or radio in Apple Orchard Cottage, and no phone reception to speak of. I put my ear against the door.

Two voices, low and happy. I couldn't make out the words, but one was Jack's and the other was a woman's. I felt my heart and stomach sink together, and knocked quickly on the door and walked away. I looked back before I went into the orchard. Jack opened the door and picked up the tray—at least I had been more than generous with the croissants and jam. He was wearing a bathrobe, and a woman put her arms around him and pulled him gently back inside. He didn't look at me.

I ran back to the house and opened the scrapbook again. There she was, *Stefanie Albury, 19*. I looked through the articles in case they mentioned a bereaved twin, but there was nothing. I wondered, briefly, if my brother was playing a prank, but it would have needed more effort than he usually gave.

I called my parents.

"Dad," I said. "There's a dead woman in the cottage."

My dad thought this over. "Call the police," he recommended.

"I can't," I said. "They won't believe me. She's walking around."

"Hmm," said my father. "That could be a problem."

"Da-ad," I said. "You aren't helping."

"You're the one who said you could handle an independent beat," he said.

"I can," I said. "I'm doing fine. I've cleared the orchard of piskie-webs and—oh, apparently there are undines in the dam, which explains so much, including why picnickers keep having shiny things stolen, so I'm going to go up there with the bagpipes as soon as I figure the dead woman out!"

"Start at the beginning," said my father.

I gave him a potted version, and when I finished I heard him hold the phone away and say to my mother, "Some idiot making deals with the devil."

My mother got on the other phone.

"Have you been involved at all?" she asked. "Bargains, pacts, deals, tentative arrangements?"

"Agony aunt," I said.

"Oh, that's alright then," she said. "It will sort itself out—think of it as consequences-based education."

"Survival of the smartest," said my father.

"Thanks," I said. "Thanks a lot. You guys are a real help."

"Go pipe the undines out of the dam," said my father. "It'll make you feel better. Give you a sense of achievement."

"Do you think they took Jack's wife?" I asked.

"They like treasure, mostly," said my mother. "They're not a very common introduced species, so I don't know for sure, but I think in the ballads they only ever took people who were exceptional in some way—brilliant sailors or incredibly beautiful, things like that."

Stefanie had been self-esteem-crushingly beautiful. Maybe even innocent.

"So you'll be safe, Tor," said my brother in the background.

"Bye," I said.

I went out on my rounds in a bad mood, but Bartok was unsympathetic. Back at the homestead, Jack appeared before I could get in my ute and head up to the dam. Bartok pricked up his ears and grinned at Jack.

"Hello," said Jack, watching me load gear into the ute. His hair looked softer than it had the day before. "Fishing?"

"Mmm," I said, noncommittal.

"Do you do dinners?" he asked. "It says on the flier that meals are by arrangement and I know I didn't book in . . ."

"I can," I said. "But it will be simple."

"Thank you," he said. "That's fine."

"For two?" I asked.

Jack turned red. "Yes," he said.

I held his gaze until he lowered his eyes. I unloaded the fishing rods again.

"I had to take the chance," he said, evasive. Then a smile lit up his sad face. "And it's true. It's her. She hasn't changed. I don't know—I don't want to know how it's possible." There was a challenge under the happiness. "I walked up to the bend and threw the ring in, and when I turned back, there was someone walking along the bank. I thought it was you, and then I saw that it wasn't, and that she was dripping wet as if she'd walked up out of the water. I followed her up the hill and then she turned, and it was Stefanie. It's as if no time has passed at all." He was possessed by a fragile, fearful joy and I didn't want to damage it without evidence—I wasn't sure it would be good for Jack Albury, after the years of obsession. It was a sign of instability that he'd even spoken to the creature.

I made risotto, heavy on the garlic. I didn't have any evidence, but when beautiful women started returning from the dead and hadn't aged a day, it didn't hurt to be cautious. I carried the tray down to the cottage and knocked. While I waited, I studied the steps. They were wet, as was the bottom of the door. It was marked with little scrapes and grooves, and I wondered if Bartok had been making a nuisance of himself. I looked suspiciously at him, sitting behind me in the dusk, but he just kept on scratching himself until he fell over backwards.

Stefanie opened the door. Even in a robe, with a towel around her hair, she was far more beautiful than the newspaper photos suggested. It wasn't a showy beauty either, just a pure, unadorned perfection. She smiled, and I studied her for any symptoms of inhumanity, but there were none. Bartok was suddenly between us, in paroxysms of affection. I hooked him back with my heel and pushed him behind me.

"Bad dog!" I said. "I'm so sorry." I held up the basket, and saw that beyond her the little table was set and candles were burning. "It's risotto, and garlic bread, and coffee cake." I hadn't been able to think of a dessert with garlic, but the cake was decorated with little silver balls, although I wasn't sure if there was any real silver in them. She had very luminous eyes, exceptional but not alarming, and her loveliness wasn't brazen or crafted but tremulous and fragile, like light through leaves, or Jack's new happiness.

"Thank you," she said gently, and took the basket. Her hands were still damp from the shower, and her fingers were wrinkled. Her nails were short but beautifully manicured. "It's really lovely to meet you. I'm Stefanie."

"I'm Tori," I said. There was a little knot of hatred in my stomach that was only there for beautiful people. Human ones. "Tori Damson." She didn't react to my name.

Back in my kitchen, I put extra garlic in my own risotto, to Bartok's disgust. "I'm not going to invite her in," I told him. He just sat in the doorway and whined.

After dinner I rang home. My brother answered. "George," I said, "what do you know about mermaids?"

"They're like all women," said George. "They only want one thing."

"What's that?" I asked, against my better judgment.

"Shoes," said George, and cracked up. When he had recovered from his hysterics, I asked, "Are they related to undines? I'm going up to the dam tomorrow and trying to think ahead, work out some strategies that might translate."

"It'll just be a crocodile," said George.

"This is nowhere near crocodile country," I said, "but if it is a crocodile, I'll call you." George called himself a shark whisperer, but anyone can say that—the truth will only come out when they fail. I suspected it was just an excuse for spending most of his time surfing.

"Any advance with the zombie infestation?" he asked.

"Vampire," I said. "I thought. But she's not. Bartok likes her."

"You know that's not necessarily a good sign, don't you?" said George. "I told you he's daft."

"You told me he's attracted to liminal states," I said. He'd also told me Bartok was one-eighth werewolf, which wasn't a family tree I cared to contemplate. "I think she's human."

"You don't know human," said George.

"Maybe Bartok likes her because she's perfect," I sighed. "You should see her. George, when undines take people, do they ever let them go?"

"No," said George. "Never. Theirs is an undine love." He broke down laughing again. "Undine—get it?"

I hung up on him.

I went up to the dam the next day and played the bagpipes, to the annoyance of the few picnic parties. Dad says bagpipes are as basic a tool of the trade as bread-trails and walking the bounds and keeping salt in your pockets, but bagpipe music is much prettier when someone else is playing it in the blue distance, and not on your shoulder. Since I try not to practice, I almost pass out whenever I do play, but I struggled through "Bluebells of Scotland" and "Amazing Grace" and all the classics, because people tend to be more likely to forgive pipers if you play a tune they know. There wasn't a flurry of bubbles from departing water-folk. I'd have to keep coming back, try and herd them down, and when I'd made the dam unpleasant for them and the tourists, I'd start hitting the quiet waterholes, although that could be awkward. One of the backwaters had something that looked—from the corner of my eye—like a nest, very big and not belonging to any of the invasive creatures I was familiar with. If it was something rare that belonged here by rights, however alarmingly large, I didn't want to disturb it.

When I got home I could look down the hill and see Jack and Stefanie wading in the river near Apple Orchard Cottage. Stefanie's hair wasn't just blonde, it was gold. I could see the light glancing off it from where I stood. Not a vampire, then. I sighed.

There were three messages on the answering machine—a booking, a complaint about the bagpipes, and George. "It was a pun, but not a joke," he said. "I've been reading up on them and they get bored, but they stay jealous. If they get tired of something they still keep it stored up for a rainy day, and it takes strong—well, you know—to get it out of their clutches . . . Hey, Tor, why are you worried? You're riding the fences, aren't you?"

I called home. "George is out, darling," said my mother.

"Whispering to sharks?" I asked, sarcastic.

"The beaches have been very safe since he started there," said my mother.

"Mum," I said, "there have never been any shark attacks near that beach, and if you ask any of the beach babes, they'll say the beach was safer before George showed up. You do know he says he's possessed by the spirit of Errol Flynn?"

"At least he's doing his rounds," said my mother. "You are too, aren't you?"

"Every day," I said.

"Marked or actual?" my mother asked.

"Both, Mum," I said. Bartok has a thing for boundaries, and if I let him off the leash I can just trot along after him. Old fences tend to fall near real boundaries, but never exactly, so I have to walk the actual, important edges to make my presence felt, and then go back over the fences themselves to make sure nothing's broken or fallen over.

"And you still think something's broken through?" she asked.

That gave me pause. "I've been walking them," I repeated. "But what Jack said . . . And I've seen the newspaper clippings, Mum. It's his wife. Clearly something has happened."

"It might not be natural," Mum said. "Have you thought about it? It mightn't be creatures. It could be people, big-shot city . . . *sorcery*." She whispered the last word. Conservation and management was one thing, but actually doing magic was something of a dirty word in our house. That was why Mum didn't like knowing about George charming the surfer girls.

"It's natural," I said. "I'd know if people were up to tricks. And besides, there's Bartok. He only goes loopy when things or people are changing—boundaries and blood sugar levels and were-things. I don't know what Stefanie is," I added. "I got a close look at her, and she looks human. But she's been dead for years."

"You need to check your boundaries," said my mum again. "I'm not saying beating the bounds will keep things out, but it sounds like you've got all sorts of old-country creatures waltzing in, bold as brass, without a by-your-leave."

I took dinner down again. I had to knock a few times, then call. This time Jack opened the door. He was sunburned and smiling, although he also looked relieved, which didn't make sense. Maybe he was very hungry. "Sorry to keep you waiting," he said. The shower was running in the bathroom and I could hear Stefanie singing happily out of tune.

"Jack," I said. "Is everything—alright?"

"Yes," he said. "Everything is just as it should be, as it always should have been. Stefanie remembers nothing—it all seems a blur. Thankfully." He paused and glanced behind him and then said in a lower voice, "When you came down did—did you see anything?"

"See anything?" I echoed.

Jack shook his head. "Just my imagination. Or the dog, maybe." He laughed. "It's easy to imagine anything, right now. Love wins through."

"And faithfulness," I said, as Stefanie came through the living room, barefoot and with her wet hair tangled in curls of heavy gold over the shoulders of a shirt that looked like it must have been Jack's. She waved shyly.

"Thanks," Jack said, taking the food. I tramped back up to my house chewing over the problem. If Stefanie had simply disappeared for the better part of a decade by her own choice, and showed up again and she and Jack were both satisfied with that, it was none of my business. But Jack's story and Bartok's ecstasies suggested other forces were involved. The disappearance in the dam, the colour of Stefanie's hair, the frog-creature's story all pointed to undines. But to wash up so lightly right here at Apple Orchard Cottage in the middle of my territory, not even acknowledging the boundaries I'd been strengthening for months, needed something out of the ordinary run even of introduced magics. George had said—or implied—it would take strong magic to get free of the undines. Strong magic, I thought, and frog-creatures and promises and Jack's enduring faithfulness, coming back every year.

I ran the rest of the way and checked the scrapbook again. It was eight years since Stefanie had disappeared. This was Jack's seventh visit since then.

I called home.

"You know the answer to that," my dad said gruffly. "It took your mother seven years to get her hands on me and I'm still stuck. Strongest . . . meddling there is."

"Best thing that ever happened to you, dear," said my mother in the background.

"So what do I do?" I asked.

"Be happy for them," said Dad.

I didn't want to be happy for them. I wanted to be uncharitable. I brooded over Jack's story, then went downstairs to the laundry under the house and fished the pillowcases out of the machine.

Bartok whined. "I know, I know," I told him. "I'm creeping me out too." I held them up to the light of the bare bulb. I had no way of knowing who—or what—had eaten off which plate, but there was no evidence of any slimy toad-creature having slept on a pillow.

"What do you think, Bartok?" I asked. "How faithful is he? And if some gold-leaf girl like Stefanie just walked into your life, how would you feel about letting a bloated, rotten marsh-monster sleep on your pillow? Especially if your long-lost love doesn't seem to remember the details of her detour?" I thought of the slimy step the day before, and Jack letting me wait, knocking, until he heard me call.

"Idiot," I said, and Bartok, who knew the word and had been sitting innocently for the last five minutes, looked puzzled. "Not you," I said. "Jack Albury. I told him to be careful. How many strikes do you think the thing will give him?"

I was slack the next day, hoping the frog-creature would think I wasn't worried about this being my territory—I wanted to give Jack a chance to fix things. I spent the morning doing laundry and arranging books, until I looked down through the orchard and saw Jack and Stefanie emerge from the cottage. They were holding hands. I wondered what it was like to have someone serve seven years for you.

I packed up a picnic lunch and took it down to deliver to the cottage. Plates near the river—that was a chance to let a creature eat off them. I tied Bartok to a fence post as Jack and Stefanie wandered up. I wondered if her dress was the one she had been lost in.

"Lunch," I said, with my usual smoothness.

"Oh, how lovely," said Stefanie. "Thank you. It's a perfect day, now."

"We're—we've decided to go back to town," said Jack, stiffly.

Stefanie smiled apologetically. "It's so beautiful here," she said, "but Jack thinks"—she twined her fingers through his—"we both think we should go home." Happiness bloomed in her face. Of course Jack would think that. He was hiding from something.

"I hate to break the booking," said Jack. "I know what the terms and conditions said."

"About scrupulous compliance with the terms of the agreement?" I asked. It must have sounded heavy-handed. Stefanie looked surprised.

I smiled sweetly. "But I understand—these are special circumstances. But you're not heading back this afternoon."

Jack scowled. "No. We'll leave first thing in the morning."

He convinced her too late, I thought buoyantly. That was something else to be said for our splendid isolation.

"Shall I bring dinner tonight?" I asked. "On the house. I'll make extra." I put the emphasis on the last word and glared meaningfully at Jack. Stefanie looked mildly bewildered. Jack avoided my gaze.

Bartok watched the couple carry off their picnic, his eyes liquid with adoration. I sat down beside him and put my elbows on my knees. Bartok leaned against me and sighed.

"I know," I said. "Maybe I'll leave a note."

I wrote clearly and succinctly on a page of the local stock agent's complimentary notebook-and-almanac, which I always kept in my pocket: *Jack Albury. This is a friendly warning—I Know about These Things. You struck a bargain, and if you want the Benefits you'll have to take the Detriments as well. I am telling you this as Someone who will have to Clean Up After You. TD,* and took it back to the cottage and slipped it under the door. Then I went up the hill again and made myself a cup of tea and brooded until my mum rang.

"Tori?" she said.

"Yes, Mum?" I said. There was a pause.

"Well?" she said at last.

"We're waiting, breathless, for the latest development," my dad called out.

"Dear," my mother scolded him. "Let her talk. Is it a happy ending?"

"Not yet," I said. "Mum, what do I do if they mess everything up?"

"Pick up the pieces," said Mum.

That evening I took the basket down early, but didn't knock. I set the basket on the step then went up into the orchard and hid in the grass along the path to watch. Bartok sat on my feet.

The sun sank. I watched the river, but there were no ripples I couldn't account for. The orchard was peaceful. I had planned to have the old trees torn up and replaced with natives, but they were so old and neglected that I hadn't had the heart, and since I'd cleared the piskie infestation, the trees had filled again with local inhabitants. I could never quite see them clearly, but I was vaguely aware of them, busy among the twilit branches, going about their lives and happily ignoring me. Bugs crawled over my arms. Suddenly Bartok jumped up, almost jerking the lead clear. I looked at the cottage. I hadn't seen where it came from, but something large and bloated and sack-like crept up onto the step. It was bigger than I had expected. Bartok whined.

"Zip it," I told him. He lay down in a huff across my back, stinking of dog, and I was left to imagine if there was a stench of death from the creature at the cottage. It moved slowly around the basket. I had put some of the food in an open container, and as the creature lingered over it, I hoped that it was eating. Then it swung its head suddenly up and looked around as if sniffing the air. I stayed very still, and was glad of Bartok's uncomfortable and pungent warmth. The thing was giving me chills.

It shuffled around the basket and began to scratch at the door, making a sound like words. I was too far away to hear clearly. Then it stopped as if listening and slowly, sluglike, heaved its bulk down to the path. I expected it to crawl back to the river, but instead it began to work its way around the side of the cottage. Bartok whined. "It's picking up speed," I said, sat up and dislodged the dog. Already the creature was rounding the corner, its shadowy form lengthening, growing upright and more agile, slithering around to the back of the cottage where the bathroom window was.

"Bartok!" I said. "Come on!" We raced down the hill, and I expected to hear screams from inside the cottage. I hammered on the door. "Jack! Jack Albury! Open up!" It's too late, I thought.

Jack opened the door and stared at me.

"What is it?"

"Your dinner," I said, looking down at the step. There were a few crumbs beside the basket, which was a good sign. "And salt," I added, fishing it out of my pocket. "I forgot the salt."

"Why is there grass in your hair?" he asked.

"Camouflage," I said. "Jack, it's gone around the back of the cottage."

He bent down and picked up the basket. When he stood up, he didn't look at me again. "I don't know what you mean," he said.

"Yes you do," I answered.

"No," he said, before I could continue. "What I said to you the other day—I shouldn't have. I was distressed. I was imagining things. These last seven years have been a bad dream, but they're over now and neither of us wants to remember them. Thank you for the dinner. We'll be gone before breakfast. Good night."

I caught a glimpse of Stefanie wrapped in a towel, looking lovely and anxious, before he closed the door. "Is everything all right?" I heard her say, but I didn't hear Jack's answer. I walked around the cottage, wading gingerly through the long grass at the back. My hand felt something damp on the wall behind the bathroom, but the window was closed. I got back to the front. Everything seemed to be normal. I could see Jack's and Stefanie's shadows in the firelight.

"I've warned him," I told Bartok. "He's still got a chance to make this right."

I lay awake worrying about what ought to be other people's problems while Bartok whined reproachfully under the window and then I slept in. When I looked out the window in the morning, Jack's car was still parked near the cottage.

"Maybe he did the right thing," I said to Bartok. Curiosity and hope won out and I struck off through the orchard. I would start my rounds at the river and just happen past the cottage. I was still in the trees when I heard a yell.

Bartok started barking and pulled me through the orchard. We careened out onto the driveway just as Jack opened the door, stumbled down the steps and threw up. Bartok was uninterested. I raced inside.

There was no sign of Stefanie. In the bedroom, a horrible stench made me want to be sick too. A sweet smell of decay and slime and river mud. Dirty water drenched the mattress and floor, all the way to the window, which was open.

I ran out again and into Jack. He was standing in the doorway, pale. "It was a bad dream," he said.

I tried to push him aside but he didn't pay any attention to me. "She's asleep in bed," he said. "I'll walk in and she'll be there."

"No, she won't," I said. I squeezed between him and the doorframe and plunged outside, where Bartok was rolling around in the sun, and into the grass by the river. There was a trampled-down trail in the reeds, and I saw something shining and yellow-green slither along it.

"Stop!" I said. "Stop, this is my territory and I want to know what you're doing here."

The sound of rustling stopped, and I parted the reeds and looked down at the thing Jack had woken up to see. It was much bigger than a toad, and all the colours of death and decay. Its shape and limbs were contorted beyond anything recognisable.

"Undine?" I said, although I could see it wasn't. The thing flinched and blinked. It had luminous blue eyes. I looked down at its splayed, webbed hands and caught a glimpse of gold set into one finger, the decaying flesh grown half over it. In the translucent lumps and warts on its skull and back a few fine yellow strands of hair were embedded and ingrown. "What are you?" I asked.

It gave a rattling, rotting breath and whispered, "Going. I am going."

"No, no," murmured Jack at my shoulder. "No—Stefanie."

The creature heaved itself away and continued to pull itself through the reeds. I followed until I was almost knee-deep in the choked water and the creature slipped easily down. There were a few bubbles and then nothing.

The air was clear again. I stood catching my breath, and then Jack waded past me, out into the river.

"Wait! Where are you going?" I said. He ignored me and fought his way out to deeper water, staggering downstream as the current caught at him.

Behind us, Bartok barked once.

"No!" I said. "No-no-no! She's gone, Jack, you've lost her, you can't fish her out." Bartok hadn't been interested in the creature this time, not the way he'd fallen for Stefanie when she had been at the point of change, trapped between life and the river. Death, even animate death, didn't interest him.

I kicked off my boots and threw them back on the bank and jumped in after Jack. The current swept me quickly down to him and I grabbed the back of his shirt and kicked out until I got my heels in the mud of the riverbed. I really didn't want to think what else was down there, let alone whether any undines would have taken the hint and started working their way downstream. I didn't think I—or Jack, now that he'd failed at the last hurdle—would hold any particular attraction in and of ourselves, but they'd probably be annoyed. The first rule of aggressive bagpipe playing is to get out of the way of the things you play it at.

Jack didn't want to come. At first he ignored me, pushing out further into the water, and then he flailed behind him. I got my arm around his chest and tried to swim for shore, but he was taller and stronger than me and could still reach the bottom, and didn't care.

I held on to him. "Jack!" I said, spitting out river water. "Remember, you can only drown once."

"I only want to drown once!" he said, and I realised he was only swimming now enough to counter my efforts to get back to shore.

"I don't!" I said.

"Then let go," said Jack. He twisted around to face me, treading water. I clung on.

"No," I said. "I'm not going to let you drown. Not here. It's bad for business." His foot caught my leg and I went under and had to claw my way back up his shirt to get to the air. He let me push him down in the water, and I saw him sink, eyes open, air streaming out of his mouth. Through the murky water I thought I saw a twisted hand reach gently for him.

Obsessive and desperate, I'd called him. And determined enough to just let himself die. I took a deep breath and dived down after him, got hold of his hair and his sleeve and started kicking my way back to the surface. He was heavy, and he started to fight. I tried to get him in a life-saver grip, though I've never been the swimmer in the family. George's bad puns ran through my head. *Shoes*, I thought, and laughed, and then thought, *I'm drowning*, and kicked out—hard. My bare foot struck something fleshy that gave way under my toes. Jack seemed to lighten. I kicked out until the darkness began to tremble. Air or eternity, but I didn't think I could hold my breath until I reached either. Black spots were in front of my eyes, and then I broke through.

There was a lot of thrashing and a pain in my shoulder and something tore at my back, but I could feel the river bottom and I hadn't let go of Jack, and I could breathe. I tried to stand, and sank to my knees. The pain was Bartok, who had a hold of my shirt and was still trying to pull me to shore.

"Good dog," I gasped. "Good dog, let go now."

Bartok ignored me. He kept his teeth fastened in my sleeve, growling occasionally, as I heaved Jack Albury to the bank. Jack was unconscious. I wasn't sure what to do for drowning. I read too many old books. Pump his arms up and down? Thump his chest? I tried that first, cautiously, and then with a will because I was angry at him. Nothing happened. I opened his mouth and held his nose and put my mouth over his and blew in, and thumped his chest again.

"Don't! Die!" I said, punctuating the words with blows. "I wasn't kidding about the bad publicity. Don't die!"

I breathed into his mouth again, and this time his lips tasted less like river and more like salt. I realised I was crying. I wasn't cut out for working with people. I hit him hard, right below the ribs, and then water spilled out of his mouth and he rolled over, retching.

I dropped onto my back, causing difficulties for Bartok who was still holding on to my sodden sleeve, although he seemed less excited now that no one was on the point of dying. In spite of his awkward position he started scratching his ear. I was shaking and cold. My nose and throat felt scoured with silt. I could hear Jack gasping, or sobbing, or both. I lay on the bank and stared at the sky until my hair started drying and the strands blew over my eyes, then I sat up and disengaged Bartok's teeth. He wandered away. My sleeve was still wet with water and blood, but twisting to look at it I could see that the bite wasn't very bad, although the scratches of Bartok's claws on my back still stung.

Jack Albury lay with his eyes closed. He was breathing, but his lips looked blue. I shook his shoulder. "Come on," I said, and hauled him to his feet. We went back to the cottage. He didn't want to go inside so I fetched a blanket to put around him and boiled water and made tea, and Bartok retrieved one of my boots. I never found the other.

I hoped, a little, that Jack would realise that there were things in the world that he hadn't heard of, and people like my family who were expected to deal with them, but I don't know much about people. Jack Albury didn't want to realise. He had already convinced himself that the whole thing was a nightmare, a delusion, the champagne from the gift basket, or all three. I suppose if I had lost my true love twice, woken up to her living corpse on the pillow beside me and then had my landlady stop me killing myself I wouldn't have wanted to be clear on all of the details. Jack never came back to Apple Orchard Cottage, and I hope that means he moved on.

When my family called I gave them a summary, which George filled in with lurid colour. I spent several days in bed, only emerging to feed Bartok and show him some appreciation. After that I had to start all over again, herding the undines out of the dam.

I don't know how long it takes a dead woman to die. Stefanie's only crime was being so beautiful that she was more attractive to those diminished, exiled undines than their usual prey of watches and spare change. She'd been torn from the undines by the magic of seven years of faithfulness, and from Jack Albury by his not being able to keep one promise. I hope she's not lying at the bottom of the river, waiting for it to disintegrate her and sweep her away. It must be desperately lonely down there.

I often make a little extra at dinner and take the plate down to the bend of the river where Jack and I almost drowned. The food is gone in the morning, but there are many things out there that could have taken it. None of the visitors to the cottage have ever reported seeing blue eyes watching from the reeds, or a glimpse of gold beneath the water.

## *Kindling*

Minke was hungry for a great story, but no-one who came to Ye Aulde Owle ever brought her one. She served stale sandwiches, glasses of wine and whisky and listened, discontent, to the idle tales customers told.

*Ah yes. The call of the open road, the thrill of adventure.*

*Let me give you some advice.*

*Do you remember Ye Aulde Owle Café & Bar? A little before your time, perhaps. It was in that part of town—you're old enough to know the quarter I mean!—which was run by the arch-family in the days when they were the source of fear and order. It lay between the Royal Mechanical Gardens and the Crystal Valance, which even then was famed for its Ectoplasmic Peep Shows, though most of the ghosts were tricks back then.*

*A canal ran behind the Owle, a road in front. Omnibuses and wheel-horses rumbled by in dust and oil fumes. Little wind-up delivery boats and hand-punts slid along the greasy green canal. You could get the parts for them in those days, and curses were too expensive a fuel. Not like today. When we heard the grind of gears, no-one twitched and thought of war machines. No-one listened for the whistling roar of spirit-eyed Steam Tigers.*

*If you were in that quarter already, you wouldn't have avoided the Owle, but you wouldn't have recommended it by name. It had a few apathetic regulars, an intermittent procession of visitors nursing their own distractions. It was, perhaps, as perfect a microcosm of life at the time as you could have hoped for. Dull, imperfectly gentrified, fraying at the hems. Little complaints. Little tragedies. Little ghosts. Little wants and hopes. All anonymous. None staying, all going nowhere much.*

*Looking back at it now, it's touched by the light of paradise.*

Minke carried a box of empty cider bottles to the alley behind Ye Auld Owle Café & Bar. The brassy tendrils of the shop-front railings retreated into sooty stone, and the music of guitar, accordion, glasses and engines was muffled.

The boy was waiting in his boat in the canal, crestfallen, as ever. His twisting hair misted with rain.

"I'm going to sea, Minke," he said.

Minke met his gaze. This is what she saw:

*The boy did not want to go to sea. He wanted Minke. He was going to sea because she told him once that he would have to prove himself. He wanted her to think he was a hero.*

It was hard to be a hero in that alley, in that city, in that world. Maybe heroes could still be made at sea. Perhaps great white ghosts endured beneath the oily waves. Maybe a giant, many-limbed curse could rise from unimaginable depths to pull down ships and crew, all alive-o.

Minke doubted it. There were no spectacular evils in the world, and so there could be no real heroes.

"I'll come back for you," he said, as he wound the boat-spring. "You don't belong here."

"Where else is there to go?" said Minke.

She watched his vessel tick down the canal. She despised him for leaving on a fool's errand; but she envied him for still thinking the world might be big enough for adventures.

*There was a waitress at the Owle in those days who had a talent. Not for waitressing—she dropped glasses, forgot menus, made change badly and kept her job only because her aunt owned the establishment. But she could light up that dingy room with a smile.*

*No, I don't mean she was pretty. I never worked out whether she was. It was that she could look at you and see what you wanted most in the world. Maybe it was a drink—she could guess an order without fail, even if she forgot the price.*

*She told me once that there were ghosts in the attic room where she slept, although in those days before the great wars began there were hardly enough ghosts in the world to really believe in. She said these ones had been drowned in the canals by the arch-family, but she could usually work out what they wanted, and so that kept the numbers down.*

*Could she tell what I wanted? Oh, when I went into the store-room with a delivery she would smile at me like a twist of a knife, as if she did know and might just get it for me, if I pleased her. If anything in the world could please her. I'd have slain a dragon for her, if I could have found one.*

*Take it from me: don't go looking for adventure. Learn to be content with the cruel little dragons, like her, and the peace that comes before you get what you want. Before little dragons learn to grow.*

The customers of the Owle didn't even pretend to believe in monsters for Minke's sake. She looked into their eyes, took their orders, saw their minuscule hopes, their little fears, and fretted.

"Hello," said Minke, leaning on the bar in front of the busker.

She could see what he wanted. He had written scurrilous songs and displeased someone great. His guitar was cursed—that meant he had made an enemy of the arch-family, since not many others could afford a real imprecation. Now he could only play true songs, and it cost him a career—he could have been someone, too. He didn't know how to lift the curse. He would never know. Nothing would come of him, there would be no grand adventure to follow from this beginning. Just slow decay.

"Let me guess your poison," said Minke.

*I remember the light in Ye Aulde Owle was the reddish-yellow of gas and oil lamps, of streetlamps through unwashed, uneven glass. It had sticky varnished tables with mismatched vases of wax flowers, undusted. There was a tarnished gilt-gambling machine in a side-room, but no-one ever won.*

*People walked in for no great reason, sat for a while in which nothing happened and walked out again into no particular story.*

*Maybe we can get back to that blessed boredom one day. After a few restless years, a body grows weary of adventure, of the world being all firelight, curse-light, the glitter of battle and glory. The sunshine through a whisky glass starts to look both more romantic and more attainable. But there are promises to keep, roads which I still need to travel.*

*Don't start on journeys. You don't know where they'll take you.*

Minke took a shandy to a girl in the furthest corner of the bar. The girl was dressed as a tradesman, but too clean. Minke could see what she was: a wealthy girl, a healthy girl, afraid of seeing the arch-family's livery in the doorway.

Minke noted the profile on both the girl and the coins she paid with, smiled at her and gave her back the money.

"Keep it," said Minke. "It may come in handy."

The girl looked abashed. Minke could see that she didn't want pity—she wanted the rough-and-tumble of the world.

Minke glanced towards the guitarist. "When he's drunk, he'll play," she said. "Well, when he's drunker. Give him the money then, and call us even."

Minke kept her eye on them, even when she should have been washing glasses. The guitarist played a song about giving everything up, going rambling, hitting the road and freedom, and people who'd treat you kind, treat you mean, until you hit the bottle and lost it all.

It was a true song, but the runaway with the shadows in her eyes only heard the first half: the dream of the romance of the road. Hope kindled in the girl's gaze. It shone there when she gave the money to the guitarist.

It would take time, Minke knew, but she thought this might be a long game. She saw the girl speak with the guitarist briefly, shyly. Their paths lay in the same direction. They would catch the same omnibus out of town. They would travel together, unmask each other. She would learn to lend a shoulder to someone else. He would learn that truth is powerful, but that sometimes lies are needed to temper it.

Given long enough, he would one day have to ask the girl to forgive him for something, and if she did, if she wanted to, with that blood in her veins, it would lift his curse. Until that happened, they would have adventures, however small. They would see the world.

"Minke! Bar!" said her aunt.

*It's simpler now. The world is like a map drawn in spilled wine on a bar, with all the inaccuracy and convenience of that school of cartography.*

*Here, world-sawing mountains. There, dark forest. The bird-foot marks of swamp. All that blank space in between—those are the stories, spilling out of the map like fat white grubs. The dirty marks where a finger lands on the paper: "Here be steel dragons. Here is the rendezvous. This is where our band was almost lost. Here is the poisoned river. Steer clear of that valley (heavily marked)—you won't be seen again. Here are all the ghosts of your nightmares."*

*The maps were more complicated back then, in the days of the Owle. People had time to draw them, and to invent the need. You could unreel a map across the bottom of a boat and see every shoal and all the endless empty places in between were filled with neat curving lines. They didn't leave enough room for stories to fill them. Perhaps there weren't enough stories.*

*Be a cartographer. You can probably take credit for reinventing the art. Fence the world in with lines, cage it with chicken-wire contours. You'll be doing us all a favour.*

A gutter-sleuth arrived, looking for a girl, perhaps one disguised as a tradesman's apprentice. He sat at the bar and pretended nonchalance. He wore his hat low and tried to chat up Minke's aunt in a gravelly voice. Minke's aunt liked being chatted up, but she didn't know anything, and she had to break away to shout at Minke for spilling the suds bucket, to get back to the bar where she could do less damage.

The gutter-sleuth wanted whisky and lightening up. He wanted real crimes, real mysteries, not runaway brats, however much discretion they called for. He didn't want to die like his partner had, whittling his life down to nothing worth living, something so small and easily snuffed out. Not even a note left to explain.

The gutter-sleuth wanted an answer to how that happened. How to stop it happening to him. How not to get tangled up with the arch-family more than he already was.

*I remember when people went on trips, not journeys. There's a difference—when people can go on a trip again, as a matter of course, we'll know things are mending.*

*We didn't have journeys, then—all those detailed maps had little wind-dragons drawn neatly in the corners, but no-one believed they still existed to be woken. Not even I, when I sailed off to find them. I was just going on a trip.*

*It's not a journey if you travel alone (and everybody was, then). It's just an itinerary. A quick tumble from one location into another. Might as well be asleep for it. People were just like cogs and wheels on lonely little paths, bumping elbows but not looking. Fitting in just as they ought, not trying something new just to throw everyone else off-course.*

*But a journey! Well, we have enough of those now. If you go out into the night brangling and singing, if you rub someone up the wrong way, or rub along well enough with them, if you can watch their back or know you have to watch yours—that's a Thing in its own right. It lights up a little bit of the world, like fire glowing on the edge of paper. Maybe it's a light in the darkness, maybe it will set off fireworks.*

*When enough of those sorts of journeys got going, they set the world alight.*

The woman in red was looking for a ghost. It wasn't one Minke had met yet.

If the woman found the ghost, she would be able to stop seeing smears of blood on the wall. If she found the ghost, she could simply be afraid, she could forget the kick of the pistol in her hand, the shape of it under her fine silk handkerchief, the feel of the dead man's hand beneath her own as she had folded his fingers around the grip. She could remember simply how cool and careful she had been, for she had known the dead man had worked for the arch-family, and if they cared that he had died, they could afford to pay to have the smell of someone who had handled a weapon sniffed out. If she found his ghost, she could shut it up for good. She could forget the murder and remember the bruises.

She wore her diamonds discreetly. Her hair was bottle-blonde. She drank red wine. The makeup was heavy over her scars. Her lipstick, when she left it on the lip of the glass and reapplied it, was the colour of coals. Minke took the tube of it when the woman glanced away.

Minke was so careless, so clumsy. It was easy to bend down to sweep under the bar, to trip the woman up so that she fell into the welcoming arms of the gutter-sleuth. By the evening the woman in red would—against any good judgment—be his client. Neither would tell the other the full story, and they'd both find what they were looking for, eventually. They'd both get what they wanted.

Minke was satisfied with the first story she had started, but this she found more exciting. There was a salt-sour taste to deceit and murder, a gunpowder smell, that truth and music didn't hold for her.

*Perhaps that's what she thought the world was missing, the waitress at the Owle—the one I was telling you about. Maybe she wanted stories to be big, with adventures that swept down in wind and fire and carried you off. That's what she wanted me to fetch for her.*

*I wasn't whole-hearted: I went over the seas for her but I never forgot that I loved the littleness of life—the fey and elusive moments that flitted across my path, as I puttered down the canals in my delivery-boat. A glimpse through windows at people laughing in a kitchen. Half-seen dim deeds of the arch-family's employees. The sounds of barroom talk drifting out the back door. Polite morose customers who came in and went out, caught omnibuses and slept while the world rumbled by. The waitress with a tray and a laugh, both always for someone else—a girl who mopped the bar and didn't get out much more than I did.*

*Now she has what she wanted. Great and terrible rumours, gathering storms, things that chase you. And I have what she wanted, too: a storm warning, a world in turmoil and something to hunt down.*

Minke's thoughts ran ahead of her.

"You're losing your touch," said the alchemist.

"Not your usual?" said Minke, surprised.

"This is a special occasion!" he said.

She looked into his bright, unsteady gaze. The alchemist, in his shabby striped suit, smelled of chemicals. His beard was patchy with burns. When he smiled, his eyes shifted and slid as if he watched a great and amusing secret scuttle across the walls.

He wanted everyone to know how clever he was, and Minke could see that he was clever. It was that as much as the smell of chemicals which took her breath away.

The alchemist thought he had invented a perpetual motion device, and he wanted someone to build it to his specifications, to prove it to the world. He was one of many customers with similar beliefs, and Minke had learned enough from watching mad scientists to see that the spinning wheels in his mind wouldn't do what he claimed.

But the truth of it would never be known—who would invest in a scheme proposed by such a man? He was mad. Yet although his device wouldn't provide endless energy, it was dangerous and—if only it could be constructed—completely and horrifyingly feasible. Minke knew the arch-family would have given lives to get it.

The alchemist thought about power in terms of combustion and friction, kinetics, reactions and catalysts. What he thought he had discovered for a machine with its cogs and vacuums and little explosions was merely a principle he had observed in the world: knowing what people are hungry for gives power. And to be powerful is to want more power and have the means to get it. It is a cycle of desire fulfilled.

Minke thought that was a beautiful thing.

*We used to have stories, but in those all the puzzle-pieces would fall together, the good end happily, the bad less so. The travellers in those stories sang songs.*

*Our bad and benevolent governments alike were built to a modest scale—the arch-family with their conspiracies and quarrels, foreign kings with ceremony, mystery and human foibles. No great and terrible arts, no haunted air-breaking war machines.*

*To balance this, our stories had villains who wanted to hold the world to ransom, and green-black clouds gathering ominously in the west to spread their tendrils out over bright lands until brave hearts leapt to action. But we knew how those stories would end, and we kept them in books where they couldn't grow too large.*

The tin-tinkerers were regular and irascible customers. They were short-sighted and their hands had been nicked by wires and burned by solder irons.

Minke's aunt did not like them, she said they lowered the tone, but they drank well and paid well. Sometimes they sang.

They looked at Minke over great bushy beards and wanted this: to make something worthy, something grand, something of fine gold wires and blown glass frail as a bubble, something with clockwork delicate as a heartbeat and riveting smooth as ice and a fire in its chest as slow-burning as a life—not factory engines or ship apparatus, nor gaudy necklets and tiaras, but something devastatingly beautiful in its function.

Minke flirted—she was good at that too—until they began to talk to her. She admired the twisted chain on which one of them wore his watch and wished aloud that she could have something so fine. He called it bread-and-butter work, and Minke wondered wistfully whether he took commissions?

"Not for trinkets and bagatelles," he growled. Minke was too tall—she wasn't his type at all. "There is no vision, no ambition in the world," he went on. "Give me an impossible contraption, an infernal device—" His hands gripped the air with frustration. "If someone designed it I could build a machine to take the pulse of the world to the accuracy of an eyelash, and they would weep to see it. And they want watch-chains."

Minke shrugged, but she had seen the alchemist look up, bleary with dreams and beer. He had enough courage by now—Minke had seen to that—to take himself over to the tin-tinkerers' table and introduce himself, enough stubborness to withstand their mockery, enough madness to intrigue them.

His hands, with their chemical stains, would trace delicate charts on the table and he would convince them. The tin-tinkerers and the alchemist would build something remarkable together, until they fell to quarrelling about aesthetics, purpose, ownership. Then that marvellous machine would prove itself on the world, for better or ill. Built as it was for aggrandisement and born of dispute, it would most likely be for ill.

It occurred to Minke that someone who knew how to play on hearts could make use of that, if they placed themselves well.

*What she gave the world, without being asked, without most people even noticing how she did it, was something to shake it up, a beat to dance to, a sun towards which to turn. Something to set the little stories in motion, and braid them together into one great tale. A common cause, a common destination.*

Minke made matches in the bar, while her aunt grumbled and aspired to better, petty things.

Customers went out, not yet knowing their fates had been joined. Minke's heart ached. Not because she wished to find such a story for herself, or to know how each of these would end, but because she did know. She was doing no more than setting candles in paper boats and sending them out on the night tide—they would gleam beautifully, then burn out and sink while Minke stood watching in the shallows.

It wasn't enough. She wanted to join them all together into a brilliant light-show. She wanted to braid them into a great net of stories and fling it over the world. The cursed musician and the runaway, the gutter-sleuth and the murderess, the alchemist and the tin-tinkerers. Their mysteries and discoveries and inventions should not be allowed to fade gently into the night—they should set each other off, explode against each other like firecrackers, wake the ghosts of all the old stories and set them loose on the world.

*I am piping on a penny whistle*, thought Minke, *when I should be conducting orchestras.*

She could not do that from Ye Aulde Owle.

*A common cause may start a hundred stories, but to weave them into one took a common enemy. Someone to throw a spanner in the works, to steal the inventions of quarrelling conspirators and spill blood for sleuths to sniff after, to cross the paths of young lovers with those of their pursuers. To tangle the threads, to take advantage of situations. Someone who wasn't tied into one little story, but could stand up and pull the strings of all of the characters. Someone to elbow out empty places on the map, stir up ghost-eyed dragons, set fire on the high mountains, raise storm clouds, start wars. Someone to take over the world.*

*Someone to call out a hero.*

*Here is my advice to you:*

*Don't start out to be a hero. If you must find a story, make it a little one, with someone content to stay near home. Find a cause and a goal which hardly anyone else shares. Don't add fuel to the fire. Dampen it. Turn your back on the flames. Starve them. Make a little light and let it die out when its time comes.*

*Set up petty, predictable bureaucratic villains as your government.*

*Be comfortable.*

*Make a difference.*

*Stay at home.*

*No, I can't stay any longer. I've been tangled in this story for too long. I have tigers to hunt, dragons to slay. An old friend to find.*

ᯈ

There was an empty, sleepy world outside Ye Aulde Owle Café & Bar, and Minke had a gift she didn't want to waste.

"No-one will hire you!" said Minke's aunt. "Where else do you have to go?"

"I've everywhere else to go!" said Minke.

"What about that nice delivery boy who said he'd come back for you?"

But Minke had forgotten the nice delivery boy. She slung her bag over her shoulder and pulled on her boots.

The road lay before the door.

# The Splendour Falls

"Didn't Clare get in late?" said Paul as his housemate slammed the door shut behind her, setting the guitar behind it jangling.

"She has to learn the world doesn't revolve around her," said Brenda. "Come on, buses wait for no lawyer."

"I'm not one yet," said Paul.

"Won't be one at all if you don't get to work on time," said Brenda, who was a year ahead of him and already admitted.

She set a smart pace and Paul followed, the loose ends of his tie flapping while he tried to button his shirt, one hand hampered by his briefcase.

"That briefcase looks ridiculous," said Brenda, without looking back.

Paul was too busy walking and buttoning to argue. It wasn't yet seven and the sky was already vicious blue, the air hot and heavy with humidity and the cloying scents of summer flowers and burned bacon. His shirt stuck to his back.

"Wait up," he said. Brenda kept walking. Paul set the case down in the grass so he could knot his tie. As he straightened up he saw a woman. She was standing in the side street, between sagging overgrown fences and the neglected sides of houses where rubbish spilled out of wooden boxes. Weeds and vines tumbled over walls and verandas and strangled mango trees and clotheslines, a dense carpet of yellow stars and orange trumpets, red bells and the long curled bone-coloured arabesques of honeysuckle.

She was standing barefoot on the cracked and burning bitumen, in the merciless sun that lit her up like a flame—hair on fire and her long flowered dress glowing like coals.

Paul stared, the ends of his tie forgotten in his hands, while the sun sent sweat sliding down his back and shins, and let the image of her be seared into his mind, together with the smell of softening tar and the damp beneath verandas and the thick perfume of summer gardens. She was so bright that when she stepped into the shadow of a leaning fig, she vanished as completely as if she had been extinguished.

"The bus!" shouted Brenda from the top of the street, and Paul grabbed his briefcase and ran.

There was no way to track her down. He had no name, no clues and she did not turn up again as other people seemed to, over and over like bad pennies in this small city. But he did not forget her, and he began to look—at photographs, in newspapers, pictures on the television, as if he could recognise her again from that one glimpse in a sunny street. He looked at clients, at passersby, into every alley and lane, and the more he looked the more often he thought he caught a glimpse not of her, but of her having passed, of eddies of wonder in the dull world.

There were colours among the trees of the overgrown parks that sparked brighter even than flowers or birds. There were shadows about the wooden lacework of high balconies that detached themselves and were part of a deeper, more vibrant darkness that threaded through the night, and lights in the water that were not true reflections but seemed to glance up unbidden out of the river. There were lions of brass and stone in niches and parks and fountains where he had not noticed them and which seemed as he searched to organise themselves into arcane hierarchies. There were people who seemed for a moment marvellous or mysterious or terrible, then turned and were again part of the workaday world. He turned on his heel a dozen times a day and each time he saw the hint of a world which he began to think must always have existed beyond the edge of his vision, unnoticed.

The memory, these discoveries, made the long hours of paper and ink and files and cases bearable, like a ray of light into a dark cave. But he could not find the woman.

"You're getting twitchy," said Brenda, interrupting her own story.

"I'm in love," said Paul, without intending to. He had been looking into the afternoon crowd at the bar, keeping an eye out for yellow hair. He had tried to describe the woman to Brenda, but he could not come up with a better description than that and she had been merciless.

"Well, something's wrong with you," said Brenda. "You were ignoring me completely."

Paul struggled not to run outside, into the darkness and mystery of the night, away from the bar with its smoke and beer and sweat and crowded young professionals crushed elbow to elbow, sweating in their polyester suits.

"I'm sorry," he said dutifully. "You were saying?"

"It worked. He bought it for me—a gorgeous piece of machinery. Either his secretary picked it out or he bought the most expensive one they could sell him. And next day, as if nothing had happened, he asks if I could help him with a letter and I said that I hadn't spent seven years at uni to drop everything when he had some dictation and both the typewriter and I were too damn expensive and too damn beautiful to be wasted on that."

"You said that?" said Paul, who knew he didn't have the nerve to stand up to Brenda's supervising partner.

"I was mad," said Brenda. "And we'd had a bit to drink at lunch. So yes, I pretty much said exactly that."

"And then," said Paul, fascinated.

"What could he say?" said Brenda. "I'm too damn expensive and too damn beautiful to fire."

"Too smart," said Paul.

Brenda snorted. "Smart has nothing to do with it. For the first few years you're worth nothing to the firm. The only security you have is how many you can take down with you."

"I'll remember that," said Paul. "Don't let me make an enemy of you."

"You're too nice and too honourable, Paul," said Brenda pityingly. "You're doomed."

But Paul's attention had already wandered.

"You're looking for your mystery girl, Paul," she said.

He snapped back to reality. "I'm sorry," he said.

"Never apologise," she said. "It leaves you open to liability and ruins the drama of the moment. You know my opinion, I know yours—let's leave it there."

"I wasn't paying attention—" he began.

"No need to fear a woman ignored," she said. "It's the ones who get to keep their hooks in you you need to keep an eye on."

"She's not!" said Paul. "She's never even spoken to me!"

Brenda shrugged and was pointedly silent. Paul cast his eyes over the heaving crowd again and saw, as he suspected Brenda could not, patterns in the crowds that matched eddies he had seen among the mangroves along the river's edge, patterns like the whorls on a fingerprint.

"It is rather splendid, isn't it," said Brenda. "Just the sheer chaotic humanity of it all. I mean, I know it's all a seething hotbed of lust and ambition and anarchist plots and organised resentment and mindless drug-fuelled attempts at dancing but really, if you take a step back, there is a beauty to it."

"Does it make any sense?" asked Paul.

"About as much as modern art," said Brenda. "My mum says it's living proof the world is going to hell in a handbasket."

"She sounds sane," said Paul. "Last time I asked my mother for advice she announced that the spirits of the forefathers will haunt the resting places of their lost children."

Brenda frowned. "Save my seat," she said. "If we're going to talk about your mum, I need another beer."

She slid off the stool and elbowed her way grimly through the crowd. Paul's mother had met her and told Paul, in front of Brenda, and despite Paul's careful explanations that Brenda like Clare was his housemate not a girlfriend, that Brenda would do well enough for raising grandchildren but that she had an aura of insensitivity and no vision at all into other planes. Brenda didn't visit again.

Paul sat on the stool and leaned on the windowsill and fished in his pocket for a cigarette. If he could have trusted her to be rational, he would have asked his mother about this—the golden girl and the tracery of mystery that seemed to be drawn across and on and *with* the city.

And she would sit in her living room, where the light fell through the coloured windows onto dyed throws and the plaster head of Tutankhamen, and the Venetian Tarot cards and say—over gingernut biscuits and tea—that "it" had been waiting, and that it was a curse or a blessing or a Sight, and that would not help at all.

He glanced back to look for Brenda and her blunt dismissiveness and saw the woman.

She moved through the crowd as if she were more a part of it than everyone else, as if she knew exactly where everyone was and approved and managed to walk through without being elbowed or trodden on or having beer spilled on her. No one seemed to register that the dim light shone on her as if there were no crowding bodies in the way, or to see that the eddies which moved through the press had their origin—or their end—with her.

"Hi," said Paul before she passed. He searched for something to say. "Do you want a seat?" he asked, and slid off the stool and said without thinking, "I've been looking for you."

To his relief she looked more flattered than disturbed.

"I saw you in the street, up the hill," he said inanely. "You were standing in the sun." But perhaps it had not been only the fall of the sunlight. Perhaps another light had played around her as it seemed to now. She moved as if to go by.

"Wait," said Paul. "Can I see you again?"

"You've managed it twice," she said. "Chances are you will a third time."

"I'm Paul," he said, before she could walk into the crowd that was already parting to let her through.

"Yes," she said.

"Well, will you tell me your name?" he said, sure now that all that was bright and beautiful was on the point of slipping through his fingers.

She smiled as if pleased. The crowd became more boisterous and Paul was faintly aware that it had delivered Brenda to his side.

"What will you give me for it?" asked the girl.

"A seat?" said Paul, then realised it had been taken and Brenda was standing with a beer in each hand looking royally annoyed. "A beer?" he said.

The girl raised her eyebrows. Paul knew he wasn't good at this, but he was bargaining for something more than just a name. Dicing with destiny.

"What do you want?" he asked, and laughed. "My first-born child?"

Brenda snorted. The girl laughed aloud. "Does that line ever actually work?" she asked. She spun away and then, as she was enveloped by the crowd, she called over her shoulder, "It's Kismet."

The patterns in the crowd grew fainter and lost their focus.

"You're an idiot, Paul," said Brenda conversationally.

"I got her name, didn't I?" said Paul.

It was like learning a new language, learning to see the world he followed Kismet into, learning that the patterns of the streets and the buildings, the pedestrians and even the cars had meanings, and that where other people left footprints or paper trails or nothing at all, Kismet and the ever-elusive people like her left all the brilliance and sordidness of the city.

There was no one to share it with. Brenda already thought he was unbalanced and he did not want his mother to confirm it.

And he could not find Kismet. He could guess where she had been, or might be, by the brightening air or the breath of frangipani, but she was always a little too far ahead of him.

"Is she doing this deliberately?" he said to Brenda, over a garish curry and sweating wine glasses. Even in the gaudy restaurant, the clink of glasses spelled her name through the expiring sitar music.

Brenda said, "She seems the type."

"What do you mean by that?" said Paul. "You've only seen her once."

"I've seen her around," said Brenda. "It's a small city. I'm not arguing she hasn't made an impression on you, but I don't see anything remarkable and—well, she's immature. Whatever age she is, she reminds me of Clare. She's a kid."

"An innocent," said Paul.

"Oh, come on," said Brenda. "Do you just 'feel' that? She's probably figured out she can get a reaction out of guys—all right, for the sake of argument, out of *you*—and she's working out just what she can do with this power, for good or ill. From my admittedly universal experience, most girls go through that phase. Some get scared off, some swear off, some grow out of it and others never do."

"Which are you?" said Paul.

"I don't want to incriminate myself," said Brenda.

Paul thought. "It isn't fair," he said at last.

"You'll pull through," said Brenda, snapping pappadums.

"I mean it isn't fair that you keep running into her," said Paul, "and I never see her at all."

"I'm not sure you'd see her if she showed up now," said Brenda. "You'd just see some sort of pulsating aura of glowing ideals."

"It isn't *like* that!" said Paul, angry because it was near the mark. He had seen Kismet, but there was so much more to her—something not at all frail or tentative, but large and magnificent and exhilarating and a little terrifying.

"Have you tried calling her?" asked Brenda.

"I don't have her number," said Paul. In spite of the weather he had spent hours walking through parks and markets and over bridges and underpasses, trying to track her by feel and half-glimpsed signs.

"You have her name," said Brenda. "It's an odd name and a small city."

"What should I do?" said Paul. "Go to the middle of the bridge and shout 'Kismet! Kismet! into the night?"

Brenda shrugged. "Beats what you're doing now."

"And what's that?"

"Brooding," said Brenda. "And fascinating as that is to observe, I think I'll excuse myself for a moment."

She left Paul contemplating the ruins of their dinner. He pulled out a cigarette, lit it, stared at the smoke and then stubbed it out again and saw through the dispersing swirls a yellow sundress.

It was Kismet, but she was not looking at him. She moved past the gold-embroidered hangings, and he realised she was heading for the door.

He jumped up and bolted after her, but a party of diners effortlessly, innocently got in his way and he *knew* she was doing it deliberately. When he reached the street outside, there was no sign of her, not even a hint in a breath of wind.

Paul got back to the table, too late to stop it being cleared. He ordered fresh drinks and they arrived at the same time as Brenda.

He drank until the world no longer seemed to have any overarching pattern or coherence at all, and until Brenda was disgusted and left him to find his own way home. He walked until he reached the bridge and went to the middle of the walkway. Headlights flew by on one side and lights slid beneath the surface of the river on the other. They belonged to another city below and behind the one he had thought was normal. It was a city of lights and reflections, ceaselessly shifting and changing and moving in ways which had little to do with the overgrown concrete-wood-and-bitumen city he had known. Now he stood halfway between the two.

"Kismet!" he yelled. He held out his arms to the night above and the sky—if it were sky—reflected below and shouted again, "Kismet!"

There was distant laughter from the riverbank and he dropped his arms, sobered slightly by embarrassment, and saw Kismet.

Unless she had been standing in the shadows of the framework, he didn't know how she could have been so close so soon. She walked up to him and he saw she was barefoot.

She leaned back with her elbows on the parapet and said, "I was beginning to think you wouldn't call." There was a mischievous delight in her eyes. She reached out and grasped his hand. "You're warm," she said. Her hand was much cooler than the sluggish night air. He handed her the jacket he had carried.

It was a very ugly jacket. Kismet was stunning in spite of it. Whatever Brenda said, Kismet wasn't ordinary. He wondered drunkenly what combination of countries had delivered up such a captivating being. Somewhere northern and old, he thought. East of England, west of China. Somewhere wild and full of trolls and haunted forests, with bears and princesses with yellow-silver hair and dark eyes and translucent skin.

"What do you want for it?" she asked.

"Go out with me," he said. Her smile shifted and became one of endearment and satisfaction. She slid her arm through his.

"Then let's go," she said.

"Where?" asked Paul.

Kismet gestured out to the starred darkness of the suburbs. "Out," she said.

They walked through streets and parks and scrubby wildernesses that were state forest and gardens and vacant lots. They walked past shuttered stores and pubs spilling patrons into the night and falling dim and silent as well. Past public pools and private hospitals and down narrow grassy lanes barely wider than an armspan. And Paul saw what he had only suspected—that the streets at night shimmered and moved as if with a midday's heat-haze, and the shadows were alive and some became only stormbirds or bats and others became an old man with a wheelbarrow ("He lets the bats out," said Kismet) or a trio of tall women with dirt-coloured hair whose arms seemed inextricably entwined about each other's waists and who stared unblinking as Paul and Kismet passed. ("They are my aunts, and they are jealous," said Kismet. "Of us?" said Paul. "Of everything. They can never have what they want, you see, and they wanted the world.")

Possums tightrope walked along power lines overhead and from under tin roofs pale geckos chattered and shrieked. The air was warm and still like wine, and Paul could see although there was no moon.

He told her the little there was of himself, his work in the firm. "I think, sometimes, I should dream of something bigger," he said, ashamed of her amusement.

"What do you dream of?" asked Kismet.

"This, I think," said Paul. "It's been sneaking up on me most of my life. Things I've seen out of the corners of my eyes. Reflections that weren't quite right, things like oily hands in the river. And you."

"You see a lot, don't you?" said Kismet lightly. Paul's mother had warned him it wasn't wise to admit to everything you see. It could bring trouble from those who didn't believe, and from those who did.

"I'm going to be a lawyer," he said glumly. "Like Brenda. I'm going to spend the rest of my life dealing with clauses and terms and conditions. It's dry as dust and the offices smell like instant coffee and old smoke and mouldy paper, and the lights and the fans hum. And I dream that there's something more interesting and bigger right here. Something wilder—red in tooth and claw, even—right here, and that if I look out the window, if I squint just right, I might be able to see it."

"Who taught you to dream like that?" asked Kismet.

"My mother," said Paul. "She's not quite . . . right."

"Most of them aren't," said Kismet. "There are lots of those in my family. Many grandmothers and aunts and cousins. Golden boys and girls and black sheep."

"'Golden boys and girls all must—'" said Paul, then stopped, embarrassed.

"I'm a black sheep," said Kismet. "I don't care about them." She spoke coolly, and Paul envied that, for he couldn't manage not to care. He lived in fear of his father's quiet disappointment, Brenda's vocal disapproval.

"But we rather specialise in black sheep," Kismet added, with an impish grin. She pointed to a dark street and said, "That street leads nowhere we wish to go tonight. But in sunlight, the light falls through the trees like stained glass and I can follow it home."

"Where does it lead now?" asked Paul, but Kismet only shook her head and repeated, "Nowhere you wish to go."

Paul did not know if he could find it again. He did not even know anymore which side of the river they were on, and yet he did not feel lost. The centre of all he had known was no longer a fixed point. It had splintered and grown feet and wings and each point shifted, spinning out and about him and the city like stars in a galaxy, each with its own loops of light and influence, tugging and pushing at the edge of each other's spheres. Some were bright beings, sending great crashing currents around, turning streets and weather. Some were smaller, their power in the interplay, the effects they could have on their larger neighbours, the shifting of attention or a conversation (for words and glances were a part of the landscape of this deeper city, as surely as the pylons on the mountain, the spiked bridges, the bronze lions). Others were lightless, mysterious, pressing down on the world invisibly and inexorably.

"Why can I see all this?" asked Paul.

"You didn't know where to look," said Kismet, "and you weren't standing in the eye of the storm." She slipped her arm through his again and stood so her face almost touched his. He could not feel the warmth of it, but he could feel her yellow hair as it blew against his neck. She was one of those centres, and standing there he felt night and starlight, streetlights on streets, headlights on leaves, even the breath in his lungs and the blood in his veins, align themselves in relation to her. There was nothing beyond this to dream of—the exhilaration like the crest of a turning wave, like falling into the wind, all the unfurling power and beauty of the city at night centred on the yellow-haired woman beside him.

"What are you?" he asked.

"I don't know yet," said Kismet. "I am from a very old, established family, but I'm still new to this."

"A stealer of hearts?" suggested Paul.

"Perhaps," said Kismet, and kissed him. "Perhaps of something more."

They turned a corner in a park and were in a cutting beside a highway which became a winding street on a steep hill. Kismet trailed her hand along a picket fence and Paul, following, did the same and brought his hand away abruptly. The blunt palings were sharp as broken glass and his hand filled with blood. Kismet waited for him on the top of the hill, which was no longer a street but a lookout which oversaw the river and the sleeping city below. She held out her hand, lined with fine scratches, and put it palm to palm against his.

"Holy palmer's kiss," said Paul, and where Brenda would have scoffed, Kismet held his hand and turned into his embrace, so that she stood with her back against his chest, looking down over the city. The sky was already grey. His hand stung.

She left him at daylight and he walked through the trees and pale gilded shadows into the hot early dawn in the square in front of the city hall, with its statues of lions and kings far from their native land, and its wakeful pigeons glistening like fool's gold. Without her, he was grounded, bound to the surveyed streets, but he found his own way home, seeing the glint of possibilities at every turn, seeing the world spin in the great dew-hung labyrinths of webs which draped yards and trees, seeing throughout the echo and image of Kismet like a benediction.

He arrived home and slumped on the veranda stairs, drinking in the scent-laden air and the songs of birds like falling water. Brenda nearly fell over him when she opened the door.

"Good grief, Paul," she said. "Where have you been?"

"Out and about," said Paul. But that was wrong. He had been through and behind the fabric of things. "I've been out all night before."

"For three days?" said Brenda. "If you hadn't shown up today I would have called the police."

"I'm sorry," said Paul.

Brenda sighed. "No need. Frankly, it's quieter with you gone. It's turning up like something the cat dragged in that bothers me. You lower the tone of the whole street."

She frowned and squatted down to look at his face. She studied his eyes.

"I'm not *high*," he said. "And I'm not sick."

"That depends on how you define it," said Brenda. She put the back of her hand against his forehead. "You're probably cooler than you should be. And your clothes are soaked—did you run through a sprinkler on the way home?"

She hauled him to his feet and inside. The world spun and shifted on its myriad, unseen axes. Brenda let him drop onto the daybed in the annex, with its bare boards and coloured windows. "I'm phoning you in sick," she said.

"It's Saturday, Bren," said Paul. He let the light play across his fingers.

"It's Monday," said Brenda. "Do you think I dress like this for comfort?" She saw his hand. "What did you do?"

"Cut it on a fence," said Paul.

"Great," said Brenda. "It's probably covered with possum piss. I'm calling myself in sick too." She stamped out and came back with her shoes off and with an ice-cream bucket of water milky with disinfectant. "Stick your hand in and keep it there," she said. She went off and he could hear her on the phone, something about dodgy curry and that she'd be in later if she could drag herself upright but Paul was probably down for the count.

The disinfectant stung and he could see the pain ripple back up the beams of light and wondered if Kismet could see it. Perhaps. The world had broken open and it was full of wonders.

Brenda came back. She had changed out of work clothes and taken off her makeup and had the first aid box. She bandaged his hand and said, "Well, you won't be playing the guitar for a bit, that's a mercy."

He pitied her, unaware that the hum of the traffic was the breath of a living thing and the hieroglyphs of the jacaranda shadows had meanings. "I won't play it again," he said.

"It's only at one a.m. that I mind it!" said Brenda.

"No," said Paul. "I was never going to be that good."

Brenda stood with her arms crossed and looked down at him. "You were with her."

"I'm going to marry her," said Paul.

"I'm happy for you," said Brenda dryly. "When is the joyous event?"

"As soon as she can arrange it," said Paul. "Maybe next week."

"Fat chance," said Brenda. "I know weddings. I've been in weddings. It takes *months*."

"Her family has ways and means," said Paul, and closed his eyes.

"Lord, you're serious," said Brenda. Paul remembered Brenda could not feel the wheels and gears, the limbs and mind of the city already turning slowly and inevitably to that purpose.

"I asked, I think, and she said yes."

"To a penniless articled clerk with a bad run in pick-up lines?" said Brenda. "What did you have to give her in exchange?"

"My dreams," said Paul. "She liked them, and I don't need them anymore. You don't have to talk me out of this."

"I don't think I'm in a state to try," said Brenda. She walked out through the orange-carpeted living room, already hot despite the early hour and high ceilings, through the kitchen and into the fresh air of the overgrown backyard. She sat on the steps with her elbows on her knees.

Paul found some dry bread and butter and brought it out.

"What is she?" said Brenda. "How did she manage this?"

"They're very influential family," said Paul. "They're not like ours." He was starving.

"Speak for yourself," said Brenda. "But your family—a *week*?"

"I'll tell them later," said Paul. "They'll understand. You're the closest I've got to family anyway."

"I'm flattered," said Brenda, but the sarcasm was gentle.

"Want to give me away?" grinned Paul.

"I'll never do that," said Brenda. "But I'll stand up for you, if you want it."

"Yeah," said Paul. "I do. Be best man?"

"As long as I don't have to dance with any bridesmaids," said Brenda. "And on condition I get to speak to her before the wedding." She stood up and looked at Paul wolfing down the bread.

"You shouldn't give away your dreams," she said.

Paul glanced up at her. "But they've all come true."

Paul returned to work, to jibes, to Brenda's keen observation. But he was part of something larger now. There was a point to this labour. There was Kismet, and the city that echoed her when she was not with him.

"You owe us a new housemate," said Brenda at lunch.

"I'll advertise," he said.

"I know a few people," Brenda conceded. "Maybe Clare's boyfriend will actually start paying." She paused. "I met her, this morning."

"Kismet?" said Paul.

"I was on my way back from a settlement and she found me," said Brenda. "What does she do, Paul?"

"I imagine she'll go into the family business," said Paul. He was hungry for news of her, though he saw her every evening and even apart the brilliance and promise of her filled his mind. "What did you say to her, Bren?"

"That if she was in this honestly, I wished you both luck. But if I was right, I knew her type and she should watch her step and remember that she was no better than other people and couldn't just use them for her own ends, and she'd do well to remember that."

Paul sat very still. "And what did she say?"

Brenda squinted into the light across the river. "Among other things, that she was from a very old, established family and I said I knew, and so was I, and she and hers really didn't want to cross me and mine. And then she said you were in love and would be married no matter what anyone said and I asked her what you saw in her."

Paul waited, angry and curious.

"She said," continued Brenda, "That you saw past her and saw possibilities and wonders and futures. That you loved her for who she could be. So I said I hoped she lived up to it."

"She'll be furious," said Paul. "It's true about her family. They could hurt you, you know."

"I know," said Brenda. "But I think she knows she doesn't

need to. I'll give her that—I don't know what she's in this for, but she's not a fool."

The wedding was held in the city gardens while bells rang ascending into the sky from all the steeples on all the hills of the city.

"I don't know these people," said Paul, panicking.

Brenda's face was already red with sun. "You will soon enough," she said. "They're certainly an odd assortment. No one can say she doesn't take after them."

"Brenda," he said.

She waved her hand. "I'm still in shock."

It was not the indisputable oddness of them that confronted Paul: the intertwined, envious aunts, the barrow man uncommonly scrubbed, the bright and solemn women in broad veiled hats, the men—dapper or stolid or brooding—and even some who seemed, as shadows passed them, to flicker between human form and birds or swarms of wings. It was the rolling power which came from and surrounded them until the air and the earth was alive with it. The crushing awareness that all the city was centred here today, and all the force spun out from it almost perfectly aligned. This was not exhilarating. It was terrifying.

"And here's the bride," murmured Brenda.

Paul had thought he would sense Kismet anywhere, but here in the crowd of witnesses she was barely a glimmer of light, a tug like butterflies in the pit of his stomach, and he was jealous for her. She should and would be more.

Time elided. She reached him and put her hand to his, palm to palm. Though red welts still ran across his, hers was smooth, and again he found himself in the eye of the storm, felt Kismet's strength and stubbornness and pride, and was proud for her.

The words of the service were unfamiliar and at times even the language seemed to stretch into something unrecognisable. He would have glanced at Brenda for reassurance, but he held Kismet's gaze and she smiled, and that was a spell he would not break.

They seemed to have slid outside time, there in the green shadows and the sunlight.

In answer to a distant question he said, "I do." The words came again, and Kismet hesitated.

Paul held her hands and waited and she said, quietly, "Do you like what you see?"

"You know I do," he said. "I adore you."

"What would you give for me to say I do?" she asked, earnest as if it were part of the vows, while her hair burned bright as fire beneath the old, old lace.

"Anything you ask," he said.

She leaned closer, so close he could have kissed her, and whispered, "Would you give your sight?" she said.

"*Paul!*" hissed Brenda.

"It's yours," he said, "If you want it." What else was there to say? The whole world had been turning to this overwhelming question.

"I do," said Kismet.

Then they did kiss, and time began again and Paul opened his eyes to blinding light and the oppressive steaming heat of a summer afternoon that brought sweat to his scalp and neck and back without even the relief of a breeze.

There was no weight of power, no swirling vortex of shifting worlds. There was the gardens, the trees, the hot blue sky building itself up to clouds at the horizon, the city squatting squarely on its thousand foundations. There was a motley group of wedding guests sniffing and smiling and sneering. Odd, but unremarkable.

"Paul?" whispered Brenda, but he looked at Kismet. Her hands were still in his, but there was no more weight or power in them than in his own, and for a moment he did not recognise the woman in the heavy veil. She was unchanged and yet altered utterly, and for all the hours he had gazed at her he might have been seeing her for the first time—a small woman with a blunt, wide-mouthed face and sharp teeth and dark eyes, a woman who seemed as much bound by the laws of nature as himself. A woman who was only—herself, and nothing more.

"Kismet," he said, shaken by the stillness, like a sailor come unexpectedly ashore. "What's happened?"

"Your wedding gift to me," she said, and touched his face. "The hope, the potential, the wheeling world—all that you could see." She was fiercely happy. "You have given me the world."

"And me?" he said.

"You have what you bargained for," said Kismet. "You have me. Am I not enough, my love?"

And it had to be, for there was nothing more to wish for, and all the magic had gone out of his world.

Paul looked for it, for a while. But though he knew it had been there, he could find no glimpse or hope or dream of it returning. The trees were only trees, the houses only outdated architecture steaming and rotting in summer and keeping no wind out in winter. Nothing was greater than the sum of its parts or moved to a pattern he could trace. The river cast back only his own reflection, and the bridges and the sky. And in months, and years, he ceased to search because there was never a spark of hope, no dream to lighten the long days.

There was only the mundane city, the office, the summer, and Kismet whose power and glory was beyond his sight, and always would be. A world thin as paper, with nothing behind it and nothing worthwhile to wish for that had not been vowed away.

# Acknowledgments

My thanks and love go to the following:

My parents, who appreciated the value of a good short story, and kept a rotation to replace our family novel reading on nights when visitors were staying over.

Angela Slatter, whose incisive advice made so many of these stories so much better, and whose friendship and example encourages me to keep writing. My ongoing development as a writer over the ten years of stories in this collection is heavily attributable to Angela.

All the friends (and housemates!) roped in on very short notice to provide last-minute edits, proof-reading, vocabulary assistance, audience, and encouragement. Aimee Smith and C. S. E. Cooney represent geographical (and temporal) extremes of this much larger group.

All the editors (and proofreaders and typesetters and illustrators!) and publications where these stories appeared, and the hand they had in shaping and presenting these stories. Many first appeared in Australian publications, which represent a long-standing and valuable network of Australian colleagues and friends—as does the Vision Writers Group, my first critique group, out of my time in which came so many friends and connections, and whose feedback influenced the earliest of these stories. And of course, Alex Adsett!

Outside Australia, I must single out Ellen Datlow, who edited "The Heart of Owl Abbas," and then as editor of *Flyaway* let me get away with constructing a novella almost entirely of short stories.

The tellers and retellers of fairy tales and other stories of enchantment. There are many influences on this collection, overt and covert, but in these stories I owe particular debts to Charles Dickens, Diana Wynne Jones, Ruth Parks, Robin McKinley, Anna Tambour, C. S. E. Cooney and Angela Slatter (and to D. L. Ashliman's translations).

Science fiction, fantasy and horror short story writers, all of you—I've always loved the form, but I've been engaged in a very large short fiction reading project for the last eighteen months, and my respect for your craft and the possibilities of the form has deepened astonishingly.

And most particularly Kelly Link and Gavin J. Grant—not only for how they shaped (through feedback and publication) "Skull and Hyssop," or for their foundational, enduring and multifaceted impact on my career as an illustrator, but also and especially for their friendship.

# *Publication History*

These stories were previously published as follows:

"The Heart of Owl Abbas," *Tor.com*, 2018.
"Skull and *Hyssop*," *Lady Churchill's Rosebud Wristlet* #31, 2014.
"Ella and the Flame," *One Small Step*, 2013.
"Not to Be Taken," *Bitter Distillations*, 2020.
"A Hedge of Yellow Roses," *Hear Me Roar*, 2015.
"The Tangled Streets," *Bloodlines*, 2015.
"The Present Only Toucheth Thee," *Strange Horizons*, 2020.
"On Pepper Creek," *South of the Sun: Australian Fairy Tales for the 21st Century*, 2021.
"Annie Coal" is published here for the first time.
"Undine Love," *Andromeda Spaceways Inflight Magazine* #52, 2011.
"Kindling," *Light Touch Paper, Stand Clear*, 2012.
"The Splendour Falls," *Andromeda Spaceways Inflight Magazine* #41, 2009.

## *About the Author*

Kathleen Jennings lives in Brisbane, Australia, and was raised on fairy tales in Western Queensland. She is a British Fantasy Award–winning writer and World Fantasy Award–winning illustrator, and has previously been a translator and a lawyer. She is the author of an Australian Gothic novella, *Flyaway,* and a poetry collection, *Travelogues: Vignettes from Trains in Motion.* She has an MPhil in creative writing (Australian Gothic literature) and is currently a PhD candidate at the University of Queensland. She has also illustrated extensively in the fantasy field.

ALSO AVAILABLE FROM SMALL BEER PRESS

"The core of the book is a cleareyed survey of the complexities of Black American experience, distilled in a few lines from the title story: 'I hated the powers for what they had done. But I learned the pride. That I was of a people who could take all the hate and poison of this world, and laugh, and go dance on Saturday.'"
— Amal El-Mohtar, *New York Times Book Review*

"The landscapes of Elwin Cotman are mythical, searching, and stimulated by haunting fanaticism." — Jason Parham, *Wired*

PHILIP K. DICK AWARD FINALIST · NPR BEST BOOKS OF THE YEAR

paper · $17 · 9781618731722 | ebook · 9781618731739